WEI

WEIRD SPACE

A. M. Wiley

KDP ISBN: 9798860283268

Cover illustration and design by: Daniel Wiley
Printed in the United States of America

For Heather

Table of Contents

Introduction

Weird Space has been over thirty years in the making. It began as an impromptu story I told my friends in the woods of my hometown in 1992. Surrounded by skeptical, ten-year old peers, I learned the basics of storytelling: beginning, middle, climax and cliffhangers. I discovered how to hang lanterns on important plot points and avoid gaping plot holes.

I infused inspirations like Star Wars, Peter Pan, Little Rascals, Red Dawn, Explorers and E.T., but the story really came to life when I inserted my friends as the characters. The premise was simple: by day we were normal elementary school kids, but by night, we snuck out to become the secret crew of an ancient starship. We flew on missions, hunted monsters, rescued the girls on which we had crushes and had skirmishes with the local bullies, the Big Boys.

I was painfully aware of my audience and could see when they began drifting or getting bored. In these moments I would raise the stakes, slip in a reversal, or kill one of them off. I let the narrative go wherever was needed to keep my audience invested and I remember falling madly in love with storytelling when I sensed some of my audience believing in and caring about the idea as much as I did. Making this kind of connection was a magical feeling and I've been chasing it ever since.

When I was twelve, and at the behest of my mentor, my aunt Anne, I sat down and filled two notebooks with the first draft of the origin story. It was the first time I called it *Weird Space*.

Over the years, the story stayed close to my heart, even as my friends, immortalized as characters, drifted away. Weird Space wasn't just a fun story, it was what I wished was true about myself, my relationships, and my world and I still can't drive through the small town I called home without feeling a deep sense of numbing nostalgia.

For that reason, I spent all the years after childhood trying to make the story a reality. I wrote it as a screenplay, a short story series and made many failed attempts at crafting the novel. None of it worked and I began to process what it meant letting the whole thing go away. It felt like the death of a loved one.

It took a global pandemic and a few vivid dreams to set me on the right path. Suddenly, a story that had given me so much joy and heartache over my life spilled out. I frantically wrote the messy first draft in a matter of months, but I spent the last three years obsessively revising it. I can hardly believe that after thirty years, it's finally done and that there are two more stories on the way! This is more than a story to me. My goal was to find a window from adulthood back into childhood fantasies, hopes, and dreams as well as explore my greatest fear, growing up. The characters in this novel are based on the same real friends I told those stories to in the woods, thirty years ago, but I have changed their names... mostly. This story gives insight into what was dear to me, but I hope you use it to rediscover what was once dear to you and that you might remember what it was like to be a kid.

Sincerely,
Andrew Michael Wiley, 2023

Author's Disclaimer

Please believe this is a work of fiction. It is not real. It never happened. All the names, characters, places, events and incidents in this book are either the product of the author's imagination or used in a fictitious manner. Any resemblance to actual persons or events is purely coincidental.

This is *NOT* based on a true story...

Prologue

1992 . . . In Another Dimension

The Zoltarian dimension was the last to fall. It contained a small and beautiful galaxy. The planets were so close the Zoltarians connected them by encased bridges. Wanderers once camped along these star roads as they hiked to the different planets.

Their dimension gateway was in the sky over Zoltar's capital planet, where the people had been peaceful, productive members of the interdimensional council. But the star roads that once glowed with the lanterns of travelers were now dark appendages, connecting planets with no light. Star vessels, great and small, drifted lifelessly through the close galaxy.

The Dimension Warriors had marked Zoltar lost. All nine dimensions had fallen.

The large Zoltarian portal flashed blue and spat out what looked like a firefly. It zipped erratically, trailing a twinkling tail of sparks. It nearly collided with one of the star roads before banking sharply.

To see it closer, the firefly was a wide, rectangular, eight-passenger ship—an A29 Cruiser, to be exact. The bronze-plated spacecraft was like an aged memorial or something ancient, a worn symbol of the North Star stretched to look like a sword and encircled by nine smaller stars emblazoned on the starboard side. Its cockpit, which currently stood empty, was a half dome of windows. This was a family vessel, perfect for interdimensional travel, modified above and below with ball turrets containing stolen gremlin gutter guns and reinforced armored plating at the bow and stern. Of its modified twin engine thrusters, one rocket worked while the other choked glowing particles from the damaged intake.

Then, the gateway yawned as a giant beast broke through the portal. Bulbous like a misshapen planet, its wrinkled, purple-black skin was vivisected with rockets, gun turrets and tiny windows, launch bays, and thick plates of armor. The cyborg leviathan blinked with lights and bore mechanical, insectoid legs—part creature, part warship. Its eyes gleamed red as it chased its prey. This was Lord Malgore's Necrobeast.

The cruiser lurched wildly as its thrusters flared. Its captain, and only occupant, was a girl of twelve wearing an over-sized flight jacket, panic soaked with sweat. She clawed through the cramped fuselage, tossed about as the ship pitched and screamed with alarms. A fire sprang out from a bank of monitors by her head and she quickly sprayed it with a foam extinguisher.

She kicked a panel and the alarms died. She was about to move for the cockpit when she noticed the frayed ends of her wild black hair were on fire. She sprayed the flaming tips with foam and shook the smoke from her head.

The fires out, she punched a flickering radar screen. The fizzling display showed her ship's dot. The warship's large circle filled the screen and was closing the distance.

An automated voice warned of an "incoming." The girl climbed up into the ceiling ball turret and saw the Necrobeast had fired a green undulating orb now speeding toward her. She gasped, dropped into the cabin, and lunged into the cockpit. The orb struck the right stern, the ship convulsed, and an alarm shrieked as sparks showered her mop of tangled raven hair. The cabin lights flickered and went out. The alarm died.

She was in total darkness but for the stars outside and the growing red light of the oncoming ship. She heard no sound but her own short breaths. Taking the pilot seat, she yanked on a headset and kicked the dash controls. The dying ship flickered back to life.

"Please work—please . . . Bash, are you there?"

In another dimension, the Toren dimension, in the deep tunnel systems of the Toren planet, a group of children between the ages of ten and fifteen huddled in a smooth, brown-walled cave with a low ceiling. The bunker was dimly lit with lanterns. Blinking gear and monitors lay shoved against the walls. The kids, tattered and dusty, each hefted an adult-sized rifle. They huddled around a small screen, watching as the girl's face fizzled in and out.

A girl working the signal yelled, "We've got her, Bash!"

A fourteen-year-old boy with bright blue eyes and the cruiser pilot's same messy black hair shoved through the crowd. He grabbed the screen close to his face as the others gathered. He wore the same black fighter jacket, the North Star symbol patch on his shoulder. "Sheela! You made it!"

"I got it, Bash." Sheela dug into her jacket and removed a

3

small, blue-glowing object. Bash and the others leaned in, wide-eyed. "The key was exactly where I knew Father would hide it . . . Malgore caught the others. The key will lead me to whatever dimension Father hid the Polar Starship."

Bash nodded soberly. "Where are you?"

The cruiser jolted Sheela from her seat. The Necrobeast's spider arms had caught hold of her ship. "*Wait*, is Malgore chasing you now?"

"I can't talk right now. I'm going!"

"Going where?" Bash said.

Sheela held out the key and ran her thumb over the blue lights so that one glowing dot projected a hologram of coordinates. She read them aloud. "Tenth dimension? There's no tenth dimension."

"Sheela, come here first. We'll go together!"

She shook her head as the warship's shadow closed over her. "That would lead Malgore to you. That starship is all that can save any of us!" Sheela touched her screen. "I'll find the ship and come for you."

"For Orel." He put one fist to his heart. They all did.

"For Orel." Sheela entered the coordinates into the navigation system and aimed the ship at the Zoltarian gateway.

The spider arms were sinking laser tips into the cruiser's body, pulling it into a fleshy red and black umbilical cord from below the Necrobeast.

Sheela shoved away tears. "Stay alive. That's an *order*." She killed the feed and threw all her weight forward on the thrusters, routing all auxiliary power to the rockets. Outside, the tiny cruiser ripped from the arms of the beast and shot back through the gateway.

Chapter 1

Tenth Dimension: "Uncharted"

Drew Shipley always found it impossible not to stare at the stars, and this summer evening was no different. The dusk was hazy from the sweltering day. The smell of hot tar rose off the cooling asphalt, mixing with the symphony of crickets and the rhythmic hiss of automatic sprinklers.

As he pedaled his Huffy hard along Sweepstakes Avenue, the breeze kicked back his shaggy blond hair. He yanked a walkie off his belt and brought it to his mouth. "Micky Mouse has warts . . . over." He wobbled, trying to steer the bike with one hand. "I'm approaching Uptown. Justin, Kevin, do you copy? Over."

He could see the lights from Warfield just ahead. The town was so small it barely showed up on any map. If you were lost in a song on the radio, you'd drive right through it and never know.

Drew pumped his bony legs hard against the pedals. He

only lived a mile outside of town, but he'd taken the long way to avoid the graveyard. Tonight, he was lost in the gigantic night sky with its peach-pink horizon and deep dome of stars. He looked up again and a moment later ran headlong into a pair of trash cans. Every dog within earshot barked and several porch lights flicked on. Drew hurriedly propped up the cans, tossed in some loose trash, and shoved off.

He cut through the woods, racing across a thin footpath as the briars tugged at his pant legs and honeysuckles brushed his face. He emerged beside the hardware store and jumped off the curb onto the crowded Main Street, swerving from the streetlights and pretending they were UFOs trying to beam him up. He fantasized more on summer nights, imagining the town residents were spies and femme fatales or aliens mimicking humans.

The pasty old men in their lawn chairs outside Pete's Barber Shop shouted for him to "get a haircut." They were aliens for sure.

Drew waved but kept pedaling. "Have a good night!" he called over his shoulder.

His walkie squawked. "Drew! Come in! It's Justin. Over!" As Drew tried to respond, he veered into a row of bikes propped on their kickstands. He skidded to a stop and watched the domino effect as the bikes crashed to the pavement.

When he went to pick them up, he had a horrifying realization: These belonged to the Big Boys. The Big Boys were the closest thing Warfield had to a gang, and he was already on their hit list. He looked around and saw Jimmy Griffin and his cronies in the arcade across the street.

Drew sped away through the crowd of witnesses, praying no one had gotten a good look at his face. "We're stationed at the Druid! Over!" Justin called over the walkie.

"On my way!" Drew pedaled a few blocks and found the two boys exiting the movie theater. The heavy one was being escorted by a young male usher. The little skinny one held the walkie.

"You're banned this month, Kevin!" the usher huffed.

"You don't mean that, Bruce!" Kevin Gadoy was an enormous, pale boy with blond, greasy hair. He insisted on wearing one of four Hawaiian shirts, none of which fit him. What buttons hadn't popped off were always straining over his massive midsection.

Drew flew to a stop as the usher stormed back into the lobby.

"Kevin started performing a stand-up routine during the movie—again," Justin said. Justin Mcgrath was black and a fidgety wisp of a boy with large glasses. Like Kevin, Justin always wore the same thing, only his wardrobe was mostly all blue NASA windbreakers he got from space camp every summer. It made him look like an astronaut.

"Your pops told us you were still grounded!" Kevin said.

"Don't worry about it." Drew was looking back down Main Street to see the Big Boys leaving the arcade. They'd just seen their bikes. "Let's go get Ryan," Drew said.

Drew and his friends rode out of town, weaving through the crowd as people jumped out of their way. They passed the used bookstore and Jack and Ray's restaurant. After that were a few sparse neighborhoods and then nothing but cornfields and tangled, sprawling woods.

They came to the baseball field, a quarter mile west of town, and parked their bikes against the backstop. Ryan Wilcox stood on the mound staring down the giant batter at home plate. Ryan's Huskies were up five to zip at the bottom of the ninth, and there was no way they would be losing.

Drew waved to catch Ryan's attention. Ryan glanced at him and Drew pointed at his watch, hoping his best friend would speed it up. Drew mouthed the secret code, "Mickey Mouse has warts!"

Ryan looked away from him and readied himself for the pitch while Drew, Justin, and Kevin began making stupid faces. Ryan ignored them and pitched a laser. Strike one. When his friends blinked flashlights at him, messaging crude words in Morse code, Ryan responded with a beautiful curve ball. Strike two. He smirked, knowing he was about to win their little game. Then Kevin lifted his Hawaiian shirt and pressed his pale belly against the backstop, his flab bulging through the chain link diamonds like rising buns in the oven. Ryan choked out a laugh but tried to refocus and shook his head. The catcher was confused, thinking the sudden headshakes were a signal.

"Ryan, what are you doing?" his dad, Big Jake, the Warfield sports legend, yelled from the dugout.

Ryan stifled his laugh and hurled a pitch so hard his catcher fell back into the umpire. Ryan's team ran out onto the field to celebrate on the mound. This was his first no-hitter. Drew couldn't help feeling weird as he watched his lifelong best friend hoot and holler with his team. He'd been waiting to see when Ryan would finally figure out he was too cool for the likes of Drew Shipley.

On their way through the parking lot, Big Jake high-fived his son. "It reminded me of my first no-hitter! Jimmy Cone ice cream on me!"

The team cheered, but Ryan waved them on. "You guys have fun."

"Where are you going?"

But Ryan was already jogging up to Drew and the gang.

"Can I have your autograph?" Kevin grabbed him like an adoring fan while Justin took the game ball and turned it over in his hand.

"What was the airspeed velocity of that ball?" Justin said.

Drew approached. "You can go get ice cream if you want."

"And let you guys have all the fun?" Ryan held out his hand and they commenced with an elaborate secret handshake ending with rooster crows. "Hey, I thought you were grounded."

Drew shrugged. "Come on!"

They all jumped on their bikes and rode back through town, toward Drew's neighborhood. They turned into Angela Court, an incongruent cul-de-sac of faded bungalows, Cape Cods, and ranch houses. The court backed right up to a wavy ocean of corn belonging to the Gladhill farm.

Drew lived in a yellow split-level. His mom had grown up here, and his parents had moved in after his grandpa passed away. A garden and a fresh green lawn used to be out front, but weeds now strangled the garden and crabgrass had overtaken the lawn.

Gravel crunched under their tires as they rode up Drew's driveway. They wheeled around the side yard, behind his house, where the quiet backyard was lit only by the glow of a TV pouring out through the kitchen window. They ditched their bikes against the house, and Drew hushed them with a finger to his lips. Then he dug into his backpack and began handing out flashlights.

He whispered, "Boundaries are the same as last time: cornfield to the Pal's Run, Western woods to the creek, and no further than the Gladhill barn." Drew smacked his flickering flashlight to rejigger the batteries inside.

"I don't like the cornfield. I'm allergic to the pesticides," Justin said.

"I brought tissues." Drew checked his watch and looked back at the TV through the window.

"I'm not going near the barn. It's haunted. Robby Barrows disappeared in there," Kevin protested.

"I made that up, Kevin," Drew said. "Besides, it was just one kid."

Drew had secretly feared the Gladhill barn since he was little. He'd seen its slanted cupola and rusted tin roof from his bedroom window all his life. The abandoned farmhouse was torn down twenty years before he was born, but the field between his neighborhood and the barn was leased out for corn. Drew once heard his parents discuss the mystery around who even owned the property.

"I'm supposed to be home by now," Justin said, looking close at his digital watch.

"We're all supposed to be home." Ryan nudged Drew.

"*Guys,*" Drew said. "It's a perfect night. Why go home when we could be out here together?" They all agreed and headed across the yard toward the cornfield.

"What are *you* guys doing?" The voice startled them and Justin shrieked. They'd been caught.

Chapter 2

Ghost in the Graveyard

It was a standoff.

Drew's next-door neighbor, Kristen Miller, and her friends Sonetta Brock and Missy Allen had returned from the pool. They were leaning over her privacy fence, and Kristen was smiling wickedly. Drew had known Kristen all his life. They'd been playmates throughout childhood, but now she was a girl, a *real* girl.

"Why do you always wear that stupid hat, Ryan?" Kristen asked, her green eyes flashing in the distant streetlights.

"Uh, it's part of my uniform." Ryan spun his hat from back to front and pulled the bill low.

Justin was hiding behind Kevin.

"Yeah, well you're not in the game now."

The other two girls snickered. Kristen's skin was bronzed from weeks at the pool. She'd been the first sixth grader to attempt makeup and her once-soft features had receded to reveal the beginnings of a woman. Her mere presence terrified most boys her age.

Sonetta stood a foot shorter than the other two, her ebony skin smooth and shiny. Her puffy hair was wrapped with blue hair knockers. Her giant pink towel was wrapped tightly around her, and whenever she talked to Drew and his friends, she wore a disapproving scowl.

Missy's fair skin was burned and her wild lion's mane of strawberry-blonde hair was sun streaked. She always grimaced, like she'd just licked a lemon, and she shouted, squeaked, or squealed nearly everything she said.

Drew tried to hurry his friends along. Seeing the girls made him feel hot, excited, and freaked all at once. Girls, particularly these, made them clam up and act stupid, so it was better to retreat.

"It's almost bedtime," Sonetta called out. "Where are you *boys* going?"

"I heard somebody was grounded . . . again," Kristen said, smiling at Drew.

"Tell us where you are going or we're gonna tell Drew's dad!" Missy said.

"No, please!" Justin came swishing around from behind Kevin. His eyes were large and scared through his thick glasses. "We'll do anything. Don't tell!"

The boys looked at Drew helplessly. "Alright, fine. You just can't give away any of our secrets."

Kristen smirked. "Secrets? You're such a bunch of dorks."

They followed Drew through the corn. The group of them squeezed between the regimented cornstalks, jumping and shrieking, tagging and scaring each other. Their flashlights danced like mad fireflies up through the leaves. Drew paused several times to look up at the galaxies overhead and only came back to earth when Missy grabbed his wrist and slapped him with his own hand. "Stop *hitting* yourself!"

He looked skyward again, rubbing the sore spot on his cheek.

Kevin bumped into him from behind. "Hey, space cadet, keep it movin'!"

He couldn't see the barn, but he knew right where it was, the broadside looming on the far side of the cornfield.

"We'll start in the woods," Drew said. He didn't want to get any closer to the barn. None of them did.

He cut sharply to the right and led them into the tree line. They followed a narrow footpath, beaten down by generations of kids who'd owned the woods before them. Those kids had disappeared into adulthood. Drew had once liked the idea of following in the old footsteps, but now their names, etched into the trees, made him think of ghosts.

Drew looked back at them, a group he'd known all his life. They were all changing, too, and soon they'd be ghosts if they weren't careful.

"Hey!" Drew called out. They all gathered around him as he yanked out a strand of his hair and held it out. "We'll never grow up. Swear on the hair."

No one remembered the origin of the hair or why they swore on it. Drew promised he hadn't started it. He claimed that adults swore on the Bible, but kids swore this way. The truth was his mom, Anne, had started it. He'd simply forgotten.

"May we never grow up and become sad and work all the time and die, and if we break this oath, may we grow old and die."

"I swear," the rest repeated. Kristen rolled her eyes. Even

13

as they swore, he could feel them slipping away. They were all growing up and were going to leave him. Then he'd be alone.

They came to the edge of the woods and could just make out the barn. The large dilapidated structure was terrifying during the day, but at night, when it blended with the twisted locust and vines, it looked like a black hole.

"Can we *please* go," Missy squealed. "A kid got killed out here."

"*Shut up*, Missy," Sonetta said, her eyes wide.

"Kids disappeared in there," Drew said. "Never seen again."

"I'm positive we're trespassing," Justin said.

Kristen said, "Ryan, you're big and strong. Why don't you go in?" She glanced sideways at the lanky boy as he shifted nervously.

Drew said, "We're playing Ghost in the Graveyard. One person hides in the field and tries to catch everyone else as we get across."

"We haven't *forgotten* how to play," Kristen said.

"Not it!" Missy said. Everyone touched their noses except Ryan. He'd been too distracted looking at Kristen.

"Fine!" Ryan grunted and jogged into the corn.

Drew hustled to the far end of the field, near the barn. Ryan got to the middle of the field and counted down out loud. When he finished, Drew took off through the corn. He knew Ryan would be nowhere near him, so he took his time. He tried not to look to his right—tried not to think about the barn. He paused. Someone was near him.

Then came a whisper: "Hey, Drew."

His blood rushed cold, and he froze. Before he could switch on his light, he was punched so hard the air evaporated from his lungs and his flashlight flew into the leaves.

"Good to see you, friend," Jimmy Griffin said as Drew gasped for air.

Jimmy and the Big Boys crowded around him. "We could hear Missy for miles. Heard you knocked over our bikes and didn't bother to pick 'em up."

Jimmy spun Drew around and shoved him to the ground. Then he took Drew's arm and twisted it back. Drew groaned.

"You guys having fun?" Jimmy asked. He spoke gently, even kindly.

Drew gritted his teeth, the pain escaping in grunts and tight breaths. He could hear his friends. Ryan had caught them all and now they were all searching for him . . . in the other direction. Jimmy was twisting his arm in an unnatural motion and Drew hissed in agony.

"My bike's all scratched up. Can't let you off easy this time," Jimmy said. The others chuckled.

Drew pulled away, but they overpowered him and dragged him out of the corn to the Gladhill barn. The dilapidated homestead barn loomed over them. Jimmy punched him in the gut, and they all shoved Drew against the barn doors. He hit the warped planks and fell to the ground.

Billy, the number two, threw Drew's flashlight at him. It hit him in the head and fell beside him.

"We're gonna leave ya for the ghosts," Jimmy said, and they melted back into the corn.

Drew tried to get up but was still catching his breath. The humiliation was worse than the pain, but it all gave way to terror when he remembered where he was. "They're just stories," he repeated to himself as he went to get up.

Suddenly, he felt the hairs on his arms and neck stand up. A tingling sensation crawled up his back. His flashlight, lying nearby in some milkweed, flickered on and shone back on the

15

barn. Drew stared dumbly as the flashlight grew brighter and brighter, buzzing until the bulb blew out with a tiny pop.

Drew lay planted in the silence when his walkie crackled to life and a girl's voice blasted in and out. "Bash, anyone? Help! I'm going down! I'm going down!"

Drew crawled to his walkie and snatched it. "Kristen?"

"Who is this?" the girl responded. "Help me. I'm crashing in an uncharted dimension—" The signal cut out.

His friends were all talking and laughing their way back toward the neighborhood. This wasn't them; he'd picked up someone else's signal.

He pressed the talk button and lifted it to his mouth. "Are you in trouble? Do you need the police?"

The girl's voice returned, quivering, "Help me, please. I'm going down. I'm going down! Help me—" She cut off and Drew lay frozen in the leaves, clinging to the walkie.

Then he heard a low rumble and looked slowly to the sky, the stars. Something wasn't right. One of them winked brighter than the others and looked like it was spiraling. It grew closer and closer, glowing bright blue as it fell to earth. Then it crashed in the tall evergreens behind the barn, and a murder of crows erupted into the sky. An ethereal blue light haloed the barn and a low humming sounded before it went dark and quiet again.

Drew had forgotten to breathe. After a moment he raised the walkie to his mouth and whispered, "Hello?" Silence but for the birds but then—

"Drew?" Ryan's voice startled him over the walkie.

Drew was quivering. "Ryan, I'm at the barn. You're not gonna believe this—"

"Dude, your dad's here."

His dad fumbled with the walkie. "Home—*now*, son!"

16

But Drew couldn't move. He lay there staring at where he'd seen the star fall. He could see nothing now—no sign, no light, and no screaming girl.

Drew lay there so long Ryan finally appeared, leading his dad to him. They were calling for him, but he didn't hear them. He was having a moment, one of those where you wonder if you're insane. For Drew, this meant thinking the daydreaming had finally gotten the better of him. He was now talking to alien girls and seeing UFOs. Had Jimmy given him a concussion?

His dad, Steve, dismissed Ryan. Steve's tired frame was rigid as he tramped toward his son. Steve was taken aback to see Drew sitting on the ground. Drew hadn't moved or broken his gaze from the barn, pondering in dread what was behind it.

Even as Steve murmured about Drew being responsible and not living with his head in the clouds, Drew just lay there, mouth agape.

"Get up!" Steve hoisted him up.

Drew tried to speak, but he couldn't. He weakly motioned at the barn, but he couldn't form words.

"This is not what your mother would want . . ." Steve was about to launch into one of his lectures, but he deflated and wearily trudged home. Drew followed.

Flashlight tag would be over for a while, but at that moment, it didn't matter. Drew was afraid he could no longer distinguish between reality and fantasy. That night, as he lay wide awake and very much grounded for the rest of the summer, his mind kept going over the event. He had the walkie beside his bed, and he whispered into it throughout the night.

"Hello, are you there?" But there was no answer.

And there was only one way to prove he wasn't crazy.

Chapter 3

Close Encounters

"Do *not* leave the house." Steve hurriedly made himself breakfast and was spinning in circles, looking for his briefcase.

"It's by the recliner," Drew said absently. He sat at the table in front of an untouched bowl of Cheerios, glued to the morning news on their small kitchen TV. Its retractable rabbit ears pointed up like a crooked peace sign, but the signal was always snowy. A heat advisory was in effect and the carnival would be opening soon—nothing about a plane crash, a comet, a UFO, abductions . . . anything. He skimmed his dad's newspaper again. Nothing.

Steve had been storming about the kitchen, muttering to himself. He left the room and came back with the briefcase, wrestling with his blazer. "I'll be home late today, but Mrs. Miller said she's around if you need anything. She also knows you're grounded . . . again. I'll be calling regularly. Clean up your room, do the dishes, and do laundry." Steve checked his watch and started out of the kitchen. He stopped and stood in the doorway, hesitating. "Son?"

Drew pulled himself away from the news with a start.

"I just want to say . . . I need you to grow up."

"Okay, Dad."

Steve left and Drew heard the door close. He turned to watch through the window as his dad's Celica drove up the street, and then he bolted to his room. He grabbed his walkie and talked into it as he packed his backpack with M-80s—big fat firecrackers that could blow your hand right off if you weren't careful—and some ninja throwing stars.

"Come in, Ryan. Over."

A moment later, Ryan's voice came over Drew's walkie, his voice low. "Hey, what happened to you last night—"

"Ryan, shut up a second. This is important. I saw a light and it crashed behind the barn—"

"Drew! You just got grounded for the rest of your life! What is the matter with you?"

"I know you think I'm making this up, but I'm *not*!"

"Drew, if you're leaving your house, count me out. And don't tell me if you're going because I *will* turn you in. Over and out." Ryan switched off to the soft sound of static.

Drew switched off and peered out his window. The barn stood on the horizon, haunting and mocking him. The day was hot, hazy, and normal—no aliens or creatures or helicopters. He could have dreamed it.

What do ya say, Drew? Stay home, watch a movie, and stay out of trouble?

He shoved the walkie into his backpack and grabbed a cola and some chips. Lastly, he grabbed his dad's pump-action BB gun. He shook it and heard the BBs rattling in the chamber.

He went out the back and stayed low, creeping along Kristen's privacy fence. The girls were out in the backyard playing badminton. Drew ran and launched into the cornstalks before they spotted him.

To keep from being seen by whatever had crashed, Drew's plan was to take the path through the woods and approach the barn from the west. He paused to pump the BB gun to its maximum threshold and then moved cautiously up a row of corn. The long leaves slapped and gripped at him. He cradled the gun against his shoulder, aiming the barrel low, the way they did in the movies. He imagined he was on a search and destroy mission in the steamy jungles of Vietnam.

"Don't get distracted," he whispered to himself. Something was out here. Something real.

He sprinted from the field into the trees. The moist, warm air was close in the woods and the Maryland humidity hung heavily on Drew's sweat-drenched body. He moved slowly along the footpath, looking for any signs: large tracks, glowing green goo dripping from branches, little green people.

Crossing over the creek, he pushed through vines and low branches. The forest felt foreign and it occurred to Drew what might have happened to all those kids who'd once played in these woods. They hadn't grown up and left. Creatures from outer space had snatched them. Drew resisted the fear and pressed forward.

He could just see the barn now, its tin roof rising like the bow of a ghost ship. Drew knelt and listened, checking his surroundings. A strange tension lingered in the air, the hint of something beyond taste, sound, or touch. The sensation was electric, tingling through him and making him buoyant. He could sense it; *something* was out here.

He couldn't hear a sound, and the dappled sunlight and shifting shadows below the dense canopy made it difficult to see what might be lurking just ahead as he pushed through brambles and low branches. A horsefly suddenly darted at him and sent him running headlong into a newly spun spiderweb. Drew whirled around, slapped his neck, and jumped, dropping his gun in the leaves. He yanked the wad of silky web off his face and wiped it in the dirt. No spider. It was probably in his shirt.

He realized then that he was standing in the clearing in front of the barn—the barn where Robby Barrows had disappeared and where even Jimmy Griffin and his Big Boys wouldn't go. It somehow looked worse in the daytime.

He switched on his walkie and it babbled snow. He pressed the talk button, his voice barely a whisper. "Hello? Anyone out there?" He waited longer than was necessary. Once he was around that barn, he'd see it and the world would never be the same. He licked his lips, but his tongue was dry. One small leap for Drew Shipley . . . one giant leap for all kid-kind.

Drew unshouldered his gun and moved slowly to the corner. He paused, gave it a three-count, looked into his destiny, and found . . .

Nothing.

Birds chirped and the sky was blue. He spied no smoldering tree stumps, no smoking wreckage, and no government agents chasing a squat, waddling alien. *Nothing.*

Behind the barn, the ground sloped steeply away into a wall of thick evergreens. He climbed up on a lip of the barn's concrete foundation for a better view. All looked normal. He climbed higher on the ledge and went on his toes. Now he could see the area behind the trees. There was nothing there.

These were still just the woods, and he was still just a daydreamer.

"Dang," he whispered.

"Daaaang," a tiny frog voice repeated. Drew turned slowly to his left.

The thing he saw stood upright on the ledge next to him. The size of a rat, it had short-cropped white fur, big brown eyes, and drooping ears. Its tiny pink nose sniffed the air and it waved at him with one of its three webbed paws. "Daaaang," it squeaked again.

Drew screamed.

The thing screamed and its fur flashed from white to bright orange. Drew backpedaled onto a loose piece of concrete. It gave way and he tumbled down the slope. The world flipped, with the sun below him and the hill above—a jarring spin cycle of sunlight, grass, sky, barn, and mud. He hit his head, his backpack crunched, and his BB gun was driven into his hip.

He somersaulted into the evergreens and took out some low branches as he glided over a blanket of dead pine needles. Sliding to a stop, he lay there facedown, beneath a pile of pinecones. The sweet smell of sap filled his nostrils as he groaned.

He pushed himself up and froze.

Drew lay at the mouth of a trench with exploded wood chips blanketing the ground like confetti. This was not what he'd seen from the ledge. Metal crates were stacked in piles and a small satellite dish stood erect and opened upward, beeping.

His eyes followed to the end of the trench where an unidentified crashed object rested in the soft earth. It didn't have wings, but three rocket boosters yawned back at him. It

23

wasn't a plane. It wasn't anything he'd ever seen before. It was the length of a large camper. The long, hexagonal body was galvanized in dark, copper-colored armor plating.

He got to his feet. His dad's BB gun had cracked in the middle and now hung limp off his shoulder. Drew couldn't take his eyes away and a moan escaped his slack-jawed mouth. He smacked his face and ran both muddy hands through his hair. No matter how hard he pinched and hit himself, the ship was still there.

"What?" he whisper-chuckled. He then looked from the sky to the ship, at the trees, and all around, mumbling as if his friends were standing there with him, "It's still there, it's—it's—it's a *spaceship*." He inched cautiously toward it and saw black, blistering scorch marks blooming all over the exterior and a half-dome of windows at the front, but he couldn't get to the windows with the way the ship was pressed into the pines.

He reached out with a shaking hand and touched it. The surface was cool and vibrated, popping goosebumps on his arms. He laughed and his vision blurred through welling tears. He ran his hand along it as he passed back around the rockets. On the other side he paused. A gullwing hatch sat open, and a short staircase was lowered to just off the ground. A thin vapor of mist cascaded from the opening.

Drew screamed as another furry monkey creature turned orange and shrieked, "Mayday, mayday! Going down!" It waddled beneath the ship, scampered up one rear leg to the undercarriage and disappeared into the landing gear.

Drew cradled his broken BB gun as BBs spilled from the busted chamber. He flipped the barrel around, held it up like a club, and moved toward the hatch. When he got to it, he couldn't see inside. It was too dark.

He gulped and forced himself forward. He took one step at a time and passed through the hatch. The darkness paralyzed him. He soaked in the alien vessel with all his senses.

It was cool inside. He heard a low hum followed by scampering and rustling. More of those creatures rushed about. His eyes adjusted to the natural light from the cabin windows up front. The rest of the ship was cave dark. Dim lights and blinking monitors came into view like stars. The interior smelled of burnt circuitry and leather as well as metal and other things he didn't yet know about.

He crouched in a corridor with a low ceiling. Orange conduit ran along the walls between blinking panels. Wiring hung from the ceiling, the frayed ends sparking and snapping. It reminded him of Kevin's mom's conversion van. The low hum gave him the sense this thing was hibernating, very much alive. What if it suddenly took off?

Tightly knotted rigging restrained gear and gadgetry along the walls and ceiling. He crept slowly through the fuselage, pausing to gaze at a gun rack of copper-colored, rectangular guns with short stocks, their barrels lined with blue glowing dots. Beside the guns hung helmets, chest guards, visors, and shin and elbow pads. They were painted and marked and tied off with beaded string and wiring.

Still crouching, he walked a narrow track between bucket seats, screens, and consoles with blinking buttons, levers, and switches, all coming into focus through the warm glow of yellow running lights. It was a sweltering dream, and he was intoxicated. He entered the front cabin and looked up through the half-dome windows. The sunlight spilled in over the pilot's seat—a flight wheel with a disintegrating leather grip cover and a dash of what he assumed were flight controls.

Drew couldn't help it. He laughed and danced and gasped to himself as he clasped his hands and shook his head. Then he sat carefully in the large seat. Its brown, broken leather crunched and creaked beneath him. He sat for a moment, his eyes washing over the dash before he allowed himself to reach out and grab the wheel. He turned it and then pressed a few buttons on the busy control panel. Nothing happened, but he was awestruck, and tears ran down his cheeks as he laughed out loud. He felt that tingle of magic, as if he'd just discovered dinosaurs still existed. He couldn't yet articulate it, but his heart was full and his mind clear. The world was no longer dark, and his life had changed forever.

Then he heard a hum behind him. Someone was there. His full heart froze, and he felt a warm release of pee. Before he could turn around, a blast from behind struck and hurled him headfirst into the flight wheel.

Chapter 4

The Hostage

Drew woke with the sun in his eyes. His head was foggy, his ears were ringing, and his mouth felt full of cotton. He was propped against a leg of the ship, near the hatch. He heard a tiny grunt and looked down to find one of the white-haired monkey-lizards standing upright on his lap. He tensed and held his breath, waiting for it to strike, but it just tilted its head and stared at him with its bright green eyes. It bore two normally placed arms with a third protruding from just below the left arm. It held his digital watch and took a bite, chewing casually on the electronics while it looked on. Drew tried to move and found his hands were bound behind his back.

A figure suddenly blocked the sun and stood over him, nudging the monkey creature away with a gouged leather boot. Drew peered up and saw a girl unlike any he'd ever seen. She might have been his age, but it was hard to tell. She wore an oversized, burnt-black fighter jacket over a tan flight suit. Her wild raven hair spilled over a thin silver headband. Grease smeared her face and a pink scar streaked across her right cheek. She held a copper-colored pistol by her side and looked down on him coldly, piercing him with eyes the color of blue dusk.

When she spoke, her voice was low and threatening. "My name is Sheela Vestril, commander of the Dimension Warriors of Orel, and you dare try to steal my ship?"

Drew stared at her with his mouth unhinged before absently mumbling, "I'm Drew . . . I think you were on my walkie."

He heard the monkey creatures all whisper, "Deroo."

"Well, Drew, you were in *my* seat." She leaned in. "Nobody sits in my seat."

The two stared at each other a long moment before Drew figured it out and began chuckling. "Okay, I'm dreaming. This is just a crazy dream and you're not even real. But I do like the name Sheela Ves—"

Sheela raised her gun and fired—*zpat!* A blue laser struck the ground beside him, scorching the dirt. Drew looked down at the scorched earth. He'd felt the laser heat and now smelled the burning grass.

This isn't a dream, he thought.

"I shot you with a daze charge—the next one will be lethal. Now, where are the gremlins? Are there any slore pits nearby? Do you have any food?"

Drew was now wondering if he'd simply gone insane when a terrible cramp gripped his leg. He twisted and kicked, trying to stretch out before the cramp flipped his muscle.

Sheela leapt back and aimed. "Don't move!" she ordered.

"Sorry, cramp!" Drew grunted.

Her eyes darted around and then fell back to Drew. Her

28

face went pale, twitching as fresh drops of sweat mixed with the grease and soot. "You're not a Dimension Warrior, and if you're still alive it's because you must be working for Malgore." She aimed and her finger hugged the trigger.

"Wait!" Drew screamed and startled a blue jay from a nearby tree. The bird launched into the air, shrieking. Sheela spun and fired. Blue lasers hit several pines, but the bird escaped.

She dove behind a crate and peered up, hunting for the bird. Her back was turned, and it took Drew a moment to realize this was his only chance. He struggled to his knees, trying to stay quiet, but came face to face with one of the monkey creatures.

"Deroo!" it chirped.

He glanced back at Sheela and the two locked eyes. She looked even more frightened than he felt, if that were possible. She took aim and blasted. Drew lunged into a roll, everything spinning as lasers struck the ground around him.

He collided with a tree stump, biting his tongue. His vision was still spinning when he saw her leap up and advance. She took several steps when suddenly she slowed and wobbled on her feet. She gave her head a tight shake and blinked hard. She tried to take another step when her eyes rolled into her head and she fell to the ground.

Drew looked from the girl to the ship and back again. *It isn't a dream. This isn't a dream. And it isn't my imagination, either.*

His heart thudded in his ears and all his senses were overloaded. As he stared at the girl's motionless body, his ears picked up the blue jay's distant shrieking and the sizzle of sap from where the lasers had struck the pine trees. The girl, Sheela, hadn't moved after she hit the ground.

The monkey-lizards—he'd spotted five of them—were

29

peeking out from the undercarriage of the ship and the hatch, whispering, "Deroo, Deroo."

Run! His brain finally caught up. He rolled to his knees and quickly staggered up on unsteady legs. The cord around his wrists was too tight and he wasn't waiting around to free himself. He took off at a sprint up the hill, around the barn and headlong into the corn. He imagined her chasing him and expected to be shot in the back.

When Drew Shipley burst from the corn like a headless chicken, it was late morning and his hands were still bound. He angled his body and slid between the rotting rails of his old fence. He fell into his backyard and fought awkwardly to his feet, his mind racing—*spaceship, alien girl, police, Dad!* He was almost across the yard when a voice stopped him dead.

"What are you doing?"

Drew looked and saw Kristen leaning over her fence, holding a tennis ball. She wore an expression of confused amusement. Cooper, her golden retriever, jumped up beside her, snatching for the ball. She tossed it over her shoulder and Cooper bolted. Kristen folded her tan arms across the fence rail and waited for an answer.

Drew was still heaving, his senses shot from the lasers and monkeys, "I just saw . . ." He couldn't talk. Where would he even begin? "I just, huh . . . I . . ."

No. He didn't want to begin. Beyond the panic and endorphins, something deep inside stopped him. At that moment, Drew Shipley realized he had the biggest secret anyone had ever had, and he wasn't giving it to Kristen Miller. Kristen cocked one eyebrow and tapped the fence railing impatiently.

"Jimmy," Drew finally said.

She frowned. "What?"

"Jimmy and the Big Boys. I snuck out and they caught me again." He saw Kristen's eyes drop to his crotch. He looked down. The stain from where he'd peed himself was faint but still there.

"Oh." Kristen grimaced and looked back at Cooper. "Where's the ball, Cooper?" The ball was in his mouth. She turned away from Drew and back toward her dog. Drew would have been humiliated but for the secret. He started to move for his house—

"Hey!" Kristen called.

He turned back.

"Do you want me to untie you or what?"

He backed up to the fence and she leaned over and tugged at the cord. After some doing, Drew felt it go slack, and he pulled his hands free.

"What is this?" she asked.

Drew finally got a look, holding the cord out. The cable had a clear jacket and a weave of multicolored wires running through it. He'd never seen anything like it.

"I don't know. They must have stolen it from Willy's junkyard. Got to go!" Drew tried to saunter casually for the patio sliding door, but his strut became a speed walk. He felt Kristen watching him, but he forced himself not to look back.

Once inside, he yanked the heavy curtain across the sliding door and backed into his tiny dining room. He felt woozy from all the heaving and gasping, and he couldn't think. He stared at the cable as he paced around the coffee table in the cramped TV room.

"What is happening?" he repeated in a whisper. He spotted the phone on the kitchen counter. "She tried to shoot you, she's dangerous." He went to the phone. His hands were shaking so badly he could barely dial.

A monotone woman answered, "Nine, one, one. What's your emergency?"

He grunted and his mouth hung open and wordless.

"Hello?"

The secret. He couldn't give it up. He slowly lowered the handset to the cradle.

He teetered for another moment before running and flinging open the refrigerator.

"What are you doing? What is wrong with you?" he shouted at himself.

He filled a plastic grocery bag with cookies, bread, a can of tuna, a pack of American cheese, bologna, a whole jar of Peter Pan peanut butter, and two packs of candy cigarettes. He changed his pants, filled his grandpa's old army canteen with tap water and slung the strap over his shoulder.

Taking up the plastic bag, he peeked out the curtain and through the glass sliding door. Kristen was no longer in her backyard. He exited, shut the door, and hustled across the yard, cursing himself.

Chapter 5

The General

Drew crept around the barn on tiptoe. He'd changed his mind five times on his way across the cornfield and each time he'd forced himself back toward the barn. He saw the blue jay—he assumed it was the same one—perched on the barn's rusted cupola.

"I know," he conceded in a whisper. "I'm back."

He descended the hill and ducked beneath the pines. There was the ship and there she was, right where he'd left her, face down in the grass. Her gun lay near her right hand. As Drew approached, he leaned down and picked up the gun. It was solid, cold, and had real weight. Holding it gave him chills. He looked around and decided to hide it beneath a nearby log.

He returned to her and gently tapped her with his foot. She didn't move as he dropped the plastic bag and knelt beside her. He touched her shoulder. The black jacket was hot

33

from the afternoon sun. He nudged her with his hand. Still no movement. Drew sucked in and held his breath as he carefully placed his hands on her arm and hip. He slowly pushed her onto her side and brushed some of the dark hair from her face.

She was pale and her greasy skin had a green hue. He unscrewed the canteen's lid, held it just above her mouth, and poured a little water onto her lips. The water dropped into her mouth and ran down her cheek. Her face twitched, and suddenly she choked and bolted upright.

Drew fell back and scooted out of striking distance. Sheela's eyes fluttered as she licked the water off her dry lips. At the taste, her eyes shot open, and she looked about frantically. She found the canteen in the grass, snatched it up and inhaled it so that excess water spilled from the sides of her mouth and down her flight suit. She stopped to gasp for air and then drank more.

After downing the canteen, she went limp and hugged the green container to her chest. Then she spotted Drew and crouched like a startled animal. Her right hand flew to her holster, and when it came up empty her cobalt eyes went wide.

"It's okay! I come in peace!" He'd practiced this line on his way across the cornfield but said it with more panic than he'd intended. "I'm not gonna hurt you."

She grabbed a sharp stick and held it up like a switchblade.

"Whoa!" Drew seized the plastic bag as a shield and then looked at it. "I brought food!"

She narrowed her eyes as Drew dug into the bag and came up with a soda. He pulled the pin and she jumped at the pop-fizz. He took a sip to show her it was safe and held it out. Her lips quivered as she studied it and, finally, she reached out and snatched the can. She looked it over, sniffed it, and took a small swig. Immediately, she began coughing and gagging as she waved at her tongue.

"Acid!" she gasped.

"No, it's just the carbonation," Drew said. He saw the sugar taste kick in and she drank it down, not even stopping to breathe. When it was empty, she tossed the can aside and crawled for him. Drew was about to spring up and run when Sheela grabbed the plastic bag from him and ripped it open.

Sheela didn't stop until she'd eaten everything. She paused once to heave, as if about to throw up, and then quickly finished gorging. The ground was soon littered with plastic wrappers, a hollowed-out jar of Peter Pan peanut butter and two empty packs of candy cigarettes. She burped and looked back at Drew as though she'd forgotten he was there.

"Where's my dazer?"

Drew hesitated. "Are you gonna shoot me?"

"Are you going to make me?"

Drew shook his head and pointed at the nearby log. She quickly went and fetched the gun. Then she nodded for Drew to follow her. When he stood up, she grabbed and dragged him to the ship and pressed him roughly against the armored plating. She turned and scanned the trees.

"Where are the adults? Do you have a camp nearby?" She continued her lookout while her free hand searched him, shuffling through his clothes, his pockets, up through his hair. She looked back at him, looked right into him, and whispered, "Are you being used as bait?"

Drew shook his head.

"Sometimes they use us as bait," she muttered hatefully,

and her eyes traveled back to the perimeter. "What kind of predators do you have here?"

Drew stepped back from her searching hand. "Predators? I don't know. Fox or foxes . . ."

Drew noticed her jacket had a pin on the right breast pocket with blue glowing dots. A star sword symbol was emblazoned on the left shoulder, surrounded by nine smaller stars. She seemed older, but her youthful softness was visible the longer he looked through her grizzled sheen.

"This is a genuine R7 Dazer, and it fires polar plasma. So don't cross me."

Drew nodded. She holstered the dazer and kicked open one of the metal crates. She removed what looked like a folded umbrella, but when she opened it up, Drew saw it was a satellite dish the size of a large pizza.

"My home dimension is Orel, one of the nine dimensions."

Drew nodded, pretending to keep up as she set up a three-legged stand and placed the dish on it. "My coordinates led me here. They say I'm in dimension ten." She looked back at him. "But that can't be right. There is no tenth dimension. So where am I?"

Drew couldn't believe he was saying it. "You're on Earth."

She shook her head. "Never heard of it." She looked up at the sky and angled the dish.

He shook himself and pointed at the ship. "Look, this is impossible! I don't think you're a dream, but there are not nine other dimensions. This world is it. There's nothing beyond it!"

She connected a white box with blue buttons under the dish, and it started beeping softly. "Why do you think that?"

"It's what we're taught. And how does no one else on Earth know about other dimensions?"

She considered this as she continued with the gear. "Somebody knows. Why is all this hard to believe?"

"Because those things only exist in dreams."

"Deroo," a monkey creature whispered from a nearby tree. Sheela didn't acknowledge it.

"What are those things?" Drew pointed at the monkey.

"*They*," she exhaled wearily, "are Talk-Talks. I'm assuming you don't have them here?"

"Not that I know of."

"They're everywhere in Orel and pods of them like to hibernate in *cargo holds*!" she hollered at the creatures. "You don't know they're there until you've left home. Then they hatch, eat all your food, toy with your navigation system, and repeat everything you say!" She kicked dirt at them. "It is nice to have someone to talk to on long jumps until you realize you're talking to yourself."

"Yourself," several of them repeated.

"They are good for warning you about slores. It's the only word they say on their own."

"Slores?" Drew began, but Sheela wasn't paying attention. She'd noticed something and quickly crossed the clearing to the trees, where Drew had originally fallen through. She knelt and picked a copper disk the size and shape of a hockey puck from the red-brown needles.

"Blast. How did you manage to break my Oren wall?"

"Your what?" Drew approached from behind.

"I wasn't finished with it, but it should have hidden my camp from your direction." The disk had small prongs on the back and Sheela slapped it against the tree. Then she ducked into the ship and returned with a sack. "I don't have much

37

time. I'm here to find my father's starship. It's the only weapon that can defeat Malgore."

"Malgore?" Drew asked.

Sheela paused on her way past him and dropped the sack. She stared at him as if he'd slapped her. Then she approached until she was very close. "You haven't heard of Malgore?"

Drew shook his head. "That's what I'm telling you. I've never heard of any of this."

Sheela looked at him as though *he* were the alien. Then she looked at the trees and sky like it was the first time she'd seen them. "He hasn't found this place yet."

She snapped back into motion with renewed urgency. Drew followed her as she hauled a sack of gear into the clearing and dumped a load of blinking, beeping, moving gadgets on the ground. She dug through them and came up with an armful of the copper disks. She tossed a disk at Drew.

"Attach it to that tree there." She pointed to an evergreen adjacent to him, pulling the small prongs from the backside of one of hers and driving it into the sappy bark. She slapped it with her palm, and it hummed, projecting a shimmering amber light.

"Listen carefully," she began. "Someone opened the lost gate—the one holding back the Outer Darkness."

"You're kidding," Drew managed as he followed her lead, digging his puck into the opposite tree. When he slapped it, the amber light traveled between the trees and connected, making a shimmering wall. Sheela was on to the next tree.

"The law forbade anyone from opening that portal, but someone defied the council." Sheela punched another disk hip-high into a stump and paused. Her eyes grew distant. "My father, Mayzon, and my Uncle Jay tried to close the gate, but it was too late. Most have never seen Malgore . . . but I have.

There is not a more terrible creature in all the dimensions and all the worlds. He'd been waiting a thousand years to escape. But Malgore and his army of slores, gremlins, and other monsters were not the worst thing."

She went back to the pile for more disks, and he followed. "Malgore released parasites to control the minds of the adults—parasites connected to him, to his mind." She grabbed up the remaining pucks. "Hold out your shirt," she ordered. Drew spread the hem of his shirt into a basin, and she dropped them in. He walked along behind her as they ducked below the ship to the trees on the other side, and the Talk-Talks repeated the name Malgore in hushed reverence.

She continued, "The parasite didn't control those below a certain age. We don't yet know why, but our parents became our enemies overnight and chased us out of our homes. He used the adults to hunt and capture us and built an army with them."

The blue jay squawked nearby, and Sheela pulled her gun and crouched. Drew crouched with her, transfixed by her story. She stood after a moment and holstered her gun. "We can't fight this army because we'd be killing those we love. Our parents, grandparents, friends, countrymen . . . they're all his now."

"The parasite doesn't control kids?"

She leaned in close to his face. "No. He prefers to feed on us, the young ones."

Drew shuddered.

They finished planting disks in a circle around the ship. With each disk activated, the amber light coursed, shimmered, and undulated around the entire camp. Sheela went to the ship, to a panel beside the hatch, and pulled it back. She tapped a code into a keypad behind it. The disks responded and the light waves encircling them faded away.

"Was that a forcefield?" Drew asked.

She looked at him funny. "It's a standard Oren wall. It shrouds your camp." She took him by the arm and nudged him just beyond the disk perimeter. The ship and Sheela disappeared, and he was looking at a wavy duplication of the surrounding trees. This was why he hadn't seen the ship from the barn!

Her arm shot through the projection and pulled him back inside the Oren wall. "And it alerts you to certain predators," she said. They returned to the pile of gadgets and he helped her toss them back into the sack.

Drew paused again to gaze at the cruiser as the sun glinted off its beautiful, tarnished exterior. It looked like a great beast. Sheela caught him staring. "The cruiser is very old. Generations of my family have used it to explore the worlds of every dimension."

She finished and tossed the sack by the stairs. She then removed a tool from the sack and set about working on the rear engine boosters. "I escaped with many young ones from Orel. We took our parents' ships and fled into hiding." She scraped at the gunk around the rocket, grunting as she talked. "We found young ones like us from the other nine dimensions, and I formed a coalition. We call ourselves Dimension Warriors."

She clenched her jaw, her eyes hardened, and she began to stab and slash at the blackened area. She caught hold of herself and wiped away sweat. She turned to him. "I must get back to them, but I *need* that starship." She went back to scraping the rocket.

Something tingled and welled its way through Drew's stomach. It pumped through his heart and cleared his mind like the sun through morning mist. He'd felt it when he first saw the ship and when he first saw Sheela. For the first time in a long time, he felt hope. "I can help you!"

She paused and looked him up and down. Then she chuckled. "I don't think so. I suggest you head back to your camp and forget you ever saw me. If Malgore finds this place, your world is finished."

"But I know this place. I know Warfield, the people, and anything else you might need to know while you're looking for your dad's ship."

She grunted as she worked, "So *you* want to be my liaison?"

"Your what?"

"When someone guides you through a dimension you've never been in before, they become your liaison."

"Yeah, I'll be that!"

She left the rocket boosters and went back to check the dish. "A liaison is bound to you; your life is in their hands. They must be trustworthy, intelligent, and strong. They always put you before themselves. They're brave in the face of danger and forsake their own people to protect you." She glanced back with her dusky blue eyes. "You're just a child."

"Hey, you're a kid too."

She advanced on him until they were close. "I'm the leader of the Dimension Warriors." She left him and headed for the stairs. "I have to fix my ship and start the search."

"I can get you more of that soda and food and stuff."

She paused to consider this but then kept walking. "I'll be gone before I need food again." She ascended the stairs and disappeared into the ship.

Drew saw the blue jay return to its perch in the evergreen, and suddenly he had an idea. "I think you should move your basecamp!"

She poked her head from the hatch and sighed. "You're still here?"

Drew shrugged and began to walk away. He was about to pass through the Oren wall when: "Why move my base?"

Drew turned and pointed up at the blue jay. "You're outside, in the open." He turned to leave.

"You know of something better?"

Drew pulled back one of the barn's heavy doors and beckoned Sheela in. The stale smell of dry earth filled his nostrils. Shafts of sunlight slanted down between the warped planks and lit up drifting dust moats. Swallows fluttered up in the eaves. Loose hay blanketed the floor from when massive bales had been stored there years before, but the barn was now one of Warfield's empty, forgotten relics.

Drew turned back to Sheela and saw her taking it all in.

"No one uses this place?"

"Nope. Everyone thinks it's haunted."

She sighed, pursed her lips, and nodded. Then she looked at Drew with a kind of disappointed concession. She straightened and said, "Approach."

Drew wasn't sure how close "approach" meant, but he came and stopped a foot from her. Sheela reached out and pulled him closer. She took his forearm with one hand, and he held hers with his hand.

"Do you swear on your life to counsel me well and true and serve as liaison to the Dimension Warriors in our fight against Malgore and his evil army?"

Eleven Talk-Talks served as witnesses, peeking in from the door and whisper-repeating the oath as Drew nodded and said, "I do." Without warning, she pulled his forehead to hers. Her skin was warm, and her headband was cold and hard.

"This is what we do in Orel when we make a pact. We're now linked," she said, releasing him.

Despite his shock, Drew felt a warm pride kindle in him. His chest swelled, correcting his posture. He wasn't Drew Shipley from Warfield, the daydreaming, grounded loser, victim of Jimmy Griffin and afraid of the Gladhill barn. He was the kid from his own fantasies, liaison to General Sheela Vestril, special counsel to the commander of the Dimension Warrior Coalition—and her bodyguard.

Chapter 6

The Secret Base

The Talk-Talks waddled in. One of them licked the wall, tapped the wood with a webbed claw, and took a bite of the barn door. Another one peed just inside the door, and this appeared to assure the others the space was safe because they spilled in and searched about.

Drew helped Sheela pack gear into the crates and haul it onto the cruiser, but to Drew's disappointment, Sheela still couldn't get the cruiser flying. He'd sat beside her at the controls, poised and jittery with anticipation, but the engines only groaned, and sparks shot from various panels in the cabin.

"I'll work on that," Sheela said. "We're gonna have to carry the gear."

They spent the afternoon hauling crates and sacks into the barn as well as setting up a radio station and radar dish in the hayloft. Sheela then crawled about the rafters, running cables. She shot a hole in the roof with her gun and shoved the cable connectors up and out onto the rooftop. Talk-Talks scuttled about her, chasing the swallows. Drew tried to follow her, but the darkness and height made him dizzy.

Minutes later, Sheela had him up a rickety ladder and on the roof helping her mount pizza-sized satellite reflectors. Drew clung to the sagging cupola as Sheela ran along the roof's narrow ridge. He froze several times, swallowed his panic, and forced himself to keep moving. All was going well until he was on his way off the roof. He missed the ladder's top rung and fell ten feet into a tangle of honeysuckle and brambles.

Back in the loft, Drew nursed a sharp pain in his elbow and pulled thorns out of his shirt as Sheela tinkered with the boxy radio, turning dials and flipping switches. The transmitter blinked yellow lights at her.

She plugged in a thin headset with a mic. "Scar one, Kilroog Secetor Tenthia." She repeated this several times.

"Are you speaking code?" Drew asked.

Sheela didn't answer. She listened, her eyes distant and searching for the faintest of signals. Her left hand slowly turned the dial one full rotation, and after a pause she shook her head and exhaled. "We'll keep trying. We need to get word to Bash and the other commanders."

They set up the copper disks around the inside of the barn doors, creating an Oren wall so that from just outside the doors the barn appeared empty. She took him out along the perimeter, along the cornfield and trees, and showed him how to set up invisible laser fences that would alert them to anything or anyone approaching the barn. Finally, they planted short-barreled, copper-colored laser rifles just inside the barn doors at the front and back.

Once she declared the new basecamp ready, they went to work on the cruiser, pounding away at the engine and repairing wiring. Drew followed with tools, and she called out for them as if he knew what they were. She would eventually grab the one she needed so as not to keep explaining.

When they exited the ship, the sun was dipping below the trees, leaving the clearing pink and hazy.

"Do you have a scrapyard for ships? We're gonna need to patch up some booster injectors and the flare reset."

Drew thought how Justin would love finding these parts and he was suddenly struck. He'd been so distracted he hadn't thought of his friends. "We need my—uh—engineer! His name's Justin Magrath."

"Is he just a kid like you?"

"Yeah, but he's trustworthy and smart! We also need Ryan Wilcox. He's a legend around here." Drew didn't say sports legend, but you know. "Oh, and I'll also alert Kevin, Kevin Gadoy. He's definitely Dimension Warrior material. I mean, we all are."

He could see she was skeptical, but she nodded. "You're my liaison. Go retrieve them."

"Tonight?"

Sheela nodded. "There's very little time and I need to show you all something very important, as long as you're sure we can trust them."

Drew started off but stopped and ran back. He snatched up the glowing, blinking screwdriver from her belt. "Can I borrow this?"

"Just remember: Don't tell any adults."

"Right." Drew saluted and then said, "Oh crap!" The Talk-Talk had eaten his watch, but he knew his dad would be home any minute. "I'll be back later!" He took off at a sprint, stopping only to pull the barn door shut behind him.

Drew ran into the backyard and panicked when he saw Steve through the kitchen window. Then Drew noticed Steve still had on his sports jacket, and he was pulling two TV dinners from the freezer.

He's just gotten home. Drew slipped in through the patio door and met his dad coming out of the kitchen.

"Hi, Dad!" Drew's response was over eager. His dad was slouched and tired.

"You didn't clean? What did you do all day?" He set his briefcase down.

"I slept a lot. Sorry about that."

Steve studied him. "Why are you so sweaty?"

"Oh, I started cleaning when you got home. Remembered when I saw your car."

Steve sighed until he noticed a few picture frames lying face down on the end tables. "Son, stop laying the picture frames down."

Drew looked about, trying to seem aloof. He had laid the frames down, was now laying down pictures of his mom everywhere.

"We need to talk about this. It's part of growing up," Steve began. "The world isn't fair—"

Drew felt a sudden, desperate explosion. "Dad, I lied. After you went to work, I snuck out to the old barn and found a girl from another dimension. She's running from a giant parasite, and he controls her parents and all the adults, and she needs my help."

Steve's tired eyes went vacant, and he mumbled something about comic books. "Keep cleaning up. I'll make dinner." He trudged into the kitchen and popped two TV dinners into the microwave.

At least they weren't talking about the picture frames being face down or about growing up.

Chapter 7

The Crew

This was supposed to be the greatest summer yet. The four of them—Ryan, Drew, Justin, and Kevin—had spent the drab, gray school year making a top-secret plan. During class they sent each other coded messages with meeting times and locations. The rule was you could only call a meeting with the secret phrase, *Mickey Mouse has warts*.

If one of them said it, the others had to drop what they were doing immediately, no matter where they were or what they were doing, and head for one of several secret meeting locations. After school they escaped to Justin's basement or Kevin's backyard or Ryan's garage and would pick up right where they'd left off the day before.

They had designed a treehouse—and not just any treehouse. This treehouse would span multiple trees and be camouflaged so it couldn't be seen from the ground.

Justin was the keeper of the documents and schematics.

They'd planned to string catwalks between the various platforms from which they would rain down water balloons filled with pee on attackers or girls. Kevin would keep it stocked with junk food, and Justin would hook up power using an old car battery. Ryan would oversee security and bring his binoculars to watch for enemies. They would take turns in the crow's nest. Drew would be the storyteller in residence. He had said you couldn't have a treehouse without a storyteller.

They'd dubbed it Operation Eagle's Nest.

But the plan began to spring leaks all over as summer neared and Ryan's dad enrolled him at sports camps and spring training. Then Drew's mom finally succumbed to her cancer, and he'd been perpetually sneaking out and getting grounded ever since. To add insult to trauma, Jimmy and the Big Boys had set fire to all the wood scraps they'd spent months collecting from Willy's junkyard, and like that, the greatest plan any group of boys ever had went up in literal smoke.

The summer felt over before it had begun. Justin had shredded the plans and enlisted Kevin to help spread the confetti among different trash cans throughout Warfield. Justin was still paranoid that someone would piece it back together and steal their idea.

Now it was just the two of them. Tonight, they were hunched in Justin's cramped room putting the finishing touches on a Rube Goldberg apparatus that spanned the whole room. They'd built it from Lego and Erector Set pieces, Kevin's mom's hair dryer, a bowling ball, Justin's old toddler slide, dominos, his dad's record player, counterweights, and his mom's pantyhose. At the end was a catapult scoop with an action figure cradled and ready to fire.

Justin had spent hours calibrating it and testing each part of the chain for weaknesses.

They had it aimed at the door for when Justin's sister tried to bother them.

"You know," Kevin said, sprinkling Cheetos on a Pop-Tart and trying to eat it in one bite. He continued with his mouth full and orange cheese powder poofing off his lips, "We could have just locked the door."

Justin's windbreaker swished as he moved from one section of the apparatus to the next. "She knows how to pick the lock."

"How?"

"Dad taught her. He taught all of us."

"Oh right, after you locked yourself in the bathroom during your birthday and missed the whole thing and peed yourself even though there was a toilet right there. Is that why?"

"Yes, thank you, Kevin."

"No problem. Hey, aren't Missy's scrunchies so stupid? She wears like eight of them when she does that unicorn ponytail off the top of her head."

Justin swished as he scrubbed his glasses. There was no condensation; it had become a nervous tick. When Justin didn't answer, Kevin reached out for the first domino to start the Destroyer, as they were calling it.

"Don't touch!" Justin whirled around on him. "I have it calibrated."

"Want to watch a movie after this?"

"No! After this, we wait for Shelly. We didn't spend two days building this just to walk away." Justin went back to a portion of the Destroyer, a joint made from Erector Set pieces that had come apart.

"Oh. Okay," Kevin said. Justin shoved him away from the dominos or "the fuse," as he referred to them. Kevin waited. He was trying to be good, but what would someday be diagnosed as ADHD began rippling through his body. The little plastic soldier reclining in the metal scoop at the front of the Destroyer was mocking him, begging to be launched. Shelly wasn't even home; she was in the next town away, at a skating rink. Kevin began tossing Cheetos into his mouth and then throwing them at the dominos. One finally hit its target and the chain reaction was set.

"No!" Justin shrieked.

Kevin grabbed him, holding him back from stopping it.

"I just want to see if it works!"

Kevin held Justin up in the air and the two watched as the Destroyer destroyed itself: the bowling ball rolling off the slide, snapping the pantyhose and smashing the record player, which knocked over the lamp. The catapult fell, launching the action figure at Justin. It hit him in the stomach. Kevin put him down and Justin plopped, dejected, on the floor. He put his head in his hands as the Destroyer slowly ate itself to death.

Kevin sat beside Justin and placed a meaty hand on his bony back. "What's wrong, Jus?"

Justin was trying to hide that he was wiping tears from his eyes, but the windbreaker didn't absorb them. "Just go home, Kevin."

A soft, snowy crackle rose from the smoldering remains of the Destroyer. "Shhh, you hear that?" Kevin asked.

"I'm not in the mood," Justin said.

"I'm serious." Kevin crawled on all fours, searching through the rubble until he came up with the walkie. "Is someone there? Over." He turned up the volume so the snow filled the room.

"Kevin, switch it off," Justin said.

He went to take the walkie when Drew's voice came over the speaker. "Mic . . . as . . . arts." Drew broke up over the shotty transmission, but he was close. Based on the range, he must have been in Justin's neighborhood.

"Drew? We didn't copy. Over," Kevin said.

Then Drew's voice came over the speaker loud and clear. "I said, Mickey Mouse has warts!"

Kevin and Justin followed Drew dubiously as he dragged them to Ryan's house. Ryan's bedroom window was on the ground floor of his split-level house, but he refused to pull back his curtain.

"Mickey Mouse has warts," Drew called out. Ryan's face appeared in a slit between his curtains.

"You're gonna get us all in trouble, Drew!"

"Mickey Mouse has warts."

Ryan yanked open his window. "I have a game tomorrow morning."

Kevin said, "Ryan, he's acting really weird. He keeps smiling at us like he's gonna kill us or something."

"Why did you guys follow him?"

"He said the phrase." Justin shrugged.

"And we didn't have anything else to do," Kevin said.

Ryan sighed and looked apologetic. "Go home, Drew."

Ryan closed the window, but before he could shut his curtains, Drew pulled the glowing, blinking screwdriver from his backpack and held up the greasy copper tool. Its soft yellow light along the shaft and blinking blue buttons reflected off Ryan's window and illuminated several stunned faces. Kevin and Justin gasped. Ryan leaned in for a better look. Drew pressed a button and the head of the screwdriver rotated and separated slowly, changing shape.

As they walked through the moonlit corn, Justin studied the tool. "He found this at Willy's."

"Yeah, but what is it?" Kevin asked. He snatched it from Justin and wielded it like a tiny sword.

"It's just an old . . . wrench someone customized with lights," Justin reassured him.

Ryan and Drew walked ahead in silence. Ryan was stiff, fists balled up tight. Before he leapt out the window, he had grabbed his Huskies hat and pulled it low, shrouding his eyes in darkness. For Drew's part, he was quivering with anticipation. His lips were dry and his stomach flipped. His bowels had gone liquid, but messing his pants was not a concern. Even with the ancient technology Justin and Kevin were tossing back and forth behind him, Drew felt a stab of anxiety, worrying that he'd dreamed the whole thing.

"It's solitary confinement. It made him crazy!" Kevin said.

"It's been one day!" Justin argued. "I stay in my room for weeks."

"Exactly," Kevin said.

As they neared the barn, the banter turned to hushed protest. When they arrived at the old structure the others stood back toward the cornfield, ready to run for cover. Drew sensed their shock as he strolled right up to the doors. He turned at the last moment, feeling compelled.

"Guys, this is it. If you're not prepared to have your lives change, walk away now."

The three boys exchanged glances, but all nodded back for him to continue. Drew took a deep breath and pulled back one of the tall doors. It was black and quiet and empty inside. None of them looked surprised except for Drew.

"What?" Drew shouted.

Kevin groaned, "Dang it, Drew!"

Ryan dropped his head and spat in the dust.

Justin shouted, "Drew, why are you torturing us? 'Mickey Mouse has warts' is only for the most important things! You're the hope-crusher!"

Drew felt a rush of panic until he remembered. "Oh, the Oren wall!"

"The what?" Ryan was flushed. "Drew, grow up!"

Ryan led the others back toward the corn. Drew chased them down. "No, please, just step inside the barn—just for a second—right inside the door!"

Kevin said, "Next you're gonna want us to clap to bring a fairy back to life."

Drew blocked their path, grabbing them. "Please, wait!" They started shoving and yelling at each other.

A blinding white light stopped them dead. They looked at the barn, shielding their eyes. Searing luminance blasted through every gap and crack in the warped barn walls. The heavenly light shot upward through the copula and rusted holes in the roof as if a nuclear bomb had detonated inside. A wind rushed around and beneath them, up through their clothes and hair, like the world was inhaling. Ryan's ball cap blew off and Kevin's Slim Jim fell from his open mouth.

The light shimmered and drifted out from the barn doors and then, as quickly as it had come, it died, leaving the afterglow of a UFO. Drew's eyes adjusted and he saw the cruiser hovering over the clearing. The ship lowered to the ground and the downdraft kicked up a cloud of loose, red dirt. The landing skids lowered as spurts of steam hissed off the bow and stern. The low hum of the engine thundered through them.

Then, without warning, the ship's outboard lights died, the engine cut out, and the cruiser fell to Earth with a crash.

As the dust cleared the gullwing hatch flew open and Sheela ducked out. "I've almost fixed the down thrusters and exhaust nozzle, but she's hovering again!" She hopped off the stairs and joined Drew. "Where's your crew?" Sheela asked.

Her crazy hair was blown about by the ship's exhaust steam, and low yellow running lights beneath the cruiser's undercarriage gave her a halo. Her oversized flight jacket hung open and her snub nose pistol hung off her hip.

Drew looked to his right to see his friends clinging to each other. Justin's glasses were fogged, his mouth gaping and contorted. The potato chips Kevin brought had exploded in his panicked grip and chips now covered him like confetti. Ryan removed his hat.

Drew felt it was his cue. "General Sheela Vestril, this is Ryan Wilcox."

Sheela approached Ryan and looked him over. "I've heard you're a legend in these parts." Ryan couldn't speak and Sheela looked back at Drew, confused.

Drew ran over and worked Ryan like a puppet, lifting his friend's limp hand to take her forearm. She took his forearm in the proper Orelien greeting. She released him and Ryan looked after her as if she were a ghost.

She moved on to Justin. "I'm, um . . . I'm, uh . . ." Justin bumbled. He was shaking so badly his windbreaker swished, and his fogged glasses slid down the bridge of his nose.

"This is Justin Magrath," Drew said.

She nodded. "Good! An engineer."

As he had with Ryan, Drew helped Justin with the greeting. Drew then dusted the chips off Kevin and presented the large boy to the general. Kevin's moon face twitched, the facial muscles jammed between horror and joy.

"Kevin, Kevin Gadoy," Kevin said, his brain repeating the greeting his mother had rehearsed with him in kindergarten.

"Hello, Kevin, Kevin Gadoy," she said with a nod. "You're big. We will need your strength."

"Kevin Gadoy," Kevin repeated.

After introductions, each boy reckoned with the revelation in his own way. Justin cried for a while, Kevin couldn't stop laughing, and Ryan rounded the cruiser, touching it and then pinching himself.

Sheela gave them a tour of the ship. They crawled through the busy fuselage. An overhead bin above the navigation station fell open and a bundle of Talk-Talks spilled out. Kevin leapt back and shrieked. The Talk-Talks mimicked him, all of them waving their furry little arms and shrieking.

"Space monkeys!" Kevin shouted.

"Space monkeys!" the Talk-Talks repeated.

Sheela sighed at the interruption.

Justin cautiously approached them. "Orange primate"

"Deroo, Deroo, Deroo," they repeated as they perched in various bins around the cabin to observe the newcomers.

Ryan and Kevin looked through the various bins, shelves, and rigging. Justin fiddled with the gadgets he found scattered around.

Drew noticed Sheela staring out the cockpit into the cornfield. "My father was here once."

Drew found himself beside her. Even sleep-deprived and fried up like a piece of bacon, Sheela was alive and unguarded unlike any human he'd met. Apart from the tangled hair, beat-up flight suit, and gun, he could easily imagine who she had been before her war. Waves of longing and sadness and fear and hope lapped against him as if he were her shoreline. He blinked, and he was no longer looking at Sheela.

He was looking at his mom.

That's who Sheela reminded him of. That's who he saw in her black jacket with a streak of grease across her cheek. She was looking away but then looked up at him and smiled like the picture on his dresser—the one he kept laying face down. He blinked again into Sheela's blue eyes. She was looking at him strangely. Drew looked away.

"Can we fly?" Kevin dropped to his knees. "Please, that would be flipp'n amazing."

"I'm sure you've flown in ships far newer than this," Sheela said.

"You really don't know where you are, do you? Has Drew not shown you around?" Kevin asked.

"No," Sheela said, looking to Drew. "But he did say you're all trained warriors, ready to join the resistance. So I assumed you have ships."

The boys looked at Drew, who said, "What I meant was we can handle anything you throw at us. We're a . . . primitive society. But we are warriors."

"Good. I can only use fighters at this point." Sheela looked at Justin. "Engineer? The cruiser needs immediate repairs."

"That's you, Jus!" Kevin nudged Justin forward. Justin dropped the gadgets he'd been discreetly toying with and reported to Sheela with a cockeyed salute.

As Sheela went through the repair list with Justin, Ryan grabbed Drew and held on tightly. He hadn't stopped shaking his head and blinking since entering the cruiser. The unshakable local legend was shaken.

"How is this possible?"

Drew smiled and shrugged. "I always knew something more was out there. You guys just never listened."

"Why does she think we're warriors?"

"I don't know. She needs our help, and I told her we're here."

"I hope you know what you're doing," Ryan said.

"Everyone to me," Sheela said. She explained the parts she'd need them to retrieve. It turned out their worlds—some technological advances, creatures, and interdimensional travel notwithstanding—were remarkably similar.

Justin bounced with elation. "We can go to Willy's junkyard tomorrow. It'll have everything we need!"

"As liaison, I say we get the cruiser back in the barn," Drew said. But what he really wanted was an excuse to fly.

"Everyone hold on to something," Sheela said as she dropped into the pilot's seat. The cracked leather creaked as she settled. Her hands washed over a bank of switches. The engines hummed again, pulsing through Drew like a rapid heartbeat.

Kevin shouted a high-pitched, "Yeehaw!" from the back as the ship lifted off.

Drew stayed next to her.

"You're touching my chair."

"I'm just looking."

"You haven't flown before. Have you?"

"Not one of these."

He noted how carefully she moved the wheel and how calm she looked. Flying was second nature. They hovered across the clearing and in through the open barn doors.

"If you need another pilot, I'd be willing to learn."

"Just make sure your team retrieves the parts we need."

Before they landed, Drew knew his goal was to be the

pilot. His world had been preoccupied with groundings, growing up, and death. *This* was what he wanted.

Just as they began to touch down, the engine suddenly died. They were all launched into the air as the ship fell two feet to the planked floor. Sheela hopped out of her seat as the others picked themselves up. "That'll be fixed tomorrow! Everybody off!"

They exited, and she showed them the barn basecamp she and Drew had set up. The dark, musty-smelling space softly beeped and blooped from the radar and radio station. Talk-Talks scurried among the rafters, chasing the bats. The open area was shadowy but filled with blue and green blinking lights and luminous cables snaking along the floor from low humming power bricks to the radio, satellite dish, a makeshift lab, and a stack of crates filled with gadgets.

While his friends explored the barn, Drew took a closer look at the lab. Four crates, two on each side, were stacked as table legs with an old, cracked windowpane as a tabletop. Sheela had found the window at the back of the barn somewhere and placed a muddy yellow light below to shine up through the window. On the window's surface were rows of various plants in petri dishes. She'd rigged an apparatus above the table that suspended a boxy device with a lens connected to a large screen—a microscope.

A wolf spider the size of Drew's hand scurried around a small terrarium. Blue-white electricity sparked across the lid to keep the frantic spider from escaping. A handwritten note beside the tank said "Slore?"

She had dissected several other insects and their bodies lay open in a row: a praying mantis, cockroach, and a hornet. Drew saw a moleskin journal open beside them, full of carefully written symbols and runes.

"I want to know what I'm up against." Sheela was suddenly beside him. "Your dimension has life I've never seen before." She nodded at the scurrying wolf spider. "But that concerns me."

"Yeah, they bite really hard," Drew agreed. "What's a slore?"

Sheela was about to speak when the boys interrupted them. The others were still beside themselves, pointing and running from one station to the next like a toy store.

Drew pulled them beyond the doors to show them why they hadn't seen it all before. He told them about the Oren wall and the projection disks. From just outside the doors, the barn looked dark and empty.

Drew finished with the Oren overview and handed the tour off to Sheela. She led them to the loft radio station. "We have a dimension dish on the roof scanning for any signal from my brother or any of my other commanders. They are spread throughout different dimensions, all waiting on my word. Kevin, I'll need you monitoring that day and night." She tossed him a black box the size and shape of a Walkman with a red, sweeping circular light on the casing. "This is a palm comm. Keep it with you. You'll get a green signal light if the dish gets a good signal. Keep talking. They might not be able to always respond, but they may hear you. Notify me immediately."

Kevin held the receiver to his mouth like a microphone and did his best radio announcer impression. "Kevin, Kevin Gadoy coming to you *live* from Warfield's haunted barn. I'll be playing all the classics for you Dimension Warriors out there, so don't be shy. We want to hear from you with your favorite requests."

Sheela allowed a brief smile. "Very good."

She turned to Justin. "Engineer, you and I need to finish repairing the coupling between the cruiser's primary accelerator and the rear thrusters. You're in charge of our scavenger hunt tomorrow."

She turned to Ryan. "I need your speed and knowledge of the area to plant portal seekers." She showed him a crate of palm-sized dishes, like aluminum flowers, with blue blinking lights at the center of the dish. "Plant them high and switch them on. They're crucial for our mission," Sheela said.

Ryan dug through the transmitters and then looked around him. "I'm sorry, what is our mission and why are you here?" he asked.

Sheela frowned at Drew. "You didn't tell them?"

"I was getting there."

Sheela directed them to sit on the surrounding crates. Drew shoved his hands in his pockets and leaned against the side of the ship, eager to see their reactions. "Buckle up."

Ryan shot him an amused grimace. "Sit down, Shipley."

Sheela started from the beginning about the other dimensions and her own world, Orel. She told how someone had defied the council and found and opened the hidden gate, a portal to the Outer Darkness, guarded by the Graystar Sentinels. She told of the star-eater, the worm from beyond space called Malgore. He escaped through the gate with his creature horde and sent forth a parasite across the dimensions that controlled everyone above a certain age.

Sheela and her brother acted fast and managed to help young ones from every dimension escape and come together to form the Dimension Warrior Coalition. She explained how they were being hunted by astro gremlins and slores and captured by their own parents to become food for Malgore.

The boys were very quiet. Sheela got to the end and Ryan

slowly raised his hand. His brown eyes were dark and troubled. "But why is Malgore chasing you? Why are you here?"

She beckoned them into a huddle and spoke just above a whisper. "I have something Malgore needs to destroy us all. And it's the only thing that can destroy him."

The boys all leaned in and watched as Sheela reached deep into her flight jacket and removed the small copper key with a row of blue glowing dots along the shaft. It fit in the palm of her hand. The blue light gently pulsed, illuminating their faces against the darkness.

"This is the key to the Polar Starship. It's an ancient ship, constructed with long-forgotten technology, and it houses a Polar cannon, the only weapon that can destroy his Necrobeast. I was told it can create its own gateways and is faster than any ship ever created. The legend is that Polar was used long ago to lock Malgore away in the Outland and seal off the gateway. It is the only thing he fears and the only thing that can save our worlds now."

"And your dad—he hid that ship here, in Warfield? Ryan asked.

"It was too powerful a weapon and my father feared it would tempt others to use it for domination and destruction. He wanted to promote peace among the dimensions."

Justin blinked, quivered, and licked his lips. "I assume it's big. Where would he hide something that big?"

"Up your butt," Kevin muttered.

"Up *your* butt and around the corner," Justin fired back, and they shoved each other.

Sheela said, "Malgore continues to conquer worlds with his ever-growing army, and my Dimension Warriors cannot hold him back. If I don't get this ship, all is lost."

"How do we find a flipp'n starship?" Kevin asked.

"The key is pulsing blue, which means the ship is close—very close. But I'm sure he hid it behind a portal. The portal seekers will help us find the gate and access the ship. The seekers will also tell us if any astro gremlins or slores come through the same way I did. I don't think they followed me, but we'll want to be sure. This is all why we must connect with my brother, Bash. I need him and the other warriors to come here. I can't pilot the Polar Starship alone."

"What about us?"

They all looked at Drew, and Sheela cocked an eyebrow. "What about you?"

"Teach us . . . to be Dimension Warriors. So we can help you."

She shook her head. "You want no part of this. Trust me. I'm only here to get my ship and leave before Malgore finds your world."

Drew frowned. "But we can help."

"Deroo, Deroo," the Talk-Talks whispered from the rafters.

"This isn't your fight." She put the key back in her jacket. "But I can use your help while I find my ship. Will you all help?"

Justin scrubbed his glasses and looked up at the cruiser. "I'm still not convinced this is actually happening, but yes."

"Heck yes—" Kevin suddenly sucked back his gum and nearly choked to death but waved a hand to indicate he was in.

Ryan spun one of the portal seeker dishes on his finger like a basketball. "The three of us are on portal seekers, Kevin's calling Bash, and Justin's fixing the cruiser. What's Drew doing?" Ryan gave Drew a wry smile.

"He's my liaison."

"Like your boyfriend?" Kevin screwed up his face.

"No!" Drew said.

"What's a boyfriend?" Sheela asked. She looked at Drew, saw him blushing, and shrugged. "The sooner I get my ship and go, the safer you will all be."

They'd talked long into the night about their plan and would start first thing. They were going to tell their parents they were building the treehouse in the woods and would be out there until the end of summer. Some nights they would need to camp out. They mapped out a circle around the town of where to plant the seekers and then, according to Sheela, they could pinpoint the Polar.

Drew took Justin's walkie-talkie and shoved it in her hand. "If you need anything, just press here." He showed her the talk button.

She nodded and clipped it to the backside of her belt.

He stepped backward through the Oren wall and Sheela disappeared. The barn looked dark and vacant. The only thing to reassure him it hadn't all been a dream was the dish poking through the rooftop.

Chapter 8

The Slore

The Necrobeast was docked in the Orelian dimension, clinging to Orel by a long, slimy umbilical. Its groan shook the planet as it opened its chasm mouth, displaying teeth the size of buildings and a tongue that writhed like a great snake. Orel was a tangle of colossal, majestic trees, their intricate roots bound to form the planet and their wide canopies stretching nearly to the atmosphere. The Necrobeast sucked the planet's resources, water, and wildlife as astro gremlins, stationed on Orel, fed the umbilical. Around the beast were small cruisers, once a part of Orel's Golden Fleet. They were crewed by men and women now under Malgore's control. The fleet sat in formation, awaiting orders.

Aboard the Necrobeast, Malgore's massive form crawled through the blood-lit cave of the main deck. The walls pulsed and gleamed with veins, for the main deck was built into the creature's brain. Astro gremlins scurried here and there, trembling in terror as Malgore passed. People, adult men and women, sat at stations with blank stares.

A gremlin approached Malgore but stayed away from the clawed tail dragging behind him. Malgore peered through the narrow window. Orel was there, a beautiful city of trees.

"My little darling, Sheela, escaped. Where did she go?" Malgore's guttural voice echoed through the chamber.

"We know not, oh king. We've released your slore scouts into every dimension. One of them will find her."

Malgore glared through the port window, poised and brooding. "We must find her before she finds the ship."

Back on Earth, a sparking hole yawned in the sky over Warfield. It spat a black and bloody pod, like a rancid egg, flaming through the atmosphere. The egg missile struck the southern end of town in the scrap metal section of Willy's junkyard. The shockwave shattered car windows and blew loose trash against the rusted chain-link fence.

Steam billowed from the crater and the van-sized egg glowed and crackled with heat. The previously stacked tires melted in chocolate rubber pools around the crater's edge. As the egg cooled it began oozing, and a creature hatched, breaking through the slimy shell.

A pack of junkyard mutts bounded over heaps of scrap metal and slid to a stop, hackled and growling at the thing breaking its way from the booger-shelled egg. The creature scuttled from the crater and beneath a pile of garbage. The three dogs nervously rounded the undulating mound, whining and glancing back toward Willy's office trailer.

A thin, pale extremity sprouted stiffly from the trash pile and rose four feet high, coated in a gooey membrane, its long body glinting in the perimeter lights. The tip of the pale thing opened to reveal a gentle-looking eye with a wide, black pupil, like that of a cow. It blinked at the dogs and made a cooing sound from down below the trash.

The dogs drew near, snarling and snapping so the eye closed and ducked down out of sight. The dogs moved in for the kill when a clawed arm shot from beneath the trash, glinting in the moonlight. It speared the closest dog. The mutt screeched as it was yanked beneath the surface of the trash. The other dogs went to bolt, but it chased them and made quick work.

In its resting state, it looked like a giant arthropod. Its shell was shiny black, like a black widow, but it hunched and walked like a crab. It stretched each clawed leg and flattened itself like a cockroach. It studied one dead dog and then rearranged its own body, its exoskeleton clicking and grinding until it was vaguely the shape of the mutt. It waddled around the yard, practicing on four legs.

The screen door on the trailer by the office squeaked and slapped shut.

"What the hell's go'n on out here?"

Willy was big and stocky. He had a greasy mullet and sideburns that curled under his chin and upward into an impeccably trimmed goatee. He wore a stretched hoodie and baggy sweatpants, wielding a twelve-gauge shotgun in the brazen, sloppy manner of someone who'd had too much to drink. "Turk! Bilbo! MC Hammer! Where you at?"

He smelled burnt rubber. Willy pumped his gun with a loud *click-clack!* and stumbled off the steps into the yard. He was about to shout when one of the dogs limped out of the darkness.

"What happened, boy?" Willy began when he realized the dog wasn't his and it was . . . shiny. "Hey, who are you?"

The dog paused, still shrouded in shadow. It seemed to

be looking at him. Willy looked back.

"That's it!" His patience was gone. Suddenly, the dog stood on its hind legs. It cracked and clicked into a misshapen man—the shape of Willy.

Someone might have heard a shot that night if they had been near the junkyard, but Willy was always shooting opossums, skunks, and racoons. His brother was Deputy Grimes so he could do what he wanted. And even if they strolled over and looked through the chain-link fence, all would have seemed well because even after what sounded like a scream, a figure the shape and size of Willy was strutting around the junkyard wearing a hoodie and sweatpants. He might have stumbled and wavered on his two legs, but anyone would have assumed he probably just had too much to drink. And anyone who saw would have walked away believing all was well in Warfield.

The slore flattened out again, finished eating Willy, and scuttled about the junk yard. It cleaned up, shoving one dog though the orifice on its belly while hiding the others beneath a junked car for later. It explored its new surroundings and tasted the air with a long, forked tongue. It had been sent, like its many brothers and sisters, to search for the young one, Sheela Vestril, but it didn't taste her yet. It did catch the faint scent of Talk-Talks, but this didn't excite the slore. It tasted many other interesting scents to explore and mimic while it hunted for Sheela.

The red-light sensor blinked on its back, sending and receiving signals with its gremlin handler. It crept to the fence and cut through with its razor claws. Then it made its way into the trees and across the canopy toward town.

Chapter 9

Secret Missions

Drew didn't want to sleep and paced his room instead. He had the walkie, his thumb caressing the talk button, but he never got the courage to radio Sheela. He thought about her world and the other Dimension Warriors. He thought about flying the cruiser and about what the Polar Starship would be like when they found it. His brain was bursting.

He paused by his dresser, where the framed picture lay face down. He glanced at his door to make sure it was shut and looked back to the frame. "There's more out there, like we thought. Her name is Sheela and she's from this whole other world. I'm helping her and I might get to fly a ship. I want to fly that ship so bad . . ."

He reached out to raise the picture but pulled his hand away and pushed her from his mind.

The sun finally rose above the cornfield, and Drew anxiously waited for his dad to leave for work. Steve had been working weekends for a while. They bumped into each other in the hallway and exchanged awkward mumblings. Steve gave him instructions to clean the garage and patted him on the shoulder. It almost became a hug but didn't, and then he left.

After Steve drove away, Drew ran into his parents' bedroom. His mom's things were as she'd left them when they'd taken her to the hospital for the final time, but he didn't think about this and even held his breath against the familiar scent. He went into one drawer and found his favorite shirt. He grabbed shorts, shoes, and socks. He turned before leaving and quickly grabbed a pair of underwear. Drew shoved the clothes in his backpack.

He met Ryan behind the house. Ryan was in his baseball uniform but had his bulging pack of portal seekers. "These dang things won't stop beeping. Had to hide 'em in my trash can."

"I hope Kevin and Justin aren't having a problem planting theirs," Drew said.

They divided the portal seekers into two backpacks. The two grabbed their bikes and were about to start off when they noticed Kristen, Missy, and Sonetta watching them from Kristen's porch swing.

"Where you two going?" Kristen asked.

"His game," Drew thumbed at Ryan.

"What's in the backpacks?" Sonetta pressed.

"Baseballs," Ryan called back.

"Aren't you grounded?" Kristen asked through a smirk.

"I'm allowed to the game," Drew said.

"What about yesterday?"

"What about it?"

The boys shoved off down the street.

"We saw you last night!" Missy shouted.

"Missy, shut up." Kristen shoved her off the porch swing.

They glided out of the court, cut through the park, and took the new bike path across the bridge, taking a shortcut to the ballfields. They huffed it up the hill behind the middle school, standing up on their bikes and using the weight of the packs to push down on their pedals.

They planted a seeker in the trees behind the Safeway grocery store. They planted another one on the roof of the school and were forced to hide behind a faded green HVAC unit as the janitor passed by below them.

They made it to the ballfield before anyone had arrived. The morning sun glinted off the bleachers and backstop. They skidded in the gravel, ditched their bikes against the fence, and got to work. They climbed up the ladder on the side of the announcer's box and planted one seeker on the roof. The dish had tripod legs that sprang out at the base and opened like a blooming flower, beeping softly.

"Drew?" Ryan said. "Have you thought about this?"

"All night."

"Is this a good idea, us getting involved?"

"What are you talking about? This is our destiny!"

"Our destiny?" Ryan gaped at him. "Gremlins, slores and . . . Malgore."

Drew shrugged.

"This isn't one of your daydreams or stories. This is real," Ryan said. He left Drew and descended the ladder. Drew chased after him.

"What do we do? Pretend we never saw Sheela or her ship? Forget we now know there are other worlds? I don't know why, but I've always known something bigger was out there, that there was more to life than just getting old and dying." Drew followed Ryan to the dugout. "Whatever's out there is better than here."

A few vans pulled into the parking lot and players piled out to head for the field.

Ryan yanked his bat from his bag and practiced his swing. "It's just like you said. There's no going back. You staying for the game?"

"No, I've got to make sure Kevin and Justin planted their seekers." Drew spoke low. "Meet us at the barn as soon as the game's done. We gotta find that starship."

Ryan nodded, spat into the dirt, and kept swinging.

The Warfield legend played his worst game that day. He struck out for the first time and later hit a pop fly that dropped right into the catcher's mitt. As pitcher, he walked four batters before being switched out for Bradley Shellhouse.

As Ryan sat in the dugout, he could see Big Jake fuming and hear his teammates grunting about their playoff chances going. He could see parents frowning from the stands. But it all faded to the background until all he could hear was the soft beeping from the announcer's booth. He spat again and sat there while everyone whispered about him.

Drew biked through downtown where the strong smell of water and chemicals wafted from the car wash. It was a sleepy summer Saturday, and the old-timers were leaving their breakfast at Jack and Ray's to go settle outside Pete's Barber Shop for the day.

Drew met Justin coming out of the library.

"I didn't sleep," Justin announced. He had a stack of books in his canvas tote bag. "I got Miss Tara to open up early so I could look at the microfiche newspaper articles."

"And?"

"Nothing. No anomalies. I just looked between 1955 and 1983. We could spend days or weeks going through it, but the first pass yielded no results."

"Well, Sheela's father was here at some point. There has to be some proof."

"I agree, and he's probably not the only one who's ever . . . visited."

"What books did you find?"

"Just some stuff on superstring theory and wormholes."

They talked as they rode through the Safeway grocery store parking lot. Justin trembled excitedly, twisting and swerving dangerously close to parked cars. "I want to know everything. What does her world look like? How does their technology work? Why have we only just learned of other dimensions?"

"Other people have to know. Think Area 51, alien abductions, the Bermuda Triangle, and *Unsolved Mysteries*. Now at least there's an explanation for all the weird stuff."

"And the technology! It's so ancient yet so advanced!" Justin sheepishly revealed he'd swiped the blinking screwdriver and taken it home with him the night before.

Drew felt he could soar. "See, *you* get it!"

"Get what?"

"That this is amazing. It feels like our destiny. Right? Ryan's all concerned about . . . you know, all the other stuff."

"Oh no, I'm terrified," Justin said.

They found Kevin sweaty and flushed on the south side of town. He'd mounted a seeker on the scarecrow's hat in the Griffin cornfield and planted one at the top of a tall pine tree on Owl Hill. He had the palm comm in his bag and swore he'd spent most of the night calling out to Bash and the other Dimension Warriors.

"Layton Garret and his friends asked me what I was doing. I told 'em to fudge off and chug spit."

"They didn't see the seeker. Right?" Drew asked.

"Nope . . ." Kevin rode along beside them, quiet. Too quiet.

"Kevin?"

"No way! I mean . . . I don't think so. Ah, fluff a duck, maybe."

"We'll replant it later. We have to rendezvous with Sheela." Drew pulled the walkie from his backpack. "Sheela, we're on our way. Over!"

They heard static before they heard, "Deroo, Deroo." Several Talk-Talks were fighting over the walkie.

"Interesting," Justin said.

"What?"

"They didn't repeat you. They recognized you."

The boys arrived at the barn. Ryan had just gotten there, his gray baseball uniform covered in mud splatters. He slumped wearily on his bike.

"You're early," Drew said. "Where's the mud from?"

Ryan lifted his head off his handlebars and smiled. "They called the game in the seventh inning because we were losing so bad. Told my dad I was coming out to work on the treehouse and some of my team tried to follow me. I doubled back and rode through the drainage reservoir to lose 'em."

Drew dropped his bike by the barn and put a hand on Ryan's shoulder. "I'm sorry."

"It's only baseball."

They stashed their bikes in the corn, opened the barn doors, and stared in. It appeared empty and quiet all the way to the back.

They passed through the Oren wall and into their secret

HQ. Something bubbled in the lab, and snow crinkled from the loft radio station. Shafts of sunlight spilled down on the cruiser, highlighting its muscular armor and retrofitted parts. Tools blinked and beeped on the dusty floorboards below the cruiser, and bundles of wires hung down from its undercarriage. She'd gutted one rocket and its components were strewn about.

Talk-Talks scurried about, whispering, "Deroo, Deroo."

The boys entered in reverent silence. It was all more beautiful than Drew remembered. He tingled and felt light, and while he tried to play it off, he couldn't help the tears. He wiped them quickly.

"Sheela?" he called.

She didn't answer.

They searched the cruiser; it was empty. The loft station was empty as well as the lab, the crates, the corner stall, and the eaves. They went out back and checked the roof and surrounding shrubs, but she was nowhere.

Drew felt panic. *Did someone find her? Has she been attacked, or taken away, or arrested? Have I failed her already?*

"Drew!" She startled him, coming up behind him from the pines. She was wrapped in a large piece of torn cloth, and her pale legs, shoulders, and arms were bare. She wore the bronze key on a chain around her neck. She was still dirty but had tried to wash herself in Hopkin's Creek. The scar beneath her eye showed bright pink. She had her snub nose pistol in her left hand while her right hand held the corners of the blanket shut at her chest.

"Sorry!" Drew shouted and the boys turned toward the barn. "We tried to call on the walkie!"

"I know, the Talk-Talks snatched it after you left. Did you mount the portal seekers?"

75

"In strategic locations around town," Drew said, as if he mounted seekers all the time.

"Excellent! Let's get started!" She ran into the barn, and they followed.

"Sheela, wait!"

"Wait?"

"If we're going out looking, you'll need to wear these." Drew pulled the clothes from his backpack. "They're gonna be a little big but . . . uh, I think they'll work."

She grabbed them and climbed aboard the cruiser. Drew turned to find the others looking at him.

"Were those . . . her clothes?" Ryan asked.

Drew nodded.

Sheela returned wearing a black *Terminator* T-shirt and jean shorts. His mom hadn't been much bigger than Sheela, so the clothes almost fit. Drew gulped and gave her a thumbs up as she tucked her laser pistol into her waistband at the small of her back. She then pulled the key from around her neck and scrambled to the loft.

They gathered around the radar screen and Sheela switched it on. "Okay, the seeker on the roof will connect with the seekers you planted. They'll create a readout of the sky and give us the ship's location." The screen flickered to life and blue smudges of light formed. "There's your village," she said.

"Warfield?" Drew asked as they crowded around. The splotches took on vague shapes, and soon he could see what they were—the movie theater, the strip mall, and the car wash. Pulsing dots faded into view like stars and moved up, down, and across the map. They were people and cars.

"The red dots are the seekers." She pointed to the various dots around the perimeter of the map.

"Where's the Polar?" Drew asked. "Shouldn't we see something that big?"

As the seekers swished across their section of the map, a large shape pulsed, washing out the entire screen. Every light in the barn dimmed and the radio station wobbled and wailed.

"We pinged it," she whispered.

"Was that it?" Justin said.

"Yes."

"Could it be in space?" Drew asked. "Like through a wormhole?"

"No, he just hid it somehow, but it's there!" She looked back at them. "We need to get the cruiser working. We need to get up there! He'll have left a gateway to it."

They all climbed down from the loft and followed Sheela to the ship to help with repairs when they heard voices coming from outside. The boys froze as Sheela spun toward the doors and pulled her gun.

"The girls," Ryan said.

"Friends or foes?" Sheela asked.

"Neither," Drew said. They heard the girls arguing. "They won't come in. Just wait a minute—"

Then the doors slid back, and sunlight poured in.

Chapter 10

Willy's Junkyard

They stood in plain view of the girls amid the secret base and with the cruiser glinting in the sunlight behind them.

"Hello?" Kristen called out. As Drew's eyes adjusted to the daylight, he saw Kristen, Sonetta, and Missy peering in.

They waited for the girls to scream or pass out at the sight of the ship, but they stood timidly just beyond the threshold. They were in their neon-colored bathing suits with soccer shorts and towels.

Sheela whispered in his ear, "They're just young ones. They must be safe."

Drew shook his head.

"See, Kristen! I told you! They're not here!" Missy growled. "You just made us walk all the way across the stupid cornfield to a stupid haunted barn for nothing!"

"We passed three 'No Trespassing' signs," Sonetta added.

Drew quietly got down beside Sheela. "Don't shoot."

"I have to shoot if they see us."

"They won't. They think the barn's haunted."

Kristen scanned the entire barn, her eyes sweeping right over them. She muttered, "I know Drew was out here. And last night, there was a bright thing in the sky, over the barn. I saw it."

"Yeah, well, I think you're losing your marbles," Sonetta said. "And I don't want to get in trouble for trespassing."

"I think she wanted to corner Ryan in the barn," Missy said.

Ryan blushed. Kevin suddenly hugged him and whispered, "Kiss me, Ryan." Ryan shoved him off. Drew waved at them to stop but not before Kevin bumped his head on the cruiser and cursed.

Kristen looked back. "Quiet! Did you hear that?"

Everyone stiffened as Kristen stepped to the doorway, her toe crossing the threshold. Her gun hummed. Her finger hugged the trigger.

Drew prepared to tackle her when he heard snowy whispers coming off the radio station behind them. The static danced through the eaves, refracted off the tin roof, and stirred the swallows. It was faint and ghostly.

Kristen froze at the sound. Missy grabbed her arm. "We are going, now!" Kristen didn't fight as Sonetta and Missy dragged her back from the threshold.

Sheela took her finger off the trigger and Drew exhaled. He smiled at the others until he saw it—a Talk-Talk trundling across the barnyard, chasing a butterfly. The girls spotted it. It spotted the girls. They screamed. It screamed. It ran for the barn but looked to be running at them.

The girls turned and bolted right into the barn.

They passed through the Oren wall, screaming and jumping as the Talk-Talk ran between their legs. It furiously changed colors and screeched while waving its three arms. They watched as it ran between Drew's feet and scurried up into the ship's undercarriage. They stopped screaming, but their mouths remained open as they looked around blinking.

Finally, Kristen stepped forward and pointed at Drew and the cruiser. "Ha! I'm not crazy! That's what I saw last night—"

Sheela shot all three of them and the girls dropped like dominos. Missy knocked the lab table over, freeing Sheela's collection of bugs.

The boys all screamed.

"Whoa!" Drew jumped in front of Sheela.

"You said they weren't friends," Sheela said.

"They're sort of friends. They're girls."

"Are th—they dead?" Justin stuttered.

"I just stunned them, like I did to Drew when I thought he was a gremlin."

The Talk-Talks emerged from under the ship and behind the crates. They explored the girls, licking at their hair and stealing their hair clips and scrunchies. They summersaulted across the girls' stomachs until Sheela came near and shooed them away. She kneeled beside Kristen, checking her pulse.

"Chuck a duck, what do we do with them?" Kevin said. "We're in deep sugar!"

"Sonetta's mom's a lawyer. She's gonna file charges for sure!" Justin said.

"How long will they be out?" Drew asked.

"An hour," Sheela said.

"If we get the cruiser running, we can move everything out of the barn, wake 'em up, and they can claim they saw stuff and we just pretend we have no idea what they're talking about."

"Or do we trust 'em?" Ryan said.

"Cause Kristen has the hots for you?" Kevin asked. Ryan grabbed him in a headlock.

Drew looked at the girls, sprawled out on the dusty floorboards. More people equaled more complications. "No way. This is a top-secret mission. No adults and no girls . . . except Sheela."

"They seem tough—especially their leader," Sheela said.

"We don't need 'em," Drew insisted.

Sheela nodded. "As my liaison, I'll trust your judgment. Kevin, guard them and keep trying to get my brother. The rest of us go to the scrapyard." Sheela holstered her gun.

Kevin saluted and then chased after a Talk-Talk, trying to retrieve one of Missy's neon pink scrunchies. It squealed and hissed at him.

The rest of them ran and pulled their bikes from the corn. Drew felt the clock ticking as he gave Sheela Kevin's electric blue Mongoose. They all shoved off down the overgrown gravel driveway, and Drew realized Sheela wasn't with them. He stopped and looked back to see her jump on and crash in a red cloud of dirt.

She waved them on. "I'll get it," she called out. She tried multiple times, mowing over cornstalks and rolling into a ditch full of cracked paver stones. She picked herself up while the boys waited.

Justin eyed his watch. "The girls'll wake up before we can fix the ship."

Sheela got a running start and leapt on, but her front tire wedged between two rocks. She went over the handlebars and into a tangle of rusted barbed wire. She was preparing to make a fourth attempt when Drew jumped in front of her.

"We can walk."

Sheela grabbed up the bike, refusing to look at him, and shoved past.

"Can we at least help you? We're running out of time." She sighed and nodded, but Drew grabbed her bike. "And if we help, can you take us with you?"

"Into the war?"

"Why not?"

"You'll never make it."

"And you'll never get there without this bike."

She glared at him through her greasy hair. "I'll train you, but you're not leaving with me."

"To be continued," Drew said. He waved the others over and they stood on either side as she mounted and then began pedaling. They held her at her shoulders. "That's it, faster," Drew coached. Forty yards down she pedaled faster than they could run. They let her go and she kept going.

"Now wait for us!" Drew shouted.

"Can't. I don't know how to stop!"

They found Sheela crashed at the bottom of the driveway where it connected with Pal's Run. The run was a one-lane road cutting between the farms.

"You step back on the pedal to stop," Drew said as they rode past. She jumped on and sped after them. She overtook them and sided with Drew.

"We don't have these on Orel."

"You don't say?" Drew smirked. They both pedaled faster, edging out the other for the lead.

"You can't come with me. It's too dangerous. I need warriors, not kids."

Drew huffed. "You're a kid too. And how do you know

82

I'm not a warrior?"

"Because your world is at peace."

"I can fight."

"You can?"

"Yes!"

"You could kill a gremlin or a slore?"

"Yes!"

"And you would leave your friends?"

"They'll come too. I'll convince 'em."

Sheela shook her head.

"Can I fly the cruiser?"

"No!"

They stayed on the backroads, and Justin urged them to pass through the old cemetery. "Sorry, Drew, we're low on time."

"What's wrong with the cemetery?" Sheela asked.

"Nothing," Ryan responded.

Drew tried not to look at the gray regimented headstones or at Sheela. He pedaled hard until they were ahead of it. They stayed out of town so as not to be seen, but the time was costing them. Justin rode up beside Sheela and cleared his throat a few times.

"Yes?" she asked.

"How do you travel between dimensions?"

"Each dimension has its own portal."

"Why do you speak our language?"

"Why do *you* speak *our* language?" Sheela said.

Justin thought about that for a moment. "Amazing. There must have been contact at some point. Maybe we went to you, or you came to us . . ."

Justin continued peppering her with questions. Does your world have naturally breathable air, or do you wear oxygen masks? Why the separate dimensions? What was a dimension? Sheela answered every question the best she could, and Justin was more dissatisfied than when he'd begun asking.

Because it was a workday, no adults were on the outskirts of town. They rode across Watkin's Park, and Sheela continued to take in the alien planet, her blue eyes aglow with wonder. "It feels so peaceful here."

They saw a group of boys throwing baseballs at the park, and Ryan cursed under his breath.

"Who are they?" Sheela asked.

"My team."

"Team?" Sheela said. "They're with us?"

"They can't know. Keep riding," Drew said. "As your liaison, trust me."

"Ryan!" one of them called.

"I'll catch up with you later!" Ryan shouted to his team. He glanced behind and cursed again. "They're getting on their bikes. They're gonna follow me."

"Ryan, you got to lose 'em. We can't compromise Sheela," Drew said.

Ryan nodded. "I'll meet you back at the barn." He flipped his Huskies ballcap backward and jumped his bike down a hill and into the woods.

The baseball players peeled off after Ryan. The plan had worked although they were down the fastest member of their squad, the one who could jump the fence and outrun the junkyard dogs.

Drew led them through the giant drainage tunnel. Stagnant water sprayed up from their tires and the hiss echoed off the corrugated walls.

Justin checked his watch. "We got to move!"

"We're almost to the junkyard," Drew said.

Willy's was in sight, and they rode along the fencing to an overgrown spot where someone years before had cut a hole in the fence.

They ducked in and underneath an old motorboat. They crawled around below the motor and stared out across the labyrinth of junked cars, scrap metal, and stacked appliances. All looked clear.

Drew turned to Sheela. "Get your gun ready. We'll need to stun the dogs if Willy lets 'em out."

They army crawled from under the boat and up behind the skeletal remains of a jeep. Justin scrubbed sweat off his glasses and shoved them back on his face.

"We're looking for a riding mower. Cover me." Justin was shaking as he got to his feet and stayed low, running from one aisle to another like a soldier expecting to be shot. "It's here!" he squeaked.

They crouched and ran for his spot. There it was, ten feet away, a tan Craftsman 4500. And it didn't look that old. "The ignition switch'll work for us," Justin said.

Sheela handed Drew her gun. "Keep a lookout. We'll get the switch." She pulled some beeping, glowing tools from Drew's backpack and the two of them left Drew by an old dishwasher.

Drew found himself studying the gun with its blue, dotted lights along the short, bronze barrel and the smooth, polished grip like wood. He wondered how it worked, how old it was, and what battles it had seen. The humidity and whisper of crickets began to lull him into a haze.

The junkyard was so quiet. Drew looked about. Normally Willy was kicking around, scavenging for parts to sell or shooting groundhogs with the same shotgun he threatened to shoot trespassers with. And his dogs—where were they?

That's when Drew spotted movement on the far side of the junkyard around the tires. It was one of the dogs. He looked closer and realized it was a dog he'd never seen before.

He made sure the gun was primed with a daze charge and moved to get a better look. It must have been a new stray. It was jet black and shuffling between the piles of tires so it was never in full view. It waddled like it was injured and appeared deformed. Drew placed his hand on the washer to peer over, but he felt something thick and sticky. He pulled his hand away, and a long string of purple slime came away with it. He flicked his hand, and as he did, he dropped the gun. It disappeared in the weeds.

Drew dove down and felt for it, but he couldn't feel it. He looked back for the dog. It was gone. He went back to the grass, combing his hands through the crab grass. The dog could be running at them from the east, behind the row of wrecked semis, and he'd have no gun to protect them.

His heart raced as he tore at the grass. He surveyed the junkyard again and went back for the gun, but something stopped him. He'd seen something that wasn't there a moment before. He looked back up. Thirty yards away, peering back at him from behind a crushed Buick, was one of the junkyard mutts. Only his shaggy head was visible. It must have been standing on its hind legs on the other side of the car. Drew slowly continued feeling for the gun without taking his eyes off the dog.

Sheela and Justin were yanking at the engine and making way too much noise. Drew waited for the dog to bark and bolt for them, but the mutt just kept looking at him. Drew's left hand found the gun just beneath the washer, and he brought it up and took aim. The presence of the gun seemed to interest the dog. It raised its head ever so slightly.

"Just stay put . . ." Drew whispered. And then the mutt did something that froze Drew's blood. It raised a paw and waved at him. Without thinking, Drew waved back. Then it used its paw to beckon him.

"We got it! Let's get out of here!" Sheela grabbed his shoulder excitedly and Drew jumped with a violent start. She saw him aiming and dove down beside him. "What?"

"Look!" Drew said and pointed at the Buick. The mutt was gone. Justin crouched, his bag full of scavenged parts.

"It was right there, one of the junkyard dogs."

"Then let's get out of here." Justin scrambled down beneath the boat.

Drew looked back, searching the yard. "What?" Sheela asked.

"It . . ." Drew remembered the sleeping beauties in the barn. "Never mind." They army crawled down beneath the boat and through the fence.

They were making great time. Drew felt good. He was proving himself to Sheela, not just as a liaison to the uncharted tenth dimension but as a potential Dimension Warrior. He'd even reasoned away the waving dog. Maybe it had escaped from the circus or something. He jumped his bike off a curb and rode along without holding the handlebars. He kept going, standing up and acting like he was going to stand on his bike seat.

"What are you doing?" Sheela said.

"In our dimension, we call that showing off," Justin said. "And we're gonna be late if he keeps it up."

"Let's take the woods. We can show her our tree fort on the way by!" Drew dropped back down on his seat and veered off the road. "This way'll keep us out of town!"

They collided with the woods and low-hanging summer foliage and burst through into a world of green. Drew pumped his brakes and coasted down the low sloping hill. He and his friend were the only kids who rode their bikes through the woods. They'd learned the narrow paths and knew how to duck every low branch. They'd even raced through the forest at night with minimal injuries.

"It was going to be the best tree fort *ever*," Drew had just explained their previous greatest plan ever. It sounded childish now, and Sheela's continual smirk didn't help.

"We even started setting up booby traps!" Justin said proudly.

"Booby traps?"

"You're gonna want to duck." Drew pointed out twenty yards of tightly strung fishing line, nearly invisible across the dappled, shady path. "We call that trap the headless horseman."

They ducked under it and jumped their bikes over a leafy hillock. Drew tried to stay ahead of Sheela, swerving expertly around and between the close trees. They passed below a giant, bone-white sycamore tree leaning so far over that several thick roots were exposed. Drew kept expecting it to fall and was hoping it fell on the Big Boys when it did. He looked back. Sheela was studying the tree so that she nearly rear-ended him.

"Big, huh?"

"No. On Orel, my home world, we have many great trees. They stretch up forever, so big we build our cities in them. I've never seen trees so small."

"Oh . . . well, our old fort is right up ahead."

Drew smelled the cigarettes before he saw them. He came flying around an outcropping of honeysuckle and by then, it was too late. The Big Boys were lounging on their bikes around what would have been their future tree fort. Drew hit his brakes, but not before slamming into Jimmy's second, Billy.

Chapter 11

Big Boys

Drew and Billy pitched off their bikes and landed in a raspberry thicket.

Drew's left leg throbbed, but the pain melted into panic, his brain racing. He felt a hand take his elbow and hoist him up. He winced, expecting a punch, when he saw it was Sheela. She was chuckling.

"And you were supposed to teach me how to ride?"

Drew looked down at Billy. The pale, freckled boy, head closely shaved, still lying blinking among the overgrowth.

Jimmy looked delighted, ignoring the crash and flashing them a toothy grin. He comfortably flexed and straightened his back. "*There's* my guy!" He glanced at Sheela. "Who's your friend, Drew?"

Sheela sized them all up and fixed on Jimmy. "Friend or foe?" she asked.

Drew didn't respond. He was searching for a retreat.

"I'm a friend," Jimmy cut in, "but that wasn't very friendly, knocking Billy over." None of the other Big Boys went to help Billy. They remained on their bikes as Billy clawed his way out of the weeds. He charged at Drew, but Jimmy rolled between them. "Hold up." He nodded at Sheela. "Who's the girl?"

"His pen pal from Arizona," Justin squeaked.

"Pen pal?" Jimmy made a face. "Well, pen pal, sorry you're gonna have to see this." He dismounted and flicked out his kickstand.

"So, they're foes," Sheela said to Drew.

Jimmy gestured behind him at the tree and the pile of ash where the Big Boys had made a bonfire of the materials for their future treehouse. "You guys like what we did with your old fort?

"Deal with them and let's keep moving," Sheela said coldly.

Jimmy smiled even wider. "That's a great idea. *Deal* with us, Drewy."

Drew clenched his fists and felt the blood hot in his face. The helplessness and humiliation were worse than any coming pain. Jimmy approached, and Drew took a desperate, half-hearted swing. He stumbled off balance as Jimmy snatched him in a headlock and spun him toward Sheela. From his bent position, Drew could just see Sheela's face. She wasn't afraid or angry or shocked. It was far worse. She wore a grimace of disappointment, her brow knit with confusion.

"Pen pal," Jimmy said to Sheela, "Drew and I are gonna show you our secret handshake. It's called the sleeper."

Drew fought to break free. He felt Jimmy's arm tighten around his neck.

Sheela knelt in front of him, bearing the expression of

one who just received socks for Christmas. She reached around for her gun, but Drew hissed, "No."

She stood upright and backed away. Drew struggled until the spots appeared across his vision, and he felt blackness wash over him.

He woke up on his back. Justin was shaking him awake. "How many fingers?" He always held up three and switched them to two. Drew turned his head and saw the Big Boys riding away on the mountain bike trails Drew and his friends had worked hard to create. They'd tossed their bikes into the brambles.

"Where is she?"

"She grabbed the gear and asked me for the short cut back to the barn. I told her how to go through town."

Drew sat up, his head spinning. Justin helped him slowly to his feet. Drew found his legs and waded into the tangled thicket. He fished Justin's bike from the weeds and thorns and then did the same with his own.

"I'm sorry I didn't help you," Justin said.

"It's my fight."

"What do you think Sheela's gonna do?"

"Ask Jimmy to be her liaison."

"She still needs our help—"

"Not mine!" Drew kicked his bike, cracking his shin on the crossbar. He cursed as he lifted the bike up and shoved off. Justin rolled along behind him.

"Just go back to the barn, Justin. She still needs your brains."

They rode out of the woods and into town. Justin continued following as Drew pedaled harder. "Justin! Stop following me!"

"No! I'm not supposed to let you feel sorry for yourself.

Ryan said."

The two sped uptown. "Ryan can take my place!" Drew shouted. He drifted out into the street.

"Drew! You'll get hit."

"I don't care."

"You're being an idiot."

"So!" He was. He swerved long before the oncoming car came within striking distance. He couldn't even properly kill himself. He was too weak and useless for anything.

Drew outran Justin on his way into town. He spotted Deputy Grimes's police car parked a few blocks up on Main Street. The red and blue lights were flashing. He should just tell the deputy that a girl needed help and leave this whole thing to the adults. Sheela might be safer. She needed real help. He was just a stupid kid, the stupidest kid who'd ever lived. But his final act as liaison could be turning her in to save her. People probably also needed to know there were other dimensions out there. Or maybe he'd just stay quiet and hide out in his room while his friends helped her.

Drew was so distracted by self-pity he almost ran over Sheela's blue Mongoose. It lay on the sidewalk with the front tire spinning. He slammed on his brake and looked around. He didn't see Sheela, but he did notice people looking toward the alley between Jack and Ray's and the Book Alcove used bookstore. He looked again at Grimes's squad car and noticed a scorch mark on the bumper.

Justin skidded up behind him. "Where is she?"

Drew dropped his bike and ran for the alley. The alley was empty, but he could hear Grimes's booming voice.

Drew sprinted around the corner to find Grimes yelling at a big red dumpster. He had one meaty hand on the butt of his service weapon. Grimes was coffin-shaped and topped off with a wide-brimmed hat that always cast a menacing shadow over his icy blue eyes. Sweat broke through his tan uniform, outlining his broad, muscular back. "Come out, *now!*"

Drew glanced back to see Justin peering out from the alley, wearing a mask of terror. "*Come out!* I'm counting to three and then I'm dragging you out!" Grimes barked. "One!"

Justin retreated and Drew was moving backward to follow him.

"Two!" Grimes stomped toward the dumpster. "*Three!*"

Drew heard his own small voice speak out. "Deputy Grimes?"

Grimes looked back through his shadow. His face was firetruck red and sweaty. "Get outta here, kid!"

Drew backed up but forced himself to stop. "Is there a girl in that dumpster?"

Grimes faltered. He wasn't accustomed to conversations going beyond "get outta here." "She shot something at my car. Now *get!*"

"I'm Anne Shipley's son."

"I know." Grimes's voice softened some.

"That girl's not from here. She's . . . my cousin. Can . . . can I talk to her, please, sir?"

The Deputy approached and Drew imagined himself being thrown into the back of the squad car. Grimes's voice was low. "You got ten seconds or you're both gonna get it, and I want to know what she shot at my car."

Drew went and climbed up to peer over the side. He saw Sheela crouched and shivering in the corner, her gun clasped in both hands.

"You gotta come out."

"The adults are everywhere," she whispered. "They found me."

"They're not bad adults. Please, he's gonna arrest us if you don't come out."

"I'm waitin'!" Grimes growled.

Drew climbed inside the dumpster and dropped beside Sheela. He looked into her wild eyes. "I'm still your liaison. Can you trust me?"

"They're gonna take me to him."

"No, they won't. Can you switch your gun off?"

"I need it."

"That's it!" Grimes yelled.

"Sheela!" Drew grabbed her by the shoulders.

"If you're wrong, all hope is lost."

"I'll protect you. I promise."

She ran her thumb over a button on the grip and the blue dots went out. Drew took the gun and shoved it in his pocket. Grimes's shadow passed over them, but Drew didn't break eye contact with Sheela as he helped her up. Drew climbed out first and helped Sheela over. She was shaking and gripped his arm tightly, refusing to let go.

Drew turned toward Grimes with her still clamped on him. "This is my cousin from Arizona. She has panic attacks."

"What'd she shoot at my car?"

"A bottle rocket. I gave it to her. She didn't know what she was doing."

Grimes leaned in and snatched the dazer from Drew's pocket. "What's this?"

"A toy."

"Heavy toy." Grimes tried to check it the way he'd check his weapon, turning it over in his massive hands. "What the heck?" he muttered. He pointed it away from them and pulled the trigger. Drew winced but nothing happened. Grimes tossed the dazer back at Drew.

"It won't happen again, sir. I promise."

Grimes glared down at Drew. "Stupid kids."

Chapter 12

Girl Problems

After Grimes stormed off, Sheela snatched her dazer from Drew and ran her thumb over the grip, reactivating it. She ran to the brick wall at the back of the used bookstore and peered out from the alley. Drew came up beside her as they watched Grimes get back in his car and speed off. A moment later, Justin snuck around the corner and came running.

"Holy moly, I thought you guys were toast for sure!"

"You guys gotta get going!" Drew said. "Justin, show her back to the barn."

Sheela was rooted to the ground, staring wide-eyed out at the adults as they passed by on Main Street. "There are too many of them."

Drew checked his watch; they were out of time. Then he caught sight of something and had an idea. "Justin. Go get the Destroyer," Drew said.

"The Destroyer?" Sheela gasped. Justin nodded and ran

off. Drew stood beside Sheela as she crouched low, squeezing her pistol tightly.

"I'm sorry they betrayed you, your parents," Drew said. She couldn't speak but shoved a lone tear from her eye. A minute later, Justin returned with a foot-tall soft ice cream cone, a chocolate and vanilla swirl with rainbow sprinkles.

"Try this. It'll help," Drew said.

"What is it?"

"The Destroyer," Justin said. He tipped it to her. "You lick it!"

She looked at them suspiciously, keeping an eye on the street for any oncoming adults. She took a quick lick. The sugar struck her brain, and she snatched it from Justin, lapping at the sprinkles and melting sides. She stopped only for periodic brain freezes.

"Feel better?" Drew asked. She nodded. "See that guy?" Drew pointed across the street at the Jimmy Cone with its teal-painted stucco structure and green-hooded awning. The owner, a burly black man with kind eyes and a round face, was handing another child a cone through the window. "He gave that to Justin. He didn't capture him. Justin came back. No one here is under Malgore's control."

"Yet," Justin said with a shudder.

They moved to the end of the alley and Sheela scanned Main Street, carefully studying each adult. She took note of the woman pushing the baby in the stroller and of children playing freely and even holding the hand of an old man. She finally tucked her gun into her waistband and hid it beneath Anne's shirt.

Drew retrieved the blue Mongoose and walked it to her. "You guys are late. Justin, get her to the barn." Drew picked up his bike and went to ride in the opposite direction.

"Where are you going?" Sheela said.

Drew stopped and looked back. "Ryan'll be a way better liaison." Drew shoved off down the sidewalk. He was passing the Chuck E. Cheese when Sheela rode up beside him.

"You're still my liaison."

"I failed you."

They pedaled on, and each time he tried to pull ahead she caught up. "You came back."

"I still failed."

"You're failing me now."

Drew eventually slowed, relenting, and they all rode on together. This time, he kept his butt on the seat. No more showing off.

Sheela was fascinated by the adults. As they passed the park, she slowed to a stop and watched a man with his little girl. He was waiting for her at the bottom of a slide, and she squealed as she slid into his arms. He tossed her in the air, kissed her, and held her close to him. She rested her head on his shoulder.

Drew and Justin wheeled back around and parked beside her. "Sheela, we need to go." She watched as the dad carried the girl from the slide to the jungle gym. "He's not gonna hurt her. He loves her," Drew reassured Sheela.

"I know." Sheela shoved off.

They arrived at the barn and ditched their bikes in the corn. When they ran in, they found the girls still on the floor with several Talk-Talks curled up around them, sleeping.

Soda cans were lined up on a haybale at the back of the barn, and a cluster of holes were scorched into the barn's back wall. Sheela stepped over the girls and picked up a squat, boxy laser rifle off the floor. Kevin emerged from a stall at the back of the barn carrying a busted egg crate. A young

Talk-Talk was perched on his shoulder, whispering, "Bigger target, bigger target."

"Oh, hey guys!" He hid the crate behind him.

"Shooting practice?" Drew asked.

Sheela examined the gun and then looked back at the cans. All four of them stood, untouched. She frowned.

"The gun's defective!" Kevin said. Sheela took aim and squeezed, blowing up every can on the ledge. They exploded in sprays of creamy bubbles. She handed Drew the rifle.

"We'll work on marksmanship later. Let's get in the air." She and Justin headed for the ship, Justin carrying the backpack of scavenged parts.

"Did you get anything over the radio?" Drew asked as Kevin inspected the remnants of the blasted can.

"Ah, nope, but I did reenact the 1989 World Series voiced by Kermit the Frog and burped 'The Star-Spangled Banner.'" Drew gave him a look and Kevin shrugged. "What? They're kids like us. From the sounds of it, they probably need a laugh."

"And what about them?" Drew nodded at the girls.

"Not a peep, and I managed to get all their hair clips back.

"We're gonna move the base and then leave 'em on those beach chairs on Kristen's deck. Then we'll pretend we've been playing video games in Justin's basement."

Kevin pinched Drew's cheek. "You are so smart. Yes, you are!"

Drew shrugged him off. "It's critical the girls don't ruin this for us. They cannot see this stuff ever again and we can never give up that it's real."

Kevin saluted.

"Get back to the radio. I'll be helping on the ship.

"Where's Ryan?" Kevin asked.

"Getting chased by half his baseball team."

Kevin started climbing the ladder to the loft when he paused. "Wait, what?"

Drew checked on the girls, making sure they were breathing and placing handfuls of hay under their heads for cushioning. He ducked beneath the cruiser's undercarriage and found Justin's legs dangling from an open compartment. He looked up into the ship's guts. Justin held back a tangle of clear cables with different liquids running through them while Sheela used a red-glowing torque wrench to remove the thick bolts around a galvanized panel. She tossed the bolts to Justin. Each one fell and bounced from his hands so that he had to frantically snatch and hold them to his chest.

Sheela lowered the heavy panel to Drew with one hand, but the weight took him by surprise and nearly caused him to fall through the hatch. The removed panel revealed an entrance to a duct system. Sheela tied her wild hair up, and they followed her, crawling single file into the duct. She gave them the tour, explaining how polar plasma made interdimensional travel possible.

They located the hover jets, and Sheela ripped out and showed them the fried coupling. She explained the hover technology as Justin flooded her with questions. They fixed the several sections using the replacement parts from Willy's. The technology was somehow intuitive. The engine looked ancient with runes and symbols carved into the conduit. Sheela explained how the cruiser's engine told a story of her people, of their advances and explorations. She knew which parts her grandfather had installed versus her father.

Drew could see Justin was as much in love as he was—almost. Time ceased as they crawled about, patching damaged wires and cables with bandages that melted and restored the flow of electricity and plasma. They finally crawled from the bowels of the ship, smeared in grease.

"Should we test her?" Drew asked with a smile.

Sheela nodded, and they raced each other for the side hatch. They reached the opening at the same time, yanking each other back. Sheela laughed; it was the first time Drew had seen her laugh. She shoved Drew against the entry and looked into his eyes, about to say something but losing her words. Drew felt weird and electric. He blushed through his greasy cheeks, and Sheela released him awkwardly.

"Guys! I've got something!" Kevin screamed. He was perched in the radio loft and got up to lean over the edge. As he did, the headset connected to the radio jerked his head back. The radio toppled off the shelf and crashed. "Frankfurters!" Kevin shrieked. He rushed to prop up the radio.

Sheela left Drew standing in the small archway and scrambled up into the loft. The radio was dented on one side and a smashed LED light flickered. Sheela squeezed in beside Kevin and pulled the headset jack out of the plug so the signal played through the speaker. Drew and Justin climbed up behind them so they all could listen.

It was garbled and snowy, but something was there. "I was just about to respond!" Kevin said and went for the talk switch. Sheela grabbed his hand.

"Don't," she hissed. She turned up the volume on the receiver.

"Icto bor, icto bor tul." The voice was barely audible above the interference. Everyone shuddered as it repeated, low and scratchy.

"Who is that?" Drew finally asked.

Sheela frowned, listening. "General ShinFar. It's a recorded message. He's speaking to me, saying I won't escape him." She snorted. "He wants me to turn myself in."

"You know . . . gremlin language?" Justin asked.

As she listened to the message, a satisfied smile formed. "They're trying to scare me out because they don't know where I am."

"You know him?" Drew asked.

Sheela remembered what appeared to be a happy memory. "Oh, yes. I vaporized his brother." She looked at Kevin. "Make sure to stay off this transmission. If you'd responded, they would have been here within hours."

Kevin looked wide-eyed from Sheela to the radio and back. He pushed away from the station, but she placed a hand on his shoulder and shoved him back. "I need you here. Just don't respond to any gremlins . . . or slores."

Drew heard some Talk-Talks repeating something down below. "Before they see us— before they see us—hurry."

Drew spun around.

The girls were gone. The Talk-Talks were rolling about, repeating, "Before they see us!"

"No! They're gonna blow our cover!" Drew jumped from the loft. He hit the ground hard but got up and limped out the door. The girls were sprinting across the yard to the cornfield.

Ryan was riding up the dirt road. "Ryan, stop 'em!" Ryan pedaled hard and cut them off before they reached the corn.

"We can explain," he began, but the girls nearly ran him over. Sonetta kicked his shin and Missy shoved him. Ryan fell trying to get off his bike. Kristen paused, looking like she might help him.

Drew caught Kristen by the arm and she slapped him

away. "You kidnapped us and shot us!"

"We're calling the cops!" Sonetta shouted over her shoulder.

Missy grabbed Drew by the collar. "You're all aliens!" She punched him and Drew saw stars. By the time his vision cleared, the girls were long gone.

The boys rushed into the corn and found the girls running toward Kristen's house. The girls sped up and screamed, "Somebody help us!"

"We're not gonna catch 'em. We're in so much trouble!" Kevin whimpered.

Then a powerful downdraft washed over the corn. The cruiser soared over them and lowered itself right in the girls' path. Sheela appeared at the hatch. "Round 'em up!"

The boys caught up to the stunned girls. Drew took Sonetta's arm and she panicked, trying to bite him. Kevin and Justin tackled Missy and they fought them on board. Drew pulled Sonetta on behind them, pleading with her, "We're not gonna hurt you!" She wasn't buying it.

Ryan had Kristen in a bearhug and hoisted her up as she struggled against him. He stumbled with her to the hatch and Sheela helped yank her in. Sheela shut the hatch and ran for the cockpit. "Drew, with me!"

She dropped into her seat and he dove into the seat beside her. Sonetta was smacking the back of Drew's head while Missy pounded on the hatch. "Let us out!"

Drew looked out the starboard side of the dome cockpit. He saw activity in his neighborhood. Cooper was barking and Kristen's dad had come out on the deck, shading his eyes to see the thing sitting way out in the corn.

"We're gonna be seen!" Drew said. "Get the Oren wall on!"

"It's warming up. We're not invisible yet!" Sheela flipped switches and tried to get them off the ground.

"Can we hover at this height?"

"If our new parts work."

The cruiser hovered low enough in the corn that only its back emerged above the wavy tassels. "Stay low and head for the woods!" Drew pointed ahead of them.

Kristen charged Drew and pummeled him with her fists. "Sheela, go!" Drew ordered.

Sheela pushed the throttle and the cruiser launched forward, mowing down corn in its path. Drew, Kristen, and everyone else went airborne and landed in a heap at the back of the fuselage.

"Where after the woods?" Sheela called back.

Drew was in a tangle of arms and legs. Kevin was on top of him and Sonetta's foot was in his face.

"Up!"

Chapter 13

A Whole New World

Drew felt a rush as he was pressed to the floor. Sheela was smiling "Here we go!"

Drew looked toward the cockpit as sunlight poured in, the rays so bright the crosshatch disappeared. Then the cruiser tilted away from the sun into nothing but deep blue sky.

"I guess it's fixed!" Sheela said.

Drew shoved his way from underneath the pile and rushed to the cockpit. He clung to Sheela's armrest and looked out, awestruck. The others crowded around. Sheela banked them to the right. The town of Warfield twinkled up, its church steeples and traffic lights catching the sun. It looked so small.

Sheela soared through the golden, sunlit clouds. She swept down over the Blue Ridge Mountains and over the next few towns, circling back to Warfield.

"They'll see us!" Justin gasped.

"The ship has an outboard Oren wall," Sheela explained. "It didn't used to. Bash and I installed it to help with sneak attacks and rescue missions."

"So we're invisible now?" Drew asked.

"That's affirmative."

"Take us through town." Drew smiled and looked back at his friends.

They swept down below the tops of the store fronts, just above the cars. To people on the street a strong gust of wind tossed about newspapers, blew off hats, and caused Deputy Grimes to spill coffee down the front of his uniform. Sheela slowed and hovered over the Druid Movie Theater. They watched as people looked about for the source of the squall.

They took her from the north side of uptown to the outskirts of the south side, over Willy's sprawling junkyard labyrinth. They took her east to the schools. They flew over and stole the flags off the flagpole of their middle school. From up here, Drew's universe looked so small. They'd toured his entire world in ten minutes.

Kristen shook herself. "Who else knows about this?"

"No one. It's a secret and if you tell anyone, I'm gonna let Sheela vaporize Cooper."

Sheela glanced back at Kristen with a smirk.

"Sheela, let's drop 'em off," Drew called back.

"No way," Kristen said. "Take us back now and I'll let Missy tell everyone in town what's going on." She looked at Sheela. "Vaporize my *dog* and I'll vaporize you!"

Sheela chuckled. "I like her."

"What do you want?" Drew asked.

"To help find that ship," Kristen said.

"Speak for yourself. I want to go home!" Sonetta said.

Kristen turned on her. "This is the craziest thing you're ever gonna experience—ever—in your whole life. You want to spend the rest of your lame summer by the pool while these *boys* get to fly around helping alien girl?"

Missy and Sonetta looked at each other and Drew watched them concede as his heart sank. The *girls*? They couldn't be trusted and they'd get in the way. His goal of joining Sheela and leaving felt further away.

"If you're all in, let's get started!" Sheela said. "You're about to see the greatest starship ever created. Drew, switch on the seeker station." He looked dumbly at the dash controls and Sheela gave him a subtle nod to a yellow switch. He flicked it, and she took the Polar key from around her neck and plugged it into a slot. "Commencing the seeker lock." Blue and purple searchlights appeared through the domed window, sweeping over the town and up into the sky.

"What are the lights? Drew asked.

"The seekers you planted," she said. "Call out when you see a portal. The seekers will reveal it. It'll look like a patch of purple against the sky."

Everyone joined in, crowding each other to see who might spot it first.

"How's it hidden?" Justin asked.

"My father probably created a fold, a space between dimensions. It was the only way to ensure no one ever found it. We're looking for the gate to that fold."

Sheela rotated the ship slowly, but as they all peered up and out, no purple doors glowed against the blue. Sheela stood and shoved through them back to the radar station. They followed her, bumping into each other. A 3D readout of the town appeared on the dish and a large blue pulse flashed—the Polar Starship hiding in plain sight.

"I don't understand! It's right in front of us!"

"Where?" Sonetta asked.

"The key shows me it's here, but the seekers aren't seeing a portal."

Kristen leaned into Drew and whispered, "What is alien girl talking about?"

"She's not an alien."

Sheela's breath quickened. She pressed down hard on the throttle and took them in a wide sweep of the town's perimeter. "We must not have a seeker in the right spot. We're missing the gate."

"She's talking to herself," Kevin whispered.

"Where's the door . . ." Sheela flew faster and faster. She swept up higher and higher, circling Warfield. The others looked down as they banked. The whole town was painted over with gridlines and the purple searchlights traced up with transparent fingers into the sky.

They flew around for hours. The others eventually started exploring the cruiser. Kevin and Sonetta found the medical compartment with its healing salve spray foam and instant wraparound bandages. Kevin now looked like a mummy and Sonetta was demanding he stop wasting the supplies. Ryan lowered the ball turret below the ship's undercarriage and jumped down through an irised hatch. Kristen squeezed in with him and the two were stuck, staring down at their town. Justin was in the rear, playing with various gadgets that hung from rigging, and Missy coaxed one Talk-Talk to sit on her shoulder by feeding it sticks of Juicy Fruit.

Drew had remained beside Sheela as she flew them around and around, scanning the golden clouds and deepening purple sky. He'd been waiting patiently for his moment. She hadn't spoken in a while but was chewing her cheek fervently. Behind them, the Polar's ghostly outline pulsed on the radar, mocking them.

"Do you need a break?"

Sheela started and looked up at him. "You're not flying."

"It would help to have another pilot—"

Her glare stopped him.

Missy ran up, several Talk-Talks clinging to her like baby monkeys. She hit Drew in the shoulder and grabbed him excitedly while gnawing on a massive wad of gum. "Justin and I found goggles that help you see through walls!"

Drew caught sight of her Minnie Mouse watch. It was nearly seven o'clock. "Oh crap!" Drew flipped the yellow switch and the blue seeker overlay cleared from the cockpit window. The mountainous clouds in the distance were now bronzed by the setting sun. With the blue tinted window, he hadn't noticed the day disappearing.

"Sheela, unless we want to explain all this to their parents, we need to get everyone back for dinner."

Moans of protest sounded throughout the cabin.

"I'll stay!" Justin called from his small table at the back of the cruiser, deconstructing random gizmos to study their blinking, glowing guts. He wore the goggles he and Missy had found.

"No, you gotta go back," Drew said.

"I don't eat dinner until eight!" Sonetta said.

Kristen poked her head up through the porthole on the floor. "They'll think we're at the pool. Relax, Shipley."

"I'm not going home!" Kevin called from the radio station. "My mom won't check my room for a couple of days."

"Hey! Everyone's gotta go home!"

They all paused to look at Drew. Ryan climbed out of the turret. "This from the kid who always wants us to sneak out?"

"Yeah, well, this is different. This has to stay secret."

Sheela nodded. "I'll drop you all off and continue the search."

"I'll stay," Drew said, and Missy smiled and chewed extra loud.

"K-I-S-S-I-N-G," she murmured in a singsong tone. Drew tried to cup her mouth, but she jerked away and continued whispering the letters.

Drew gave them all their alibis: The girls had been at the pool, the boys, building the treehouse.

Sheela dropped each kid off at their own house. With the Oren wall, the ship was invisible, but they couldn't do it with people around. She opened the side hatch and extended the stairs. They had to make sure no one was looking and, one by one, each kid made a run for it.

Kristen and Drew were last.

Kristen jumped down onto her deck. "Mom, Dad! Back from the pool!" she called through the back screen door.

"I'm serious. I'll stay." Drew eyed the Dimension Warrior jackets in a compartment at the back, each with the patch of the North Star sword and ring of stars.

"Not necessary." She guided the cruiser over Kristen's backyard and up to Drew's bedroom window. He stepped down the stairs and shoved open his window. He looked back at her. Sheela was hunched wearily against the dash controls, bathed in light from the setting sun. She was still wearing his mother's shirt.

"Sheela?" Drew said. She looked back through greasy strands of hair. Her eyes weren't bright blue but heavy and dark, and she was chewing a stick of Missy's Juicy Fruit. "We

110

will find the Polar. I won't quit." He descended the staircase from the hatch.

"Drew!" she called.

He looked back.

"We'll pick up the search first thing tomorrow . . . and your training. We'll see if you Dimension Ten kids are worth your salt." She winked at him. When he didn't move, she nudged the wheel. The ship jerked and he fell off the stairs and in through his window, landing hard on the floor.

He scrambled up and looked out. The ship was gone but the nearby tree trembled from its downdraft.

Training! It shot through him like electricity. He saw Kristen in her bedroom. She smiled at him in the soft glow of her lamp light. She shook her head, bewildered, and shut her shade.

That night, over TV dinners, Steve actually talked. He said how someone had driven a truck through Gladhill's cornfield. The cops couldn't figure it out because there weren't any tire marks and the truck—they thought it must be a truck—hadn't driven into the field or exited.

Steve chewed his Salisbury steak, shook his head, and chuckled. "They said it was a straight line, cut right through the corn for half a mile before the tracks stopped. How's that possible?"

It was the most his dad had said in a while. Then he actually made eye contact and Drew dropped his fork. Steve was really looking at him. "Did you see anything weird today?"

Drew shook his head as he ate his dinosaur-shaped chicken nuggets.

"They opened up the old barn too."

Drew sucked back a piece of breaded chicken and started

choking so bad Steve reached over and slapped his back.

"Anything in the barn?" Drew gasped.

Steve shook his head. "Grimes said they opened it up, but it was empty." His dad chewed a while longer and said, "Want to go have a look at the field?"

Yes! And maybe I can tell you, and you can be the one adult to keep it a secret and help us! Drew couldn't manage a word. His brain was tired and stretched.

His dad nodded. "Well, you're right. Probably not a good idea. I just know it's something your mom would have loved. I'm sure the two of you would have been all over that field."

They finished their meal in silence.

Drew dragged himself off to bed and slept below the dream state, in a deep, dark exhaustion.

The sun was gone and the June bugs pinged off the streetlamps. Jimmy Griffin straddled his bike on the curb in front of Drew's house. The Big Boys had heard about the cornfield incident and were here to investigate. The cops turned them away, but they snuck back in and walked up the long strip of mowed cornstalks. The others had laughed and hocked loogies in disbelief, but Jimmy had walked along silently, thinking.

He'd looked up and spotted Drew's house and remembered the mysterious girl. He remembered she'd been wearing Drew's mom's shirt and a weird, oversized jacket. He remembered her blue flashing eyes. She hadn't been afraid of him. In fact, she'd reached around to her back, like she was going to pull a weapon.

The other Big Boys all went home, but Jimmy drifted through Drew's court. He rode up at sunset, looked around, but didn't see Drew or Kristen or the new girl. He slowly wheeled around the court to go meet the boys uptown. Then he spotted something that made him slam to a stop. His tires slid over gravel. He missed his footing and fell hard. Scrambling to his feet, Jimmy looked back to what he'd seen.

Drew Shipley had appeared in the sky, above his house, standing in midair.

He'd leapt into his bedroom window.

Chapter 14

Dead Friends

Drew slept in, his dreams dark and ocean deep. He'd finally had to swim to the surface and force himself awake. He ran to the barn as soon as his dad left and was still groggy when he found Missy sitting on the lid of an old, sealed-off well. The Talk-Talks were rubbing their heads on her legs like cats.

"You're late and we're missing one of the Talk-Talks," she said, her brow furrowed.

"Missing—missing—missing," they repeated.

"Oh. I'll tell Sheela," Drew said. He slipped in past the Oren wall to find everyone else waiting by the ship.

"You're twenty minutes late!" Justin said.

Sheela brushed past him to the ship. "Let's go!" she said as she threw on her jacket. She assigned them stations as they entered. She came to Drew last and paused.

"Copilot?" Drew said.

She frowned.

"Hey, you said training."

"Not that kind."

They hovered from the barn and ascended straight up into the sky. Drew took the seat nearest to her, observing the ignition sequence and her careful touch of the wheel. As they soared over the town Drew reveled in the smells, the hum of the engines, and the sight of a deep blue horizon. It all felt like home. He wondered if he'd been born on Orel and somehow ended up here.

Ryan lowered the floor turret, opened the hatch, and jumped down inside. "Target practice?" he asked Sheela, sticking his head up through the porthole.

Sheela looked back and smiled.

"This is gonna be better than a batting cage," Ryan said.

She flew them low along the Blue Ridge Mountains, checking the radar for any large living creatures but seeing none. She nodded at Ryan and he discharged the gremlin gutter guns. The recoil pounded through the floor, thudding in their chests. Pulsing balls of red light slammed a bald hillside, and when the clouds of dust cleared, craters remained.

Missy climbed up into the ceiling ball turret and fired up into space. They crowded under the cockpit's window and watched the red balls disappear into the atmosphere. They applauded and high-fived, and Drew caught Sheela laughing with them, but he saw her smile fade as though the happiness caused her pain.

She flew them into a valley and cycled through the gunnery stations. She called out targets: weeping willow, outcropping of rocks, abandoned car. Missy was a natural, hitting every target. By the end she and Ryan were chiding each other, him taunting her from the floor while she rained insults from her perch above. No one else came close to their targets.

"I'm taking bets!" Kevin called out. "Ryan versus Missy!" They emptied their pockets while Sheela brought them back around to the clearing with the rusted car.

Drew felt someone grab his elbow. He glanced back to find Kristen behind him.

"Who are you betting on?" Drew asked, but Kristen tugged him away from the group.

"I need to show you something," she said.

Drew followed her back to the navigation station. The station was partially enclosed, like an arcade flight simulator, and built into the wall where it could retract to make more space. The whole ship was like that with bays and compartments that could fold up and disappear into the wall to make room for other stations or seating. She climbed in and yanked him in after her. They were squeezed uncomfortably in a seat made for one. Instead of a screen, an open surface like a table lay before them.

"I can't believe you figured this thing out," Drew said.

"I might be blonde, but I'm not *blonde*, Shipley." Kristen hit a few buttons and put one hand to a dial. Light poured up from the table and down from the ceiling, projecting a blue, shimmering topographic 3D map in front of them.

"Oh, cool. But we can already see Warfield in the cockpit."

"This isn't Warfield, dummy." She zoomed out, using the dial, and Drew saw they were looking at a planet. A flickering chyron identified it as Orel. Kristen pressed the dial and spun it while Orel rotated. "No, not rotate," she scolded herself for the mistake, as though she were a seasoned operator.

She punched the dial again. Instead of scaling or rotating,

she was now rewinding the map through time. The textured blue projection glitched as it rewound. Suddenly, tiny ships swarmed backward, passing Drew's face. The planet came to life with tiny city lights. Kristen stopped rewinding and hit play.

Drew looked closer. A fleet of incongruent, insect-sized ships were speeding right at him and away from Orel.

"This is awesome," Drew said, reaching into the projected universe like a god.

"Check this out," Kristen said. She zoomed in on the fleet and pressed another button on the keypad. A radio transmission crackled through the speakers behind them. A kid's voice spoke.

Drew laughed. "Sheela's gonna be impressed! What are you learning about the other dimensions?"

"Each one is a small galaxy, *way* smaller than ours, but that's not what I want to show you. Now shut up," Kristen said. "Watch."

Drew listened as a girl spoke hurriedly, her shrill voice popping through the broken transmission. Kristen nodded to the ship leading the fleet and Drew recognized the cruiser. He heard Sheela's voice trying to calm the other pilots. Their ships glowed when they spoke. A pod-like, yellow ship now glowed as it transmitted frantically. More voices. Mass confusion. Yelling and sobbing.

Suddenly, a gigantic mass dropped into the projected map. Drew pulled his hand away as if the thing was going to bite it off. At first glance, it looked like a ship, but then he saw its distorted face, its tiny red eyes and enormous mouth. Kristen zoomed out and Drew saw it was a giant beast. It sprouted thin, spiderlike arms and grabbed the yellow ship. The pilot screamed as a thick umbilical snaked from the beast's mouth and the spider arms fed the yellow ship into it. They heard Sheela yell out.

The black beast vessel fired a volley of sparkling orbs at the fleet. Nearly every tiny ship was hit and sent spiraling and sparking past Drew and Kristen's faces. One ship exploded, their transmission cutting abruptly to static. The other disabled ships were swallowed, their frantic voices disappearing one by one. Sheela's lone voice shrieked, but no one responded. Drew peered from the simulator to the cockpit, where Sheela was directing Ryan on how to hit a moving target.

"How did you find this?"

"It was up when I got in," Kristen faced him in the cramped space. "Drew, are we gonna die?"

Drew realized his heart was slamming his chest and he'd been holding his breath so tightly his lungs were cramping. He had no answer. The fear in Kristen's green eyes and her sharp grip on his arm brought him back.

He forced a smile. "She just needs us to help her find the starship. We do that and this war is over, and we're heroes." His voice cracked on the word "heroes," and he quickly climbed out of the simulator.

Drew found his way back to the cockpit, shaking off the images and screams. It had all felt like a movie or video game. Whatever it was, it didn't feel real. All he knew was this ship, his friends, and this star girl were real. Sheela steered them west, and the cockpit filled with sunlight. Drew closed his eyes and listened to the hum of the engines and laughter. The fear seeped away and he could breathe again. "Who's winning?" he called out.

"Missy, five to three!" Justin shouted. "Kevin owes me ten Slim Jims!"

Drew went up beside Sheela. She didn't look back at Drew but was gazing at the horizon. She was flying them away from the gunnery targets and back across the mountains to Warfield.

"Kristen's figuring out the navigation station," Drew said.

"What did she see?"

"Nothing. Just some maps."

She looked up at him for a moment. Drew tried not to look at her.

Kristen emerged from the navigation station. She stood behind Sheela, wiping her cheeks. Her lips were stiff and resolute. "Hey, alien girl. See the door or gateway or whatever you call it?"

Sheela glanced back. "It's very close. I can feel it."

They flew uptown for one last sweep and saw the Druid's marquee lighting up Main Street. The old theater was showing a cult classic—*Ghost of the Werewolf.*

"Have you ever seen a movie?" Kristen asked Sheela.

"It's too risky," Drew said.

"Come on, Drewfus." Kristen gently nudged Sheela with her hip. "I'll treat."

"I have to keep searching. I'll take you all home," Sheela said.

"No! Sheela, it would be *so* fun!" Missy squealed. She ran into the cockpit and yanked Sheela's arm excitedly. "You have to!"

The Talk-Talk that had snuck into Missy's backpack chirped, "Fun, so fun!"

Sheela yanked away from Missy. "No!" she screamed.

Missy gaped with her hands up. The Talk-Talks hid and everyone else stopped and looked at Sheela. She turned away to the cockpit window, her body rigid as she breathed heavily. "The Dimension Warriors are counting on me."

Drew nodded to the others and they quietly gathered their things and lined up by the door. Drew approached Sheela from behind. "The crew's ready to exit."

He heard Sheela sigh, and her shoulders dropped. She'd removed something from her pocket, a tiny black pill. She weighed it in her hand and, after a second's delay, popped it and swallowed. A second later she peered over her shoulder at Drew. "What's a movie?"

"Alright!" Kristen clapped. "She needs a shower, Drew. Your dad won't be home yet. She'll take one there." Drew tried to protest, but Kristen shoved her hand over his mouth. "*Your* house."

Chapter 15

Ghost of the Werewolf

They parked the cruiser over Drew's house, and he snuck her in through his window. The others went over to Kristen's to call their parents and ask permission.

Sheela paused in his room, looking at the stacks of comics and the model planes hanging from the ceiling.

"I know. It's a mess," Drew admitted.

"That's not what I was thinking," Sheela said.

"What were you thinking?"

She went to his desk and moved some pages about, looking at his sketches of monsters and elves. "I used to have a room . . ."

She drifted and her eyes settled on the small, framed picture on the dresser across his room. She went and lifted it. Drew's mom was wearing the *Terminator* T-shirt. Sheela looked down at the same shirt beneath her jacket. Drew saw her study the young boy in the picture, his eyes bright, smiling wide, throat muscles bulging in a lively giggle. The moment was frozen there forever.

Drew said, "Come on. I'll get you a towel. Kristen's bringing over some clothes."

Drew led Sheela to the shower in the upstairs hallway bathroom. He felt fidgety and didn't know what to do with his hands or what to say. As the two of them crowded into the cramped little bathroom, he also felt self-conscious. Was this a hovel compared to what she'd known back on Orel? She was probably wealthy or high society. She looked about the house while Drew started the shower and showed her the shampoo and soap. He left her as the small yellow room filled with steam.

Drew kept watch for his dad, terrified he might return early. Missy shoved through the back sliding door, one arm holding some folded clothes to her chest. She still wore her backpack and Drew caught a glimpse of a Talk-Talk peering out at him. Without asking, Missy opened his pantry and grabbed some raisins. She opened the tiny box and began handing the furry creature wads of wrinkled fruit.

"That thing belongs in the barn," Drew said.

"Hey, don't talk about Larry that way."

"*Larry?*" Drew screwed up his face at her, and she stuck out her tongue as she handed Larry a pack of M&Ms. Missy then stole upstairs with the clothes. "Sonetta! I need a brush, *stat*!" she hollered out Drew's window.

Sonetta bounded through the door with Kristen's pink Caboodle and a brush. She pushed past Drew and hustled up the stairs.

Kristen entered with the boys. "My dad's okay with us going and he gave me money." She headed up the stairs while the boys turned on the TV and flipped through *National*

Geographic magazines on the coffee table.

Drew anxiously kept watch through the foyer window. "I just don't want her to get caught," he was muttering when Sheela suddenly descended the stairs with Kristen.

Her once grimy skin, tanned by grease and dirt, was fair and pink from scrubbing, and her wild black mane was combed with one side pulled through a neon pink scrunchy. Kristen had tried to cover her scar with base, but it showed through, bright and angry. She wore Kristen's white floral-patterned leggings and a purple T-shirt with a shirt tie holding up one side at her hip.

She wore Missy's white Keds. Kristen had carefully applied peach-flavored Lip Smacker lip gloss and wrapped Sheela's bare wrist with several of Sonetta's multicolored slap bracelets. Sheela looked like a regular '90s girl, save for the scar and the pistol hidden at the small of her back.

The commander of the Dimension Warriors blushed and squirmed uncomfortably. "I'll try this . . . *movie* . . . but then I need to keep looking for the ship—"

Steve's car headlights washed across the living room wall. Chaos ensued in screams and hurried laughter. The kids scattered, running into each other. Kevin fell over the coffee table and tripped Missy. Larry, the Talk-Talk, went flying and landed on the kitchen counter. Drew scooped up the creature and herded them all out the sliding back door. He bumped into Sheela and dumped the Talk-Talk into her arms.

"Do I look like an Earth girl?"

"You look great—not *great*, I mean—you look fine." He winced and ushered her out the door just as his dad slumped through the front door. Drew closed the sliding door and spun around.

"Hey, Dad!"

Steve had a pizza box in hand. "How was your day?" He dropped his briefcase on the couch and lifted the pizza in a tiny celebration.

Drew sputtered to a stop and looked at the box. "Jerry's Pizza?"

Steve looked down at the thin, grease-stained box, hefting it as though guessing its weight. "I thought it was time. She would want us to have Jerry's Pizza again." He meant it as a joke, but neither of them laughed.

"Pepperoni and pineapple?"

"That's right," Steve said, his mouth trying to remember how to smile.

Drew could sense his friends waiting eagerly in the yard, and he felt Sheela watching him. "Uh . . . shoot. Dad, I'm so sorry. I kind of had plans with the guys. Can I go see a movie?"

Steve didn't skip a beat. "Absolutely! More for me!" He chuckled and held the pizza with both hands, unsure what to do with it. "I'll save you some."

"Do you want me to stay?"

"Nah! You've been doing a good job with the house, and I've been tough on you. Get out of here. Go have fun."

Drew lingered a moment and then backed out. He saw his dad enter the kitchen. He made a show of smelling the pizza and groaning with excitement. Drew forced himself to leave, and they piled into the cruiser and flew the two minutes to uptown Warfield. They parked it behind the Safeway grocery store, hidden by the Oren cover, and were careful to exit, checking for onlookers. Before leaving, Drew stacked a few discarded coffee cups in front of the invisible ship's hatch; otherwise, it would take an hour to find it.

The Druid's marquee and tall sign, ringed with bulbous

globe lights, cast a warm glow across Main Street. Teens and young couples lined the sidewalk from the ticket booth to the storefront of Jack and Ray's. Drew could hear people murmuring about the phantom wind gusts and he smiled to himself.

Sheela tensed around the adults, sticking close to Drew and pivoting so that she never had her back to any grownup. A few kids asked who she was, and Drew introduced her as his pen pal from Arizona. He couldn't help noticing the attention she was attracting from some of the older boys.

They walked into the theater lobby and Sheela looked at the crowd in disbelief. "They all look so free," she whispered to Drew. "It reminds me of how I used to be."

"I'll be right back," Drew reassured her as he and Ryan went to the counter to get popcorn.

"Sheela looks different, huh?" Ryan asked.

"What?" Drew snorted. "Yeah, I guess so." Ryan nudged him and Drew tried not to make eye contact.

They found a row of squeaky, reclining seats and sat among the throng of kids catcalling and throwing popcorn.

"Drew, stay with me," Sheela ordered, and Missy whistled as he edged past her in the row. The lights went down and Sheela reached for her laser pistol.

"It's okay. The movie's starting," Drew reassured her. He tilted the bag of popcorn to her. She shook her head and kept looking around. "As your liaison, I'm telling you to relax."

Slowly she settled back into her seat, and soon she was stuffing her face with popcorn and asking questions: What were movies? Why did people watch them? They were finally shushed by irritated adults a few rows back. She jumped several times at scary scenes and grabbed Drew's hand so tightly he thought it might snap off.

"So this isn't really happening?" she asked, unable to pry her eyes away from the screen.

"No werewolves were harmed in the making of this film," Drew said.

She looked at him and frowned.

"Dimension Ten humor," he said, and she grabbed a handful of popcorn and threw it in his face.

Kevin shoved some popped kernels in his nose and blew them at Justin. The two slapped at each other. Kristen grabbed Ryan's hand during a scary scene and held it long afterward. Even in the dark, Drew could see him blushing. At the movie's climax, there were several jump scares, and Sheela screamed and laughed. Kristen and the girls cracked up and were shushed by half the theater.

After the movie they went to Jimmy Cone where Kristen treated them to soft ice cream. Sheela devoured hers and doubled over from frequent brain freezes. They all snuck their ice cream cones into the arcade where they played Skee-Ball. Sheela took to the arcade games, crushing records on Defender, Galaga, and Pac-Man.

The kids laughed and shoved each other. They mocked and moved about, but they never separated. This world-shattering revelation had bound them together. They were a unit and they felt it. They knew they were different from the other kids.

Drew felt it as a warm tingle in his stomach, a magic levity to his mind and mood. He felt like the hero of his own movie. He imagined being followed by an old-style Hollywood film crew. Cut, print, moving on! He walked taller and imagined cameras catching every subtle look. But it was better than being in a movie. This was *real*. He could tell they all felt it, and no matter what happened after tonight, none of them would ever be the same.

At that moment, he was only afraid of one thing—waking up to find out it was all a dream and realizing his reality was being stuck in that tomb of a house, doomed to become a zombie and eventually face real death. But now was not the time to worry or feel guilty that Steve was back at the house, eating a TV dinner while an entire Jerry's Pizza cooled on the counter.

The Friday night haze of sugar, lights, and laughter blinded the whole squad to the growing number of missing dog signs tacked to the telephone poles along Main Street. Drew was so caught up thinking about Jerry's Pizza and watching Sheela transform into an "Earth girl" that he didn't see Jimmy Griffin prowling along behind them, Jimmy's dark eyes drifting between Drew and Sheela.

As liaison, Drew also missed the weird-looking kid—obscured by the darkness and shuffling in the deep shadows off Main Street—wearing a beat-up fedora and Willy's large, ratty coat in the middle of summer. The kid's large clothes were oil-stained and torn, like they'd been snatched from Junkyard Willy's closet.

The kid made soft clicking and crunching noises as he limped. He was hobbling about alone, assumed by onlookers to be physically disabled. He paused only to mimic people. He performed awkward dance moves, waved, and even high-fived no one. A few teens stopped to make fun of him, copying his walk, beating their hands on their chests, and yelling "retard," but the kid didn't seem bothered. He waved from the darkness on the far side of the street and copied them, beating his hand on his chest. This made the teens laugh harder, but eventually they got bored and left.

The hobbling kid in the big jacket ambled past the

grocery store, as if he were on a Sunday stroll, when he suddenly froze. He was a statue for several minutes before a long, blood-purple tongue slithered up through the jacket and waved in the air. The tongue quivered and moved slowly around, the tip pointing like a beacon.

The kid began a slow shamble, making a wide circle around the Safeway. The tongue kept tasting, and he sprayed something from one leg of his grimy jeans every twenty feet. He circled the area, a one-mile radius, five times before the kid clicked and crunched his way awkwardly up into a twisted locust tree at the back of the Safeway parking lot.

Later that night, they pulled Sheela from the arcade. She'd downed three Cokes and a large thing of cheese fries. She'd also attracted a crowd of older boys. They watched her destroy Pete Lusk's score on Asteroids, a five-year standing record. They demanded to know who she was and Kristen, acting as her publicist, kept saying, "Your worst nightmare." Drew had taken her gun before she pulled it out to blast a hole through the Asteroids arcade cabinet. He quickly tucked the gun in his pocket.

Sheela was drunk from the sugar rush, and her pupils were tiny dots from all the glowing pixels. She couldn't stop laughing at Kevin. He was on a roll, knocking down jokes and spasming with sudden and dangerous physical comedy. He toppled headfirst into a trashcan on their way out of the arcade and his thick legs kicked wildly so that his shoes flew onto Main Street. Drew and Ryan shoved the receptacle over and yanked Kevin out. As they slipped away from the larger crowd of kids and snuck back to the cruiser, Kevin had Sheela laughing so hard she began snorting uncontrollably and threw up her cheese fries.

Drew was the lookout, scanning Main Street. When no

one was looking, he ushered them up the alley between the dry cleaners and an appliance repair shop. The Safeway parking lot was out the other side. Drew sighed and relaxed. He'd gotten Sheela out of town safely and unseen. Then Missy grabbed his arm.

"Larry's gone!" she shouted. People on the street looked their way.

Drew power walked to her. "You're attracting attention," he whispered. "Who's Larry?"

She looked up, pouting. "My Talk-Talk."

"Which one?"

"The one with the chunk of ear missing."

"Oh crap," Drew whispered.

They separated and made a sweep of the area. Drew's heart stopped when he spotted Larry, deformed ear and all. The little creature was trundling quickly across the street. Drew made a run for him and snatched him.

The Talk-Talk shrieked, "Deroo!" Then it latched on to his right hand with a big bite. Drew stifled a yell and shook Larry off. Larry ran beneath a parked car in front of the Jimmy Cone and Drew ran for him. He dove to his stomach and caught Larry by one of his three arms. He dragged him out as the creature squealed and clawed at him and shoved Larry into the backpack before anyone could see.

Now back to the ship!

He stood and felt a hand on his shoulder. "Missy, I got him—"

He spun and came face to face with Jimmy Griffin. Drew felt his lungs collapse as Jimmy punched him below the ribs. Drew dropped the bag and Jimmy clenched the back of his neck and hauled him to the sidewalk.

"What's going on, Drew?" Jimmy was jittery and tense.

"What do you mean?" Drew was still trying to catch his breath.

"The cornfield, you jumping out of thin air above your house, that new girl. Bring me in on your secret, or I'll hurt you so bad, dude. I don't even care. I'll do you right here." He squeezed Drew's neck so that the muscles in his back and arm lost power. "I don't like stuff like this. I want to know what the hell's going on."

"Hell's going on . . ." a tiny voice whispered. Drew and Jimmy looked down to see Larry at their feet.

"What the *hell* is that!" Jimmy shoved Drew and leapt away.

"Hell is that!" Larry screamed and darted between Jimmy's legs and up the sidewalk. The crowd in front of Jimmy Cone ran over to look, and while they did, Drew slipped away.

The kid perched up in the locust tree near the Safeway had seen the Talk-Talk too.

Drew found Missy searching the garbage cans beside Jack and Ray's. He grabbed her. "We gotta go!"

"No, I'm not leaving Larry!" she said.

He pulled Missy into the alley. "We'll find Larry later. Jimmy's onto us."

Missy paused and used both hands to twist him face to face. She looked like a stern parent. "Hold on. Drewfus Shipley, are you telling me Jimmy Griffin knows what we're doing?"

"Not yet, but he's getting close."

They snuck around behind the Safeway, keeping an eye out for Jimmy. They saw the stack of coffee cups to the far-left corner of the lot. They sprinted within five feet and felt around until the side hatch slid open. The warm, low-lit interior glowed against the night and startled them. Kristen poked out.

"We lost Larry," Missy whimpered.

They were about to board when—

"Hey!" They all looked to see Jimmy speeding across the parking lot on his bike.

Drew shoved Missy into the ship. "Shut the hatch," he ordered Kristen. It slid back with a hiss.

Jimmy jumped off his bike and headed for Drew. "Where'd she go?"

"Who?"

Jimmy leveled Drew with a sweeping punch. "I'm only gonna ask one more time. What are you up to?"

Drew felt anger rising like bile. It ran hot, straight up his throat. He screamed a battle cry and jumped off the asphalt, lunging at Jimmy and swinging wildly. Jimmy backpedaled, batting down Drew's punches. One of Drew's swings caught Jimmy in the chin, whipping his head around. Drew's knuckles went numb as Jimmy stumbled back.

Drew stopped. The other Big Boys had ridden around the corner. They'd seen the hit and rode headlong toward the fight.

Drew stopped the attack and shook out his aching hand. "Are you alright?" he asked.

Jimmy looked up, his dark pupils dilated like a vampire. He grabbed Drew lightning fast and put him in a chokehold.

"I'm gonna put you out," Jimmy laughed. "You're not gonna wake up this time."

Billy meekly spoke up. "Jimmy. Forget about him, man. Let's go."

Drew felt darkness washing over him. He saw stars and his legs gave out. His hand dropped and then he felt the gun in his pocket.

To the Big Boys, Jimmy was about to put Drew to sleep, like he'd done a hundred times. This time seemed more serious because Jimmy was out of sorts and because Drew had fought back. So, it was a surprise when Jimmy suddenly went flying. The consensus later was that Drew must have hit him with an uppercut or found some inhuman strength because Jimmy soared through the air and landed in a heap six feet away.

The Big Boys watched Jimmy in awe as Drew limped off and disappeared around the corner. When they came to their senses and went to look for him, Drew was gone. Jimmy was out cold and wouldn't wake up for another three hours.

Drew entered the ship's cabin to cheers and applause. Ryan was perched in the ceiling turret and called down, "I was ready to fire a warning shot if things got bad!"

Missy punched him and Kristen shook him by the shoulders. "Hey, dummy, that was pretty cool."

Kevin lifted Drew up, slamming his head on the cabin ceiling. "You must have punched him hard. How did you do that?" He dropped Drew on his feet, and everyone slapped Drew on the back, tousling his hair all the way up to the cockpit.

Sheela was at the controls in her Earth girl clothes. Before she looked up, Drew snuck her gun into the holster hanging off the chair. Her eyes were still sugar wide, and she giggled drunkenly.

"We're missing Larry and we need to keep looking for the Polar," Drew said.

Sheela saluted and burped.

"Are you okay?" he asked.

"Yup." She set it to auto pilot and joined the girls. She

was whispering with Kristen and the others, glancing back at Drew and giggling.

Drew switched on the portal locator to search. "This'll show us Larry, or anything else *not* from our dimension. Right?"

"Affirmative!" Sheela called back.

Something caught his eye through the blue grid—a purple flash from behind the Safeway. It was big and moving fast, but when he looked back, it was gone.

Larry's not that big . . .

They flew a while longer before giving up. "We'll need to find him first thing tomorrow. We can search in teams," Drew said.

No one else was listening to him. "Sheela? Commander?" She glanced his way. "We should keep looking for the Polar!"

When he looked back Sheela was right beside him, blinking up at the grid with growing recognition. She pulled on her flight jacket and held her head, wincing. She looked down at her clothes and frowned, like she'd just woken up to find herself that way. She yanked the scrunchy off and shook out her hair. She grabbed her gun belt off the pilot chair and strapped it on. She quietly moved about the ship, checking and restoring systems.

Whatever had come over her at the movies and arcade had suddenly worn off and she was focused again. She didn't say a word about it and neither did anyone else. They spent another hour looking for the gate and came up empty.

She finally dropped them off at their respective roofs. They were leaving their windows unlocked and memorized consistent alibis. All of them were now working on the treehouse and their parents were proud of them.

Before Drew jumped out onto his roof, he hesitated and

turned to Sheela.

"What?" Sheela asked, looking back from the controls.

"What did you take before the movie? It was like a pill. Right?"

Sheela looked back to the wheel. "I don't know what you're talking about."

Chapter 16

The Right Stuff

They continued the hunt for the Polar gate throughout the weekend with no luck. Sheela was flying by night and training her new squad by day. One morning, as they soared high above the town, she fell asleep and slumped headfirst against the controls. The ship tilted downward and dropped like a rock. Their screams woke her and she pulled up before hitting the Druid. From that point on, Drew posted Missy beside her, talking, tugging, and leaning on Sheela so that drifting off would be impossible.

Drew discovered the more tired Sheela was, the more willing she was to answer questions. "What's that?" He pointed to a bank of switches on the dash.

She huffed and pointed from bank to bank. "Primary controls are there. Stabilizers, thrusters, Oren control, weapons systems, dimension jumper, navigation. These aren't your concern. Just keep a lookout for the gate."

Even as she waved him off, Drew was memorizing each bank and panel, repeating it all in his head.

He also counted the steps in her ignition sequence. Every time she went to boot up the cruiser, she discreetly flicked a switch below the dash and pressed a red button beside the wheel four times at three-second intervals. Sheela was too distracted by Missy's questions to notice him watching.

Several nights later, Drew woke with a start. He had been dreaming about running from something, and it was gaining on him. He shifted to his side and was about to drift off again when he heard mumbling.

"I'm coming . . . hold on . . ." It was Sheela, but his blood still ran cold. She was somewhere in his dark room. He peered through the midnight gloom and saw a soft blue glow just beneath his window.

"Sheela? Are you okay?"

She didn't respond. He crawled out of bed and found she was asleep and limp but for a white-knuckled fist clutching the glowing key at her chest. He went to wake her but stopped. A terrible and wonderful idea struck him.

"Ryan, this is Drew. Over." Drew was in the hallway bathroom whispering into his walkie.

"Dude, it's twelve thirty," Ryan said. "Did Sheela find the gate or something? Over."

"Come over. Over."

"I have an early practice and my dad's driving me to make sure I go—"

"Mickey Mouse has warts."

Ryan sighed.

His three friends arrived twenty minutes later and dropped their bikes in the backyard. Drew beckoned them from the roof. He'd pulled out his dad's ladder and propped it against the house.

"Drew, I need my beauty sleep or I wake up looking like a pale, fat kid." Kevin grunted.

"Hurry up. Sheela needs us!" Drew said. The cruiser's hatch sat open, suspended just above the roof like a dark portal. They followed Drew inside.

"Reporting for duty, Sheela!" Justin called out. "Sheela?" Drew closed the hatch with a pneumatic hiss. He bolted past them to the cockpit. He heard a collective gasp when he jumped into the pilot seat. It creaked comfortably beneath him.

Justin ran to the front. "You can't sit there!"

"Drew, didn't she shoot you for that?" Kevin asked.

"Ryan, tell him that's not allowed!" Justin said.

Ryan took the jump seat beside Drew. "Sheela needs another pilot," Ryan said.

They gathered eagerly as Drew reached below the dash. His finger found the switch. He flicked it and pumped the red button four times. Nothing.

"Need us to get out and push?" Kevin asked.

"Shut up, Kevin." Drew tried again—nothing. He did it several more times, his heart sinking. Justin dove in beside him, but instead of pulling Drew away, he started pressing buttons.

"I've seen her do this," Justin said.

Ryan and Kevin started pounding on the dash while Drew ran through the ignition sequence again and again.

"Start, dammit!" Justin said.

Drew finally smacked the wheel with frustration and the ship hummed to life. The panels, conduit, track lights, and flight controls lit up all at once, and the boys hushed with excitement.

Drew felt a wash of doubt but gulped it away. He reached out and took the wheel. With the other hand, he pressed forward on the throttle and the ship drifted away. They left the roof and floated over the backyard.

"Here we go," Drew said.

"Swings!" Justin said as the cruiser collided with the dilapidated playset, knocking it over.

"Sorry!" Drew said. He was shaking as he gripped the wheel. He felt lost and his brain went blank. He had a sudden urge to jump ship.

"Any day, Drew!" Kevin said.

Drew closed his eyes and took a breath. He sensed the ship, as if his blood pumped through the engine and circuitry and wiring. Then he hit the boosters.

They rocketed over the cornfield and barn and the tops of the tallest pines, the cruiser traveling faster and faster, the engines swelling and drowning out their cheers. Drew screamed with the purest joy he'd ever felt. He pulled back on the wheel and took them straight up at the stars—the stars he'd longed for his whole life. They were at his fingertips now. They would be his playground.

He leveled them out, yanking the wheel and overcorrecting as the ship jerked. He tried to bank left so they could see how high they were. The town twinkled far below. They jetted between clouds under a thin crescent moon, and Drew tilted them straight down. They were pressed back to their seats as screams sucked into their lungs. Drew pulled back on the wheel and they swept through town. The downdraft blew the lids off trashcans.

Then Drew thought of something. "I have an idea!" He took them back out over the woods, over the giant boxelder tree that was supposed to be theirs. He hovered over it and saw smoke rising. Drew could see a campfire, cigarette smoke, and the Big Boys with some girls they'd invited.

"Justin!" Drew said.

"Yes, sir?"

"Turn off the Oren wall."

Justin shook his head. "We need to stay invisible. It would be irresponsible—"

Ryan let out a rare cackle and Kevin joined him.

"Alright, fine!" Justin leaned in on the dash and disabled the Oren wall. "I'm tired of always being the *adult*."

Drew tilted downward, lowering the ship through the canopy. Jimmy and the gang all looked up as the downdraft blew smoldering logs out of their fire and across the ground. On his own, Justin activated the outboard lights, and the cruiser lit up like a mutant firefly. The Big Boys and girls were bathed in blinding light, each wearing a different mask of horror. Drew hit the boosters as they rocketed upward, but just before they launched back into the sky, they saw the whole crew fly back in all directions.

After that, they buzzed the teens making out near the fairgrounds and woke up Bruce Ellis, asleep in the Druid's ticket booth. All anyone would be able to report that night was a flying ball of light. Drew slowed them and hovered just outside of town. The boys convulsed with laughter, trying to high-five and missing each other as they fell from their seats.

Drew's laughter trailed off when the moonlight caught the top of Grimes's squad car cruising toward them. "Doesn't this guy ever sleep?"

Justin killed the lights as Drew pushed the throttle, but nothing happened. The engine moaned. "Justin, what's wrong?"

"I don't know. I don't know. The hover's still on!"

"And the Oren wall's still *off*!" Ryan dove forward and tried to switch it on. He and Justin collided and fell against the Oren controls. The ship disappeared and reappeared, hovering only eight feet over the street.

Outside, the squad car skidded to a stop just ahead of them. Grimes got out. He looked up at them and Drew's heart stopped. The giant officer gnawed on a toothpick as he pulled his gun. The boys were frozen, all twisted up and holding their breath. Grimes stared at them, but his dark eyes drifted around. He removed his hat and looked straight up. He finally holstered his gun, spat out the toothpick, and got in his car. He drove right beneath them, his lightbar only inches away from the cruiser's undercarriage. The Oren was on.

Nervous laughter and more high fives.

Drew showed off by soaring low over the fields, swooping around trees and the occasional farmhouse. He felt very self-important until he saw her, standing rigidly on the peak of the roof, her arms crossed and hair blowing in the gentle breeze. He'd forgotten about Sheela.

"Oooh, you're in trouble," Kevin said.

Drew brought the ship in over his roof and parked it near the chimney. The ship was invisible, but he could somehow tell she'd been standing there, waiting. He shut down and they exited onto the roof.

She approached wearing a deadpan expression, and her right hand rested on her holster.

Kevin shoved Drew in front. "He made us do it!"

She looked at Drew and then at the rest of them. Her voice was low. "So you want to be Dimension Warriors?"

"We can do it," Drew said.

She passed him to the ship. "We'll see," she said over her shoulder as she disappeared into the hatch.

Chapter 17

Midnight

That week, Sheela assigned Missy and Ryan the ceiling and floor gun turrets. She ordered Kristen to chart a course and send her the coordinates. Drew waited for her to give him the pilot seat but instead was ordered to watch the radar, scanning for the Polar gate.

On one mission the cruiser's systems died, the cabin went dark, and the ship rocketed toward the ground. Everyone screamed. Kevin fell from the comm link station and rolled all the way into the back of the pilot's seat. Sheela stood stoic, holding fast to some rigging and studying each person's response.

"Justin, engine failure. Run diagnostics."

"I can't! Please save us!"

"Diagnostics test, please," Sheela said.

The ground flew toward the cockpit window. Justin spun his jump seat toward a monitor on the wall. He flipped a few switches and pressed a button on a keypad. The screen displayed a line moving back and forth across an overhead schematic of the cruiser's modified dual engines.

The screen glowed yellow on his terrified face. "It says the engines are off!"

"Turn them back on, please," Sheela said.

Justin threw a big red switch beside him and the cabin flickered back to life. Everyone, including Sheela, fell to the floor as the ship lifted from the free fall.

From that moment on, no one was safe. Sheela continued to randomly sabotage the cruiser, disabling the turret hatches, Oren shield, navigation, radio, radar, flight controls, engines, and anything else. She even scorched Kevin's butt with a welding stick and ordered Sonetta to spray him with healing foam and patch him up. She called out commands and refused to answer questions. The answer was often in plain sight, and the kids began to push through the panic to stay calm and trust their training.

On one flight, Ryan was perched in the ceiling turret waiting for targets when Sheela tossed a ghost eel grenade up into his lap. It was the actual egg of a deadly ghost eel. The gremlins harvested and outfitted the eggs with tiny, black detonator rings. The detonator could blow right away or be timed, superheating and spraying the acid yoke over everything within a twenty-foot radius. This egg was timed and beeped faster and faster as a red light blinked. When it went solid red, it would explode.

"I got this!" Ryan called down confidently before he bobbled the baseball-sized bomb and accidently dropped it back into the cabin. It went down Justin's shirt. He jumped up and ran in circles, trying to find the bomb as the beeping sped up. Sheela jumped to her feet—the first time she'd looked concerned.

But right before it exploded, Missy tackled Justin and yanked the egg from his back. It was already steaming and bubbling inside. Missy squeezed the detonator ring twice and the beeping stopped a second before it would have killed them all.

Justin fell into her arms and Missy blinked, startled. She'd defused the bomb without thinking. Everyone took a deep breath and applauded. Missy tucked the egg into the front pocket of her overalls and forgot about it. A day later, while her mom was doing laundry, the washing machine disintegrated.

That started a rule of everyone being checked before leaving camp.

One afternoon, they flew directly into a mountain range of thunderheads. The sky was a wall of dark slate. Rain hit the windshield like a million hammers and blinded them. Flashes of lightning lit the cabin and the thunder rattled the cruiser's skeleton. Sheela leaned at the helm, facing back at them. She told them scary stories, old stories passed down through Orel lore.

She told them of star-eaters and the giant serpent that lived in the Red Ocean, of ancient kingdoms where people rode to war on animal-robot hybrids, and of space pirates kidnapping children of the royal court. She told them of the great flying cities and of the old vestiges of a mad inventor who created portal jumpers, bred strange creatures, and constructed time machines. Their bones and structures lay about the Talian desert and in the surf of the Red Ocean still. They all sat about the cabin, listening to her. Missy wore a bulky, gold gunner helmet as she chewed gum. Kristen sat near Ryan. Their hands touched. Ryan withdrew his quickly.

She moved hers closer.

As the sun went down, they would land the ship and check pockets for gadgets, weapons, and anything else not from their dimension. Then they ran home. Sheela claimed she slept at night, reclining in the squeaky pilot's chair. But Drew knew she was lying. He could see the barn from his window. He could see the soft orange rectangle crack open against the ink blackness of the woods. He recognized the gentle gust wash across the corn from the invisible ship. She was still flying night missions.

"Are you flying at night after we leave?" he asked her one morning.

"No, I need my sleep like the rest of you."

"It's just that I saw the barn doors open—"

"Liaison," Sheela took him by the collar and pulled him close. Her voice was low and she locked on him with both eyes. "I'm commander of the Dimension Warrior Coalition. I'll do what I like."

"What if I sneak in?"

She smiled easily. "Then you're disobeying orders and will be shot on sight." She released him.

Missy strolled by. "K-I-S-S-I-N-G . . ."

The next night, Drew lay awake waiting for his dad to fall asleep on the couch. As soon as the living room lamp went out, he went out the window and stole away through the misting cornfield.

He got to the barn and peeked in. The ship steamed and hummed in preparation for takeoff. He slid through the door and tiptoed for the ship. Sheela caught him sneaking aboard and threatened to stun him and discard his temporarily paralyzed body on his roof. Drew tried again, and she pulled her gun and fired a bright blue warning shot at his feet. He was forced to return home. As he cut through the cornfield across a well-worn footpath, he felt the warm gust of the ship as she passed overhead. He saw the faint shimmer of air pass right over his house. He cursed her, knowing she'd done that on purpose.

He did it again the next night and timed it earlier, waiting until she went off into the woods to go to the bathroom. He snuck aboard and hid in the engine room. She didn't find him until she was in the air, but she still dropped him off at his house, holding him at gunpoint as she forced him to jump to his window from the open hatch. He'd cost her crucial searching time.

"My Warriors know how to obey orders," she called out as she shut the hatch.

Drew went back the next night, but this time he snuck aboard and planted himself in the pilot's seat. "You'll have to shoot me and drop me on my roof," he said when she returned from the pines.

Sheela stood over him, gun drawn. Drew squinted and waited to wake up on the edge of his roof. But nothing happened. He opened his eyes. Sheela's hand was on her gun and she said through gritted teeth, "Not a word to the others about what you hear."

He saluted and ran through the takeoff procedure. She watched him quietly as he tried to navigate out of the barn. He bumped one wall as dust and Talk-Talks fell from the eaves onto the cockpit window. He forced himself not to look at her but focused on guiding them through the open doors. Once free of the barn, he launched them out over the corn.

When he looked up, Sheela was gone. He glanced back and saw her sitting at the comm station. She slipped the headphones on and pulled the mic to her mouth.

When she spoke, her voice was deep and strong. "To all Dimension Warriors. This is your commander. You are not alone. There is hope . . . I have located the Polar Starship."

Drew looked back confused and spun his head around again before she spotted him.

She continued, "We're prepping the ship now and are coming for you. Hold fast. Be ready. We will be victorious. Commander Bash, respond, over."

Nothing but soft static.

"Toren Unit, respond, over."

Nothing. She repeated the message from before and continued to ask for responses. She whispered promises and lies into the void, and Drew understood why she'd ordered him to stay home. He glanced back and saw that even though she spoke with confidence, her hand shook as she rotated the dial and her tears made the scar gleam in the soft cabin lights.

Looking out at an empty blue seeker map with no Polar gate in sight, Drew finally felt the weight and darkness. This was her burden every night. It felt like something he'd experienced before, something he'd blocked out. A tiny voice inside him began to prod, *What if this is worse? What if Ryan's right? What if Malgore comes here?*

She finished at the communication station and joined him in the cockpit. They flew silently across town and straight up through clouds to the very boundaries of their world. But the Polar gateway wasn't there.

After they'd searched a while, Sheela punched the wall. "It's right in front of us! How are we missing it?"

When they landed, she shoved him against the warped planks of the barn wall. Her eyes were bright and glistening in the glow of the surrounding equipment. "Do not come back tomorrow night."

As promised, he didn't tell the others about his midnight run, but everybody could see he was a walking zombie. Later that night, he fell asleep and would have missed the night mission except for a tap at his window. He found Sheela hanging upside down from his roof, looking in.

"You might as well come," she said through the glass.

This became a nightly routine. She would tap at the window and they would scramble up his roof to the hovering cruiser. Drew would take his place at the pilot seat and take off. They talked sometimes, and other times they made an entire flight with Sheela sitting at the comm station lying and playing automated, coded messages through various channels. No one ever responded. Drew caught himself almost suggesting they might all be captured—or worse.

Chapter 18

Warrior Training

She began training them on the use of body armor. It was modified, slapdash adult armor, cut to size for children: chest guards, elbow pads, and helmets. Some were organic, smooth ebony wood, carved armor, bound together with strands of emerald cord or vines. Some were lightweight, made of cool white and black metal. The armor bore symbols and markings and etching and tallies. The symbols—suns and stars and creatures the kids had never seen—represented the other dimensions and tribes. Previous owners had etched the tallies, and each one was a confirmed gremlin or space pirate kill. The armor was well-loved with dents and scorch marks, acid damage, gashes, and holes burnt clear through. Some smelled faintly of sweat, blood, and urine.

"Someone better clean these," Sonetta said, holding up a scratched and dented helmet. The others picked through the gear, putting together their ground assault look.

"You never clean them. Everyone who wears them leaves a piece of themselves in the armor."

"Yeah, like their guts," Kevin said. The girls twisted up their faces, holding the helmets away from them like dead rats.

Sheela taught them to suit up and tighten their gear. She taught them how to un-suit and properly store their gear in their designated lockers on the cruiser. She showed them how to disassemble, check, and clean their laser rifles and pistols.

"Where is my rifle's safety?" Justin asked as he rotated the squat, boxy gun.

"What's a safety?" Sheela frowned.

That week, Sheela flew them out into the mountains and taught them rifle training among the creeks and trees. They learned to use the creature detector to hunt gremlins, slores, and other Outland creatures. She taught them formations and made them hunt her. She ran about the trees or camouflaged herself among piles of dead foliage and zapped them with low-level stun bolts. When one dropped, the others had to quickly revive them. If she could get them all, they lost.

Drew had Missy, the only artist in the group, design the Dimension Ten patches. In this case, it was nearly a copy of the polar bear on the Klondike bar wrapping. The Polar Starship was hidden somewhere in their dimension, and every time they went out looking for it that polar bear image popped into his head. Missy painted the bear on their armor and on the cruiser. She even stitched the bear on a patch, and Drew used pins to stick it to his dad's Members Only jacket. They were the unofficial Dimension Ten Warriors, and because the starship ran on polar plasma fuel, they called themselves the Polars.

Justin hid out in his basement at night, attaching hover

orbs to his bike. He used rocket boosters from the cruiser's leftover parts drawer and now flew all over town. He hovered a few feet off the ground and pedaled to power the boosters. After his maiden voyage across town and back, with the Polars all sitting atop a rusted tractor, cheering him on, Justin zoomed back and grabbed Drew.

"Drew!" He trembled. His glasses had flown off his face somewhere across Watkins Park. "I'm not afraid anymore!"

The hover bike didn't have an Oren wall, so Sheela forbade him to ride during the day. Justin retrofitted everyone's bikes and even a junked couch they found in the woods. They had late night races across the fields. They even flew their cavalcade through the woods, Drew reminding them to duck the fishing line trap as they passed the Big Boys' fort, howling like ghosts. Jimmy and the others would come running, looking pale and frightened, brandishing BB guns and slingshots—but the Polars were long gone.

Sonetta emerged as director of operations. She kept careful track of the time, of continuity, and of cover stories. For a bastion of truth, she also knew how to bend it. She made them all go home for lunch and made sure to dirty their clothes and spritz them with a spray bottle to feign sweat. They were, after all, building a treehouse. She knew everyone's dinner times and bedtimes and made sure no one was late or suspicious or ever got in trouble. One slipup would blow their cover and expose Sheela. She even designated people to build a mediocre treehouse, in case the adults ever asked.

Ryan was the holdout. His dad was furious with his newfound treehouse distraction. Ryan decided to return to baseball to keep them all safe. The Polars went to his games and sat up on Owl Hill or in the stands and showed him they were there. He started playing better.

Sheela was increasingly distracted. She compiled several outfits from the girls and now took frequent "fact-finding missions" uptown. The girls introduced her to soft rock and makeup. The boys taught her pranks like fishing, where they strung fishing line across a street, tied to a pair of trash cans on either side. Several cars hit the line and dragged cans up the street. They taught her how to get around town through the storm drains and secret paths through the woods, which were the best climbing trees, and how to sneak into the pool. She loved the pool.

The kids were in and out of each other's homes, sneaking in through each other's windows and messaging each other through their comms. They were never apart, but to the adults in their lives, they looked to be having one of those summers, the type someone later writes was the most important of their lives. The adults were proud and the other kids in the neighborhood were envious, but many had given up trying to be part of the secret club.

Drew now had a big problem. Steve was always around. He seemed to know Drew was hiding something, but he wasn't getting angry about it. It was all very disorienting.

Worse still was that his dark, vacant look was fading. While Steve's shoulders still slumped forward, light shone in his eyes, like his soul was coming back to life. He didn't stare through Drew anymore but looked at him, in his eyes. It was unbearable. He was arriving home earlier from work. He was straightening the house and even making breakfast. But the worst thing was that he was talking more. He would corner Drew and ask him about his day, what his plans were, and if Drew wanted to stay in and watch a movie.

"Want to go to Ryan's game tonight?" Steve had

cornered him when Drew was on his way out the door to go with Sheela on their nightly gate search.

"Sorry, gotta work on the treehouse."

"Ah, come on. If Ryan's playing baseball, I'm sure you can take the night off too."

Drew pulled back the sliding door. "We're on a tight schedule."

Steve lingered in the kitchen. "I haven't been out in public for a long time and, uh . . . I'm kinda nervous. I could use a wingman."

Sheela would just leave without him, maybe even let Missy or Justin fly. Drew now sat on the hard bleachers with his dad and Kristen.

She leaned in. "Missing your girlfriend?"

"I just don't think Justin's ready to fly yet."

"It's good to see your dad out."

"Yeah, I guess."

Kristen saw some friends and left.

After a five-game slump, Ryan was back in stride, pitching a perfect game. But Drew was paying more attention to the action in the bleachers. People were patting Steve on the back and shaking his hand. He looked pale and edgy but forced smiles, a few thank yous, and even a "good to see you too."

A quiet voice in Drew's head said, *He'll be destroyed when you abandon him and leave with Sheela. He'll have no one.*

Drew shut the voice up. Steve timidly put an arm over his shoulder, but Drew tensed and Steve took his arm away. The two of them sat in silence.

He'll do better if I leave. He'll have to move on, start over. I'll always remind him of her.

Kristen squeezed in beside Drew and shoved a bag of

popcorn in his lap.

"What are you doing?"

"Layton and Bret bought me popcorn and I ditched 'em." She chuckled, grabbed a handful of popped kernels, and tossed them at a group of girls in front of them. When they looked back, she shrugged and pointed at Drew. "Oh, and your friends are here."

"Friends?" Drew followed her gaze and saw Jimmy and the Big Boys circling the parking lot. Jimmy had spotted him and was looking at him oddly.

The crowd suddenly cheered. Ryan had just struck out another hitter. His team fell all over themselves, cheering in the dusty dugout. Kristen jumped up and hooted as Steve cupped his hands around his mouth and shouted, "You can do this, Ry!"

Ry. Steve used to have nicknames for all of Drew's buddies.

The crowd quieted as Ryan faced off against their biggest hitter, Craig Compton. One more strike and the Huskies could keep their title. Drew saw Ryan glance at Big Jake. He wasn't playing for the title or a no-hitter. Drew held his breath, and as the crowd hushed, a sound of loud static popped and fizzled from Drew's belt.

"What's that?" Steve asked.

Kristen gave him a sharp look.

His walkie! Drew yanked the walkie off his belt, desperately searching for the volume wheel. Everyone was looking around for the source of the noise and Ryan looked back from the mound. Drew jumped up and bounded down between the rows of tightly packed spectators. Once below the bleachers, he whispered into the walkie, "Drew here!"

"Kevin, Kevin Gadoy here! Dude, I need everyone to the

barn *now!*"

"Is Sheela okay?"

"Bro, I've established contact with the others."

"Others?"

"The *others*. You are not gonna believe this. Kevin Gadoy, out!"

A *crack* shattered the silence and the crowd erupted. Drew popped his head out to see Ryan's Huskies all turned, watching a recently smashed baseball leave the atmosphere. Home run.

Chapter 19

Dimension Warriors

Big Jake stalked out into the parking lot and kicked over a trashcan. Drew heard one of Ryan's teammates shout, "What was *that*, Wilcox? You gift wrapped it for him!" The rest of his team wouldn't look at him. Ryan stood out on the mound completely alone and wavering like the gentle breeze would blow him over. He took off his hat and dropped it in the red dirt. Drew and Kristen waited for him until he finally wandered off the field, staring blankly.

Drew looked at his watch. "Hey, forget them."

Ryan didn't seem to hear him.

Kristen punched Drew's arm. "What was that with the comm link?"

"Kevin called. We got to go!"

"My dad's not gonna let me," Ryan said. "I can't work on the *treehouse* anymore."

"This is more important than him!" Drew said.

155

"Shut up, Drew." Kristen's green eyes flashed.

Drew couldn't believe they were just standing around. He searched for words and couldn't find any good ones. "Fine. I'm going—"

"Ryan," Steve came up behind them, holding his Huskies ballcap.

"Hi, Mr. Shipley," Ryan said, his head hanging anvil heavy. "Sorry about the game."

"Ry." Ryan looked up at Steve, who placed Ryan's hat on his head—backward, the way Ryan always wore it. "You were great out there."

Ryan started to say thanks when he choked and gulped back tears. Steve patted him on the shoulder. "You guys look like you're on your way to the *treehouse*." He emphasized the word and Drew tried not to react. "Have fun and be careful."

"I can't. I gotta go talk to my dad," Ryan said, trying to regain his voice.

"Yeah," Steve said, nodding slowly and looking in Big Jake's direction. "I'll talk to him. You guys go."

They watched as Steve crossed the parking lot to where Jake Wilcox was hurling baseball gear into his truck bed. When Jake saw Steve, he dropped a duffle bag of baseballs. Drew couldn't believe it. He watched his dad embrace Jake and thumb back at the ballfield. Steve and Jake had been friends since high school, and somehow, Drew knew his dad was about to call Jake out. He felt something for his dad and it was sharp and dangerous. It scared him. He waved it off.

Ryan watched them too. He looked at Drew with his subtle smile as he adjusted his ballcap. He looked like Ryan again.

After a minute, Jake looked past Steve to Ryan and nodded. Ryan nodded back and that was it. They were allowed to go.

As they rode out of the lot, Drew grunted. "I'm sorry for being a jackass."

"I forgive you. Jackass," Ryan said, swerving playfully into Drew's way.

The three of them made it to the barn late. Drew thought he saw the Big Boys, so they doubled back and took the woods.

The cruiser was parked outside with the Oren wall off. Without the Oren on, a slore or astro gremlin could detect them. Drew was about to say this when he noticed a ghostly pale glow seeping through the gaps in the barn walls.

They looked around and saw the coast was clear. Drew stepped up and performed the secret knock, three taps followed by him whispering, "Mickey Mouse has warts." The door slid back and Kevin's disembodied head floated in the doorway. He looked through the Oren wall at them.

"About *freakin'* time!" Kevin said.

They passed through the Oren wall, and Drew saw Sheela and the others standing around a waning lantern, the light flickering like a campfire. But there were more than just the Polars and Sheela.

Four others sat across from them.

Sheela beckoned him over excitedly. "Drew, come here!"

As Drew approached, he saw the others were luminous and flickering. A ray of light cast down from the comm link station in the loft. The four kids, he realized, were projections.

They were a motley crew, like starfighter Vikings. Three of them wore tattered flight jackets over incongruent military uniforms mixed with strange apparel like scarfs, shorts, and even alien animal furs and bones. They had utility belts and blinking packs with strange tools and supplies. Their weapons varied—rough, black, jagged blades and hatchets, copper-colored ancient ray guns, and boxy, painted rifles with tally marks etched along the stunted barrels.

One boy was as tall as Kevin but wiry. His body armor consisted of two decrepit skulls with fangs and horns that hung off both shoulders. He had long, greasy dark hair. A fresh scar jutted down through his right eyebrow. His eyes were dark like Sheela's, and Drew knew without being told this was Bash. He had the same silver headband as Sheela, bearing the symbol for Orel. He cradled a laser rifle to his chest, hugging it comfortably like a teenager would hold his girlfriend.

"Drew, this is my older brother, Brace. The Dimension Warriors all call him Bash. He's commander of the Orel Warriors," Sheela said.

A short, round girl in a flight cap and goggles spat. She had tight pigtails sprouting from either side of her flight cap. Drew could see she was fair with freckles sprinkled across her face like she'd messily eaten spaghetti. She chewed a wad of something in one cheek and looked like a space-age Norman Rockwell painting with her snakeskin utility belt, bulky gun, blinking gadgets, and headset.

"And this is Stormy Duegan, squad leader of our starfighter fleet and one of the best pilots I've ever seen."

In response, Stormy spat a projected wad of interdimensional chaw. It fizzled and disappeared from the projection before it hit the floor. "Stormy's from Zoltar. She actually saw Malgore fly his Necrobeast through the Outland gate and devour the Graystar sentinels."

Next to Duegan was a tall slender girl. She had strange purple pupils and thin blinking wires woven throughout her brown mane of hair. Sheela passed over her to the next kid, a

158

short skinny kid, crooked and shaking with what appeared to be cerebral palsy.

"I'm Gunter, pleasure . . . to make your . . . acquaintance," Gunter said as he fought to keep his involuntary shakes under control.

"Gunter's mother was a lead creative from Astoria. Gunter's an engineer and one of our chief strategists," Sheela said. Gunter waved off her compliments.

Sheela gestured to Drew. "Everyone, this is Drew Shipley, captain of the Polars. He is also my personal liaison to the tenth dimension. They aren't Dimension Warriors, but Drew helped me establish a base. He also pulled together the team you see here."

Duegan frowned and squeaked out, "We thought Kevin, Kevin Gadoy was the leader."

"Gadoy!" Gunter and Bash cheered. They peered back behind Drew, craning their necks to get a better look at Kevin. The big blondie beamed back.

"They've caught my show every night," Kevin said, nudging Drew.

Sheela continued, "I agreed to train them for their own protection. Kevin, Kevin Gadoy, is their communications officer. Missy Allen and Ryan Wilcox are gunners, ground assault leaders, and quickly becoming all-around weapons experts. Sonetta Brockington is director of operations, Kristen Miller is our flight navigator, and Justin Mcgrath is our chief engineer and Polar creative."

Drew saw the Polars blush as each was introduced. As he looked at his friends, their appearance in the cast-off shimmering light struck him. They no longer looked like kids. They were all becoming something else. They looked . . . grown up.

Sheela turned back to Bash. She stood tall and tucked one hand behind her back in a formal posture. "What's your status?"

The others looked at Bash as he smile-shrugged. "We're doing just fine," he said and patted his gun.

"The truth, Bash," Sheela said.

"We're holding our own," Bash said. Sheela crossed her arms and waited, staring at him.

The Dimension Warriors all hesitated before Gunter finally spoke. "Tell her the . . . truth, B-Bash."

Bash sighed. "Alright, after you disappeared, Malgore had General ShinFar and the gremlins go destroy every city in Orel. He has a big reward out for you and put it out to all the space pirates, Kreecoles and eel people. He also offered any Dimension Warrior full immunity if they gave you up—said he'd set them up with a nice little planet and let them live there and be free."

Sheela said, "And?"

"Hell, we're enjoying the new planet, right now." Bash smiled and Duegan elbowed him in the ribs.

Gunter stepped up. "We lost a few, they were questi . . . questioned, but n-none of them gave up your location."

"How many?" Sheela asked.

No one answered.

"Brentha?" Sheela finally acknowledged the tall girl.

Brentha cocked her head toward Sheela. "Deceased, two Dimension Warriors: Harding, Danyal, and Ripper, Nel." Brentha's voice was robotic and monotone. Sonetta's eyes went wide at the word "deceased" and she exchanged troubled glances with Missy and Kristen.

Sheela nodded. "Nel and Dany . . ."

Bash interrupted with a grunt, "What about you, sis? We

got your good news! Tell us, what does the Polar look like?"

The Warriors looked desperate and hopeful.

Gunter fought his spasms to force a smile. "When are you leaving to get us?"

Drew looked at Sheela. She froze, so excited to see her brother she'd forgotten about the lie.

"Something wrong?" Bash asked. "Don't tell me Dad left the engine running." His easy smile tightened slightly.

"It's a beautiful ship." Drew didn't realize he'd said it until he looked around to see the Polars gaping at him.

"Oh yeah?" Bash asked, looking back to his sister.

Sheela's eyes shimmered like pools and her gaze drifted off into the distance. "It is a beautiful ship. More beautiful than we even imagined."

Duegan hugged and lifted Gunter into the air as Gunter gave a joyful shout. Brentha smiled robotically.

Kristen and Ryan both locked on Drew, eyes wide and questioning. He gave them a curt head shake.

"Well, take us to it! Let's see her!" Bash said.

Sheela responded, "We can't do that. We don't know if this channel is secure. In fact, we shouldn't even mention the ship—not if there's a chance Malgore could find out."

The Dimension Warriors looked briefly disappointed. Bash said, "Ah, you're right. The important thing is you're on your way!"

Sheela nodded, sharpening her eyes and clenching her jaw. "We're on our way, and this time, we're going to bring the fight to Malgore."

"About time!" Bash said.

When Sheela gave up the projector comm link to go to the bathroom, Bash told Drew to take their projection away from the group. "Captain Shipley, let's have a talk."

Drew carried Bash and the other Warriors away from the group, and Bash stood beside him as if the two were only a foot apart instead of separated by dimensions and galaxies. "Thank you for looking out for her. She's got the weight of all our worlds on her. Those two we lost were close friends from Orel, from before the war. Take care of her."

"We're coming for you guys," Drew said.

Bash shook his head. "You're not gonna make it. Malgore's closing in on our position. It's not good. We have maybe a week."

"We've got to buy you time . . ."

"At least you have the Polar. Just promise not to tell her. I'm only telling you because you're her liaison. You got to look out for her at all cost. If she knew we were in real trouble she would fly out here with the cruiser and get herself killed. You need to be strategic about this."

Sheela found them. "Why are you all the way out here?"

Bash sighed. "Drew was just showing us how far he can pee."

"We all need to convene back at base. I don't know how long we'll have your signal." Sheela turned away and Bash winked at Drew.

Drew nodded.

They sat in the barn and talked about the plan. Sheela would have the Polars help her finish prepping the starship and leave as soon as possible. The other Polars listened in stunned silence. The lie had thrown them.

Sheela said, "And how are the other squadrons? Have you found everyone and brought them to the tunnel base? Amass there, consolidate, and wait on my word."

"Sounds good, sis." Bash saluted, as did the others.

Suddenly the signal fizzled. "Whoa!" Kevin shouted.

"We're getting intercepted."

"For Orel," Bash said.

"For Orel," Sheela repeated quietly.

"Love ya, ugly," Bash muttered.

"Love you too, stupid," Sheela said.

"Kevin, Kevin Gadoy here!" the others yelled as they faded out.

The signal broke. They disappeared and all was quiet and dark in the barn.

Sheela turned and looked at them all. "I know you don't understand, but I need them to feel hope. Without hope, we've already lost. I needed to . . . lie to them."

"What about you, Drew?" Kristen said. "You're the one who told 'em we found it."

"I told 'em it was beautiful. The way I picture it."

"A lie is a lie," Sonetta said, glaring at him.

"What do we do now?" Ryan asked.

The radio whistled a high sound, like a wolf howl. The projector flashed back to life and another projection lit the area. The ghostly light caught the dust moats and floating bits of hay, but where the light landed, there was nothing.

They all froze, and Drew looked at Sheela. She reached slowly for her gun. "Malgore," she whispered. "Kevin, shut off the signal before he locates us!"

Then they heard a child's giggle and a boy appeared wearing an innocent smile. His hair was parted and he wore a neatly pressed outfit. Drew frowned. Had they reconnected with the Warriors? But as he looked closer, he saw a faint beam of light arching from the top of the boy's head back to something large, something just off screen.

Everyone was startled except Sheela.

The boy spotted her. "Sheela!" his voice was playful.

163

"Where have you been hiding? Have you found the ship yet?"

He stepped toward her as if he might leave the projection to play with them. Drew could now see the silhouette of the large creature the boy was connected to leaning into the projection.

The boy spoke again, but his voice was slightly distorted. "I asked your friends, but they wouldn't say. I will find you and your new friends."

He looked around at the Polars when Sheela bolted for the comm link and ripped the cables from the back. The projection of the boy disappeared.

Everyone was quiet a long time before exhaling.

"*What* was *that?*" Kristen asked.

"Seemed normal to me," Kevin said.

"Malgore's a kid?" Ryan questioned.

Sheela said, "No, that's what he wants you to see. It's a trap."

"Reminds me of an anglerfish," Justin said.

"Sheela, your world is *super* messed up," Missy said.

As the others left for home, Sheela packed up and boarded the cruiser.

Kristen grabbed Drew. "Sheela's upset. Go with her, dummy!" She shoved him.

Drew leapt aboard as the side hatch was closing. He felt the ship lift off and drift backward. He grabbed some rigging to keep from falling forward. She didn't acknowledge him but yanked back on the throttle and blasted upward. She arced hundreds of feet above Warfield and switched on the blue map grid overlay. The seeker dishes bounced back the faint outline of the massive starship, a ghost ship.

Drew joined her. The cruiser felt dark and vacant, and Drew felt himself hyperventilating. He broke into a cold sweat. For the first time since meeting Sheela, he wanted to be on the ground. The silence dragged on as he stared out at the blue screen.

What's the point of all this? he thought. *We're gonna lose.*

Sheela stood and pulled off her jacket. She tossed it over the chair and stalked off, the blue Polar key glowing on her chest.

Drew heard the bathroom cabin hatch close and a sudden urge gripped him. He dove for Sheela's jacket and rifled through her pockets. He came up with some blinking tools and a comm link. He found an inside pocket, hidden behind a patch with the stitches pulled away at the top. He shoved his hand in and found what he was looking for. He pulled out one of the small black capsules Sheela had been taking. When she took them, she calmed; she was happy.

He rolled the hard, shiny pill between his thumb and forefinger. It was jet black, blacker than anything he'd ever seen.

Is this where you get your strength? Is this how I become a Dimension Warrior? Drew placed the pill in his mouth but hesitated to swallow it. What if it was something else? He spat it into his palm and tucked it into his pocket just as Sheela returned. She crawled up into the crow's nest.

Drew took the pilot seat, trying not to look guilty. After some time, she spoke. "Why aren't you with your family, like the others?"

"I'd rather be here." He turned toward her. "Hey. I want you to make me a promise. If I find this ship for you, you'll take me with you."

She leaned down and twisted her face. "What are you talking about?"

"Take me back to your world. I want to live there."

Her smile faded when she realized he was serious. "Why?"

"It doesn't matter. Just promise."

"Not that *you* can find the ship if I can't, but okay. If you find it, I'll take you with me." Drew left the pilot seat and reached up to make her shake.

She chuckled.

"What?" he said.

"I'm fighting to get my family back; you're fighting to leave yours."

They flew in silence, Sheela scanning the stars above through the window's radar overlay.

Drew realized after some time that she was asleep. He felt the tug of the pill. He glanced back at her and then quickly took it, dry-swallowing it without the pill getting stuck in his throat. Whatever it was, it hadn't killed Sheela. It went down easy and Drew sat still, waiting to sprout wings or spew green goo, but nothing happened.

Maybe it was just a vitamin . . .

He forgot about it as he soared above town and descended over his neighborhood, bringing the ship down and hovering over his roof. He gently tapped Sheela's boot on his way past the turret. She woke with a start, her hands instinctively grabbing for her gun.

"Nothing to report. Go get some sleep," Drew said. He sent up a salute and she nodded back.

He descended onto his roof and entered through his window. As he closed the window, he crunched his thumb. He hissed as the pain pulsed through him. He shook out his hand and started undressing. Then he paused. He looked at the small picture on his dresser, the woman and the boy smiling back at him.

He stared for a long moment because while he recognized the picture, he didn't know who she was. He went and picked up the picture and studied it, straining his brain. What was her name? The boy was him . . . now he had it. It was his mom. But he couldn't remember anything else about her. His only memory of her was staring back at him from the photo.

He put the frame down and felt strange. He felt lighter than he had a few minutes ago. The pure joy of flying was all that remained. He felt wonderful, in love. His mind drifted to Sheela as he lay down and electricity rippled through him.

I can fly. I get to fly with her every night. The thought made him giddy, and he laughed out loud. He switched off his lamp and felt the sleep washing him down like sand in a gentle surf.

A moment later, he felt a breeze. He looked and saw his window was open. Hadn't he shut it? His thumb still hurt, so yes—

A hand shot up from his bedside and grabbed him.

167

Chapter 20

Starlust

He was yanked off the bed to the floor. Sheela pulled his face to hers. Their noses touched in the dark and he felt her hurried breath. He could see her quivering in the moonlight, her pupils round and dark.

"Where is it?" Her voice was tight.

"What?" Drew realized he was in boxers and covered his nakedness with his arms.

"The Starlust! I know you took one."

Drew felt too good to lie. "I took it."

"You what?" She grabbed his bare shoulders and looked ready to reach down his throat for the pill. "I only have so many and I'm almost out."

"What is Starlust?"

"What did my brother tell you?" She shoved him hard against his bed post. "I need to know *everything*." She held him against the bed, locking his arms to his sides and staring into him with her liquid black-blue eyes.

The Starlust spoke for him. "Malgore knows where they are. They have a week, maybe."

Sheela released him and sat back. She inhaled, thinking. Then she nodded, fixing on some unspoken and difficult decision. "I'm leaving." She stood and went for the window. Drew was slow to get up but caught her before she'd climbed fully from his room. He pulled her back in.

"You can't go."

"Get off of me!"

"No! This is why Bash didn't tell you. He knew you'd fly off and get yourself killed trying to save them. You do that and it's all over—for all of us!" Drew couldn't believe he'd gotten all of that out. He felt dizzy.

Sheela pulled away but paused at the window. She turned to respond when they were interrupted by footsteps on the stairs.

"Under the bed!" Drew whispered. Sheela flattened out on the floor and rolled beneath the box spring as Drew lunged under his quilt. The door opened.

Steve switched on the hallway light. He pulled the door a crack behind him. Drew watched him through slits, his heart thumping. He tried to breathe evenly, as though he'd been asleep, but the shock of being pulled out of bed had left him breathless.

Steve shuffled across the room and paused at the dresser to pick up the frame but saw it standing upright. He made a soft sound of surprise and came to the bedside. Drew listened to see if he could hear Sheela. He couldn't.

Steve rubbed Drew's hair and hummed a tune. His dad seemed sad, but Drew couldn't remember why. A dark curtain shrouded the answer.

Steve whispered in the dark, "I'm glad you're sneaking out and living your life. She would want that." He left and shut the door behind him.

Drew waited a minute before he rolled to the far bedside, the one near the window. He peered down. Sheela had crawled out from under the bed and stared up at him from the floor. She was on her back, thoughtful and looking through him, up at his ceiling, and perhaps up beyond that through the sky and stars.

"You feel good, correct?" she asked.

"What are they?"

"Starlust capsules. Starfighters and dimension explorers took them on long voyages or when going to war. They make you forget the most painful memories but keep you frosty and focused. They help me forget my brother and my parents. They help me forget that Malgore wants to destroy me and everything I love. It made you forget Anne." Sheela gestured to the shirt she was wearing.

When she said his mom's name, the pill's potent effect subsided, the curtain slid back, and he remembered.

She sighed. "I wish they lasted longer. I've often wondered what would happen if you took more than one."

They lay there in silence and Drew allowed himself a memory he hadn't thought of for a long time. He remembered his mom lying on the floor, her hands behind her head and feet up on his mattress. She would just lie there and read him her diaries from when she was young. She would tell him wild stories about her childhood, and he would tickle her feet.

He'd blocked all of it out. He'd vowed never to think of those times. Her childhood had been so strange and he was never sure what was real or made up.

Made up.

Something struck him. Drew sat up. "Sheela!"

She was slow to look at him.

"I need to show you something!" He jumped out of bed and pulled a shirt on backward and inside out.

"No." She lay there, limp and dazed.

He realized what she'd done. "Did you take more?"

She smiled and saluted him. "A handful."

He grabbed his head between his hands. "No—not now! You have to come with me!" He pulled her up.

"I want to go to the movies," she complained.

"Sheela!" He shook her. "You *need* to see this!"

Drew had one of her arms over his shoulder and pulled her down the hall. She leaned heavily against him. Drew could see down off the balcony. His dad was stretched on the couch, an arm thrown over his face. He was still but not asleep yet.

Sheela fell to the floor and giggled.

"Sheela, no. Don't do this now." He got her up, watching his dad. He propped her against the wall and slid her to his parents' bedroom, trying to avoid the creaking spots on the carpeted floor.

They entered his parents' room, and Drew quietly nudged the door closed. He lowered her to the edge of the bed and felt his way to the closet. He slid back the door while Sheela breathed heavily in the darkness. She pulled the blue key out from her shirt, on its chain. In the blue light, she peered at a picture of Anne on the untouched, dusty vanity.

"She's very beautiful," Sheela slurred.

"I need your light." Drew went to her and pulled the necklace over her head.

"Hey." She grabbed for it but missed.

He entered the closet and shoved a row of hanging summer dresses out of the way. Hidden behind them was a box. He opened it to reveal a stack of diaries. Each spine had a year scrawled on it. He pulled several from the late sixties and early seventies. He flipped through them, feeling numb and hot. The discolored pages, the smell, the handwriting, the doodles—everything flooded back. Each page stung as he flipped them, but he kept searching. The stories were coming to him. Cracks were forming in the walls of his memory and light was spilling in.

"What are you looking for?" Sheela stumbled into the closet, peering down at the pages.

Drew found it, there in the diary from 1972. June nineteenth. His mother was eleven. There was a brief entry and a sketch of the Gladhill barn. A girl and a man were doodled beside the barn. And there was another doodle over the barn—a UFO. The cruiser.

He held it up to Sheela, and she steadied herself. She shook her head and grabbed the diary from him. She held it close, inspecting the sketch in the blue light. The two looked at each other in shock.

Drew whispered in a quivering voice, "When my mom was eleven, she told me about a spaceman she met in a place she called Weird Space. It's what she called the cornfield."

Tears shimmered in Sheela's eyes like blue pools. She gulped and let a tear fall. She looked back to the diary, combing its pages.

Drew remembered the story by heart. "She said he told her to keep a secret. He was going to hide something *beneath* the barn, and she needed to protect it. She wouldn't tell me what it was. She told me we would look together when I was eleven." He took her by the shoulders. "It was my destiny to help you."

Sheela gasped, "That's why the seekers pinged it and we haven't seen it! It's been right under us the entire time!" Her eyes were bright.

She pulled him to her and their lips connected in a clumsy kiss. Drew saw sparks, his whole body jolting.

Their lips parted and she pulled Drew to his feet. "Come on!" She was too excited to be awkward.

In his room, Drew dressed quickly and radioed the team. "Mickey Mouse has warts! We found it! We've found the Polar. Everyone to the barn ASAP!"

Outside, Kristen's dog, Cooper, was barking. Her parents were out of town, and Kristen was at Sonetta's.

Sheela stumbled about, smacking herself, trying to undo the effects of the Starlust.

"Are you okay?"

"Of course. Yes."

"What does too much Starlust do?"

"I don't know." Sheela looked at him, horrified. "What did you just tell me about?"

Drew approached her, wide-eyed, "You're joking. Right?"

She looked back, equally wide-eyed. "I know it's important, but I can't remember."

"Oh no," Drew said. "Just follow me."

Cooper was still barking when they went through the window and onto the roof. They crawled up the shingles. Sheela wobbled on her feet.

"We're almost there! The Polar! It's gonna save your people and all our worlds!" Drew said.

Cooper barked wildly now, charging back and forth along the fence.

Drew froze when he saw it. The cruiser hovered just above his roof. Sheela had been so upset about him stealing the Starlust pill and moved so quickly she'd left the Oren wall off. The ship sat exposed like an alien beacon for all of Warfield to see.

"Sheela, you left the Oren wall off?"

She crouched beside him, staring up at the cruiser in blank fascination.

"You don't recognize it. Do you?"

She slowly shook her head. He grabbed her. "Do you recognize me?"

She looked down at his hands and back to his face. She was trying, but there was no recognition. She shrank like a frightened child.

Drew felt a stab of panic. He shook himself. "It'll only last so long. It'll wear off!" he yelled at her, hoping she would reassure him.

She tugged away and he took her more gently by the elbow.

"We're good. We just need to wait for you to remember again. Then we can go find the Polar."

Cooper's barking turned to snarls. He rammed the fence, jumping and scraping against it as white, frothy saliva flew from his snout.

"Cooper, quiet!" Drew called over his shoulder. He turned back to Sheela. "Look, it's okay. We've got all night. We'll just wait this out. Let me turn on the Oren wall so no one sees the ship—"

A distant shriek echoed across the cornfield. It came from the barn.

"Slore!" It was a Talk-Talk. Drew listened as a chorus of tiny screams broke the still night. "Slore!"

174

Drew looked to Sheela in disbelief and back up at the ship. "Talk-Talks detect slores. You told me that."

She looked at him, lost, her lip trembling. "What's a slore?"

Drew looked back. The cornfield was a black mass, dead silent and still. The Talk-Talks suddenly went quiet. The crickets had gone quiet as well as the birds. Only Cooper was left. Drew watched as Cooper streaked across the yard and hurdled the back fence in a frenzy. His golden coat caught the back porch lights before he disappeared into the corn. Drew listened as the barking trailed away toward the barn.

Then Cooper stopped barking.

Drew couldn't move. His feet felt anchored to the shingles. Sheela crouched against the roof, rolled into a ball.

Drew shook himself to life. "We got to go!" He grabbed her and hauled her up to the cruiser's open hatch. Then he looked back and saw Cooper. The golden retriever was barely visible out in the darkness, but he was looking over the fence at Drew.

Cooper waved a paw. Sheela waved back. Cooper used his paw and beckoned them. Drew forced Sheela in through the hatch. He clawed his way to the cockpit and started the ship's systems. Everything hummed and glowed. Sheela huddled in a corner.

Drew couldn't remember anything in the frenzy. *How do I take off?*

A shadow dropped over his face as Cooper's head appeared in the windshield. Drew and Sheela both screamed as the body of an unusually large decapod crawled up onto the front of the ship. Its thick exoskeleton was jet black. Light from the neighborhood gleamed off its smooth skin. It looked like a crab with ten muscular legs. It tossed Cooper's lifeless body off the roof and one razor claw brought up a Talk-Talk, holding it out like a doll. It was dead and had a partially missing ear.

Larry.

The slore held it up to the windshield and danced it about, as if it wanted Drew to come out and play with it. After a moment of make-believe with the Talk-Talk's carcass, the slore tucked the animal into a cleft on its body.

The cruiser tilted as the slore climbed onto the cockpit. It passed in front of Drew and the outboard lights revealed a horrible sight. On the slore's abdomen, just below the thorax, was a distorted human face, the mouth full of long, translucent teeth. The face had no eyes, but it opened its mouth and a purple, slimy tongue emerged. The tongue slithered over the cockpit windshield, probing.

The slore tapped with its clawed legs. The tongue circled around where Drew sat in the pilot seat and then the mouth came near. The teeth fastened and crunched against the windshield. The slore braced its body. It was going to chew through to him.

"Sheela!" Drew screamed. "Help me!"

Sheela was still balled up on the floor, clutching her head. It wanted Sheela, but it was going to kill Drew to get to her. And it was going to kill him slowly. He knew that.

Drew jumped from the pilot's seat and backed away. The slore was almost through, its tongue fighting to burst the cracking glass as its teeth gnawed. Drew fell over Sheela and hit the floor. Sheela crouched beside him, screaming. The tongue squeezed through a crack, dripping slime all over the flight controls.

Drew saw Bash in his mind. *Take care of her. That's your job now.* He'd planned to run for the hatch and abandon her, but

176

instead, he forced himself up and bolted for the pilot seat.

He grabbed the wheel and punched the thrusters. The ship launched away from the roof. The slore clung to the cockpit and hissed, sending a spray of hot, purple saliva across the windshield. Drew couldn't see through the slore. An alarm sounded; the ground was getting close. They hit the treetops of the woods across the cornfield and Drew yanked back on the wheel and shot them straight into the sky.

The slore reached back with several powerful legs, punching the cockpit.

"Hang on!" Drew screamed to Sheela. He banked and barrel-rolled blindly, but the slore clenched and clung tighter. The face opened its terrible mouth.

"Sheela! I need you on the guns! It's getting through!"

A crack webbed across the shield as the purple tongue wriggled through the opening.

"Sheela!" Drew pleaded.

She forced herself off the floor. Drew opened the ceiling gun hatch. It irised open above her.

"Up there! Just pull the *trigger*!"

Sheela seemed to be remembering. She reached up into the ceiling and took hold of the foot bar. She was about to hoist herself up when the tongue squirmed all the way through the crack. It snaked around Drew's neck and yanked his head down into the controls. The ship dipped. Sheela fell, hitting her head. Her eyes rolled over white and she went limp. She slid across the floor to Drew's feet, unconscious.

Drew's throat was being crushed. His head was going to pop. He flung his arms and pulled desperately at the slippery tongue. He couldn't breathe. The saliva burned like acid and smelled like rotting meat. The more he fought, the tighter the tongue constricted. It kept ramming him against the controls. On one hit, Drew saw Sheela's snub nose gun. He reached for it, one finger curling around the barrel when the tongue lifted him out of the chair and slammed him against the ceiling. The gun went flying back into the cabin. The slore pulled him against the windshield.

Drew could hear the slore hissing audible words through the forming cracks: "Hello, darling. *Play* with us."

Drew felt himself losing consciousness as it lowered him into his chair and tightened its grip. The glass was cracking more. The rest of it would be through in seconds. Drew's hand fell to his side and felt something cool. He looked down with blurred vision. The welding tool from Sheela's belt. He took it up with his waning strength, pressed it against the slimy tongue and powered it on. The slore let loose a defining shriek as a blue, burning ball lit from the barrel.

Drew fell backward. The tongue was still coiled around his neck, but he'd seared it clean off. The slore's lime-green blood spilled in through the windshield and onto the controls. The tongue wriggled about, slithering down through Drew's shirt as he climbed back into the pilot's seat and grabbed the wheel.

He increased speed and then slammed them to a stop. The slore lost its grip and launched off the fractured cockpit. Drew watched through the splattering of blood and saliva on the windshield as the slore's crab-shaped body dropped down into Warfield. Its legs flailed wildly as it disappeared among the dark landscape.

Drew sank into shock until the tongue wriggled up his shirt like a convulsing slug and quickly coiled around his neck again. He jumped up, screaming, ripped it off, and flung it to the floor. It tried to slither up into some open conduit, but Drew found Sheela's pistol. He grabbed it and fired bright blue plasma.

The tongue exploded and the pieces made wet slapping sounds around the cabin.

Chapter 21

The Hunt

The others arrived in a hurry, celebrating and cheering because they'd found the Polar. Drew had said, "Mickey Mouse has warts" and told them to meet behind the arcade. They hadn't understood why Drew and Sheela didn't just pick them up. Justin had retrofitted their bikes and Kevin's roller blades with the hover technology, and they all glided quickly to the rendezvous point. They found the cruiser behind the arcade. Drew was there, cradling a laser rifle and wearing body armor. He was covered in green, putrid-smelling gore. His own blood was dried to his nose and burst blood vessels dotted his cheeks like freckles.

They all slammed to a stop and looked him up and down. Drew spat blood from his mouth. He was still coming out of shock.

"We have a slore," he muttered. "Justin, get the creature detector and let's go kill it."

Kristen stepped in. "Wait! You said you found the Polar!"

"Yeah, and then the slore found us."

"Let's use the Polar to kill it," Ryan said.

"Thought of that. But we don't have Sheela. It'll kill us before we uncover it, and it's gonna hurt other people. We have to protect our town. Sonetta, please go check on Sheela."

Kevin was still staring at Drew in horror. "I'm sorry, where is Sheela?"

"She's knocked out cold. It's up to us. Now get your stuff."

The others went pale, slow to react, but grabbed gear and guns. Justin returned with the detector. Sonetta checked Sheela. She had a pulse and appeared to be okay, but she was still unconscious. They lifted her to the medic bunk in the cruiser and locked her in.

The others kept asking questions. What did it look like? How fast was it? Was it scary? Was it big? Drew could only repeat as he led them forward, "Check your rifles."

Kristen blocked them, pointing at Drew. "Hey, dummy. You look like a train wreck. This is crazy and I'm not doing it."

"We don't have a choice, Kris," Ryan said. "This thing's gonna kill people."

"Yeah, like *us*!" Kristen said. She retreated toward the cruiser. "You guys are idiots if you go."

Drew sighed. "Kristen, it killed Cooper!" he said coldly and immediately felt bad.

She stopped and looked back, mouth open and ready to yell as if she were going to deny his stupid claim. But they could see her wheels turning, her green eyes drifting.

180

She muttered, "I let him out to go to the bathroom and forgot to let him back in." She stepped up in Drew's face. "You're sure?"

He nodded apologetically. She fought back tears, her lips trembling and her cheeks flushed. The others touched her shoulders, but she shrugged them off. She tossed her laser rifle on the asphalt.

"I'm done and you guys are all jerks." She left them standing there, mounted her hover bike, and took off.

"I'll go after her," Ryan said.

"No, we don't have time," Drew said.

Justin held out the detector and switched it on. He set it to slore. The glowing muddy yellow screen displayed grid lines and started thwapping. The radar was blank as it pinged a sixty-yard radius.

Drew made Justin stay beside him while the others fell nervously behind. "Kevin, Missy, watch our flank."

"We need to kill it before it sends a signal back to Malgore," Justin said.

Drew had forgotten this. Sheela had warned them Malgore would send scouts throughout different dimensions, implanted with transmitters. They fanned out and stayed in the shadows and alleys, everyone watching the perimeter.

Thwap. Thwap. Thwap. Thwap.

Ryan moved up behind Drew. "How fast are we talkin'?" Ryan was prepping for the slore the way he did when pitching against good hitters.

"Fast, big, strong. Sharp claws. Lots of teeth. Can change shape and is really smart."

Ryan chewed his lip. "So . . . no weaknesses?"

"Not really."

"Why didn't you mention this when you called us?"

181

Justin asked.

"This wasn't what we called about. We think we found the Polar, but it won't matter if we don't live to uncover it."

"Cool. And true."

Thwap. Thwap. Thwap. Thwap.

"Can we just call the police?" Missy pleaded, fussing with her armored vest and helmet.

Drew had had this same thought—*Find Grimes so he can call the army!*—when he landed the blood-soaked cruiser.

"Cops got better things to do than get killed," he said. "We have the weapons we need and we can't blow our cover now. It's up to us."

Thwap. Thwap. Thwap. Thwap.

Drew now saw what he'd missed for so long. Missing dog and cat posters. A missing Willy poster with Willy's grimy, bearded mugshot. A statement that the junkyard would be closed until further notice.

"I'm not seeing any signs of it on the detector. Maybe it went back to its dimension?" Justin said.

"Look!" Missy pointed with the barrel of her laser rifle.

They stopped in front of the large dumpster behind Jack and Ray's. It was crushed like a soda can.

A trail of trash and neon-green blood led away from the dumpster, trailing in through the back door of the used bookstore. They entered and crept down the dark, narrow book aisles. The neon blood trickled a dotted path up over the shelves and smeared along the ceiling. It pooled in the psychology section where the slore had apparently paused to glance at an old textbook.

The book lay on the floor, open to a picture of a dissected human brain.

The trail led right out the front of the store, across the

street, and around behind the Safeway. They scrambled across the street, looking in every direction. Most people were asleep, but Deputy Grimes was out lurking, hunting for his brother's killer. And the killer was close.

The Polars climbed up on the Safeway loading dock and ducked inside. It was a Tuesday night. No one was inside, and the store was closing soon. Drew led them in through the stockroom and peered through the push doors. Only the store manager and his cashier girlfriend were left making out at register one. Jazz flute Muzak played softly over the PA system.

"It's hurt. Sheela told me it'll look for a tunnel, burrow, or tight space to hide and heal," Drew said.

Drew and the others snuck in and followed the trail of green along the back of the store, across the meat section. In several places, packages of ground beef were torn open and devoured. It had ignored the hotdogs. Even in his terror, Drew thought that was funny. They moved from aisle to aisle, taking careful aim in case the slore was just around the corner. The trail of blood led right out the front of the store. The teens making out didn't see the squad of creature hunters moving, two by two, out the automatic doors.

The trail of blood stopped. They all looked up from the dead end to see Hollie Johnson, the scrubby town drunk, staring at them from the parking lot. They stared back. He was holding a bottle in a brown paper bag, looking scruffy and greasy. He was also frozen. Without saying a word, Hollie pointed.

"It went that way?" Drew asked.

Hollie nodded. The Polars started off.

"Thank you, sir!" Drew said over his shoulder.

Hollie stood, looking after them.

Thwap. Thwap. Thwap. Thwap—beep! Beep!

They stopped at the end of the parking lot and crowded around the screen. The pulse had struck an object fifty yards ahead, and they looked up.

"You're kidding me," Kevin said. They were across the street from the Chuck E. Cheese. It was closed, all the lights out.

They hesitated a long time, watching the pulse wave strike the dot.

"It's not moving. Maybe it's been neutralized." Justin gulped.

Drew realized no one would move until he did. He looked both ways and hustled across the street. His poorly fitted vest and helmet jangled on him. He pushed back his helmet and nearly dropped his laser rifle. He made it, checked his surroundings, and waved Ryan on.

Ryan followed and then the others. The front doors were shut and locked.

"Oh, well, guess we can't get in," Kevin said.

"Man up, Kevin," Missy said, shoving him with the butt of her rifle.

"Drew?" Ryan said.

The two of them locked eyes and Ryan shook his head. Drew didn't want to either, and if he said the word, they would retreat and give it all up. He was learning how Sheela felt. Leadership was lonely.

Then he pictured Sheela back in the medic bunk and found himself running around the building to the back door. The others were slow to follow, and everyone rammed into him when they reached the back. It had been torn clean off and flung into the trees. A spray of neon-green blood streaked across the wall beside the door and trailed inside. Drew's body armor rattled as he took short steps forward. He saw the security system panel just inside the door. The casing had been peeled away and the wires ripped up.

"It appears to have . . . dismantled the security system," Justin said. The detector shook in his hand as it beeped.

They filed into the back hallway, which was dark and cool from the AC. Air rattled the duct system above them. The beeping sounded in faster intervals as they neared the slore. The neon exit sign lit the whole place red. They smelled stale pizza and popcorn as they passed the employee lounge and entered the dark eatery. The animatronics stood motionless and eerie, watching them from the stage at the front of the room with their lifeless doll eyes.

Beep! Beep! Beep! Beep!

According to the detector, the slore hadn't moved. It was twenty yards away.

"When you get him in your sights, fan out before you squeeze. We don't want to shoot each other in the back. Check your settings. Make sure your rifle is set to armor-piercing. Move as one, just like Sheela taught us."

Beep! Beep! Beep! Beep!

They passed between the cafeteria tables. Drew eyed Chuck E. The mouse looked to be watching him. He wanted to blow its head off, if for no other reason than to make sure his rifle was working.

They entered the play area: a labyrinth of coin-operated rides, a ball pit, and a long indoor tunnel system of wide multicolored tubes and slides resembling a giant's large intestine. Justin scanned the room and gulped.

"He's in the tubes," Justin said.

Beep! Beep! Beep! Beep!

Drew looked across the tubes to the long green slide

185

leading into the ball pit. He knew what had to happen and he knew he was the one who had to do it. He watched, from outside his body, as he turned to the group.

"Okay." He handed Justin his rifle and took the detector. He removed his helmet and slid off his vest.

"What are you doing, dude?" Ryan only called him "dude" when he was angry.

Beep! Beep! Beep! Beep!

"I can't maneuver in the tubes with armor on."

Ryan punched Drew's shoulder. "Are you out of your frickin' mind?"

"I'm gonna enter on the far side and flush it out the green slide into the ball pit. Then you guys blast it to hell."

Drew pulled Sheela's pistol from his holster and charged it. The blue lines glowed and hummed up the short barrel. He pulled on the visor Justin had connected to the detector. The lenses displayed the gridlines through a blue haze. The dot pinged into view when it was struck by the wave. The distance between him and the slore registered on a sidebar in his visor.

Drew crossed to the tower at the far end of the room. It was the only other entrance to the tubes. The tower rose two stories, encased in mesh netting, and the only way up was a staggered staircase one had to crawl through. Drew was now big enough that it was difficult to squeeze his body up each level.

He held the gun ahead of him. He had a flashback of climbing the tower when he was younger, of feeling what his mom later told him was claustrophobia. He remembered freezing and screaming out until his dad had to squeeze up there to get him. His mom brought him back the next day and forced him to climb it again.

While other kids ate pizza, played Skee-Ball, and watched

the animatronics play a concert, Drew was facing his demons, fighting back tears, and swallowing his fear. He failed another three times. He was the only kid in Warfield forced to go to Chuck E. Cheese. He did eventually conquer claustrophobia, but that had been nothing compared to this.

Far below, Ryan and Missy dragged a table from the eatery and flipped it on its side. The assault team all crouched behind it and rested their rifle barrels along the lip. Kevin whispered, "Please, God. Please, God. Please, God. Please, God."

Beep! Beep! Beep! Beep!

Drew made it to the top of the tower and came to the mouth of the first tube. It was deep and dim, but at least he could see through the dark-vision goggles. He crouched and crawled along the tube. His knees felt wet and slick from the green blood along the floor.

He was closing in. The beeping chimed rapidly but the creature hadn't moved. Drew strained, trying to listen beyond the beeping. He came to an intersection. The dot appeared to his left. He turned his head that way but slipped in the goo pooling there. It was sticky and clung to him in lacy, thick lines.

As he tried to inch ahead, he slipped and fell face-first into the goo. The goggles popped off. He was in the dark. He felt madly for them and dropped his gun. He lay there in the pool, petrified, his eyes and ears straining in the darkness. Then he heard it, scratching. The slore was inching toward him.

It rounded a corner up ahead. He heard it hissing and wheezing. The scratches turned to scuttles. The entire tube shook as the slore sucked in its body and dragged itself toward him.

Drew spun and slid frantically over the goo. He could hear it scuttling closer and closer, closing in. He clawed madly at the sides, his legs slipping in the trap. It had set a *trap*. The slore glided easily over its own pooled blood. Drew came to the far side of the tube as one of the slore's razor claws caught his shoe. It yanked him, but he caught the side of the tube and held on as his shoe popped off.

Drew flung himself down the green slide with its spiraling drop, tumbling around and around in the dark. He popped out and splashed into the ball pit, met with a salvo of lasers from the overeager assault squad. The plastic balls burst and melted around him, and he felt trapped amid a firework display.

He swam to the surface only after he heard Ryan scream, "Hold your fire! It's Drew!"

Drew popped his head up. "Guys, it's coming!"

Following a scraping noise, the black body of the slore birthed from the slide and crashed beneath the balls. With Drew still at the far corner of the pit and the slore hidden, it was too dangerous to shoot. All grew quiet as the slore lurked beneath the surface, balls trembling and shifting like rippling water. It positioned itself between Drew and the team. It had him blocked off.

Now the balls were still. The crew inched closer, shakily aiming their rifles. They were heaving, hearts pounding, every sense supercharged. Then there was a ripple. A few balls on the far side settled. It flattened itself along the bottom.

Drew didn't move or dare take a breath.

"There it is," Ryan whispered.

It had moved away from Drew to the other side of the massive ball pit. A shiny black claw poked up from the balls, twitching and moving slowly about, searching for Drew.

"On my mark," Ryan said. "Ready . . . aim . . . *fire*!"

Blue plasma charges hit the pit, melting balls and exploding the claw. The claw burst in green blood and went limp. Smoke and a nauseating smell of alien blood and burning plastic twisted up and filled the room.

"Got ya, mother sucker!" Kevin screamed.

Drew couldn't believe it. He stood and saw the long, black, muscular arm with its razor claw. It lay prostrate over the top of the balls, scorched and oozing and still twitching. Drew sloshed toward the Polars, the balls a little higher than his hip.

The others celebrated, but Drew noticed Ryan staring silently at the twitching arm. Ryan's smile fell, and Drew knew what his best friend was thinking. The arm was detached. Where was the rest of it?

Ryan's eyes popped. "Drew, it's a trick!"

That thing used its own arm as a decoy—

Drew felt something playfully tickle his one shoeless foot. He didn't have time to scream. He was yanked below the surface so fast he lost his breath. He felt the plastic balls rush over his body as he was pulled along the floor of the pit. He couldn't see the slore and only felt its sharp grip on his foot. This was it; he was dead. They'd been no match for this Outland monster.

Then something rose in him, angry, desperate, and defiant. He'd come too far to be eaten in the ball pit at Chuck E. Cheese!

He forced his hands against the floor and thrust himself up. He shot one hand up and managed to break the surface and wave wildly before being pulled down again.

He heard Ryan bark an order and heard the *zwoot*, *zwoot*, *zwoot* of several rifles. The slore released him to shield itself.

His only hope for survival had come. He leapt up and dove for the side. Ryan caught him and hoisted him out.

The slore erupted from the pit. Plastic, multicolored balls flew everywhere and rained down. Blue plasma flashed and streaked. Drew fell into someone, someone else struck him in the head, a laser blast scorched past his leg. Missy screamed. The world flipped with a hard thud.

Drew was suddenly on his back, pinned by one of the muscular claws. Missy lay beside him. The slore's demonic, eyeless face grinned down at them, showing Missy its translucent teeth. Another clawed arm had Ryan pinned against the wall. Kevin and Justin had been shot with wads of thick ooze and lay glued to the floor. Their laser blasts had done nothing against the slore's exoskeleton.

The slore hissed and opened its mouth wide to eat Missy, who screamed, "Drew!"

"Stop!" Drew pleaded. "Eat me!" He tried to fight, but the slore pressed him hard against the cold concrete. Its teeth came down on Missy just as a plasma blast streaked across the room, blinding them. It ricocheted off the slore's armored back. The creature shrieked and reared up on its four hind legs, exposing its soft underbelly.

Drew looked up and saw Sheela in the entranceway, Kristen behind her. Sheela aimed a rifle and squeezed the trigger before the slore could shield its face.

The next plasma charge imploded the slore's pale face and couldn't exit the monster's thick shell. Smoke puffed from every joint on its body as the burning projectile ricocheted around inside, frying its guts. Chuck E. Cheese would forever smell like baked slore. The creature flung Missy and Ryan but held Drew up in the air. It shuddered and smoked and spewed neon, gooey blood. Then it blew up.

Drew hit the floor, the clawed arm twitching beside him.

They were all shaking and dazed as Sonetta checked their injuries with her medi pack. Kevin grabbed her and blubbered into her jacket. Instead of slapping or yelling at him, Sonetta held him, stroking his greasy hair.

Sheela helped Drew up. Her mouth was slack and her blue eyes showed relief. She went to say something but instead hugged him tightly.

"I guess the Starlust wore off," Drew said.

"I thought you'd be dead. Kristen showed me where you'd gone."

"Hey, dummy," Kristen said apologetically.

"Thanks for coming back."

Gurgling laughter rippled from the slore's smoldering, bubbling carcass. Everyone jumped and Kevin hit it with another blast from his rifle. The slore didn't move. Sheela, Drew, and the others approached it slowly. Inside the body was a small box. It glowed red and had a speaker from which the laughter emanated. Sheela reached in and picked it up. A string of slime followed. She shook it off and examined the box closer.

A scratchy voice said, "Hello, Sheeelaa. We found you."

"Then come and get me, ShinFar." Sheela tossed the tracker on the floor and stomped on it. The laughter died.

"Whoa! That was an astro gremlin?" Missy asked.

"They . . . they're on their way?" Justin asked as he wiped green goo off his broken glasses.

"What? But we killed it!" Drew said.

Sheela sighed and shook her head. "The tracker activated earlier when the slore saw the cruiser." Sheela suddenly grabbed him. "Was I dreaming before? About the journal?"

Drew managed a smile.

Back in the sky aboard the heavily damaged cruiser, Sheela stood beside Drew as he flew them to the barn. He pushed it, but the engines kept failing, the cabin lights flickered, and wind rushed in through the shattered windshield.

"It's like a convertible," Kevin said as Sonetta applied bandages and healing foam to his and the others' wounds, wiping them clean of the green blood. Slore blood was toxic and burned their skin.

"Where's the gate to the ship?" Justin asked Sheela as he searched the sky ahead of them. Sheela didn't respond, and the rest of the short, rocky flight was quiet with anticipation. Sheela leaned forward, tense, like she might get out and run ahead. The cruiser finally gave out over the cornfield and everyone held on as they crash-landed twenty yards from the clearing. The poor cruiser hissed, and smoke wheezed out from the rockets as they hustled off. Drew was the last out and he switched on the Oren wall so that only the smoke was visible.

Justin grabbed an extinguisher on his way out and ran to spray the engine.

Drew beckoned to him. "Leave it. We won't need her anymore."

Instead of running for the doors, Sheela looked at Drew. "The gremlins are on their way. If it's not there, we're finished."

Drew pictured his mom as a girl, seeing the ship and meeting the strange, alien man. He saw her writing it down, sketching it, and later telling a little boy the story. Drew took Sheela's hand. "It's there." He led her forward.

They pulled back the doors and passed through the Oren wall into chaos. Their base was destroyed. The slore had followed the Talk-Talks' scent and ransacked it. Several Talk-Talks were dead. A few lucky ones had hidden in the eaves, shivering miserably until Missy called them down and placed them gently into her backpack.

Sheela and Drew flipped over the lab table and cleared the gear away from the floor. They fell to their knees, feeling around the floorboards, the others looking on in confusion. Drew's fingers located the edges of something under a thin layer of hay, and they hurriedly brushed it clean. It was a trap door.

It had been at their feet this entire time.

Chapter 22

The Ship

"They found it," Ryan whispered.

The wooden trap door had an iron ring handle on one side. Sheela grabbed and yanked, but the door was constructed of thick planks, and it took all of them to pull it open and push it back. The door fell with a loud crash and kicked up clouds of dust. They coughed and rubbed their eyes as they peered through the haze. A square portal yawned up at them, so dark it appeared black. They crowded around it, shivering from the breath of cold that wafted out.

Sheela grabbed a cracked lantern and dove to her stomach, dipping the light in.

"Anything?" Drew asked.

She shook her head and got to her feet.

"Let's get some rope," Drew began, but Sheela handed him the lantern, took a breath, and jumped in.

Missy screamed, Justin gasped, and the others rushed

forward to grab her, but Sheela had already disappeared.

"Sheela!" Drew called.

No answer.

"Ryan, help me down!" He lay face down and spun so that his legs dangled into the darkness. Ryan clasped his hand and it felt like he might pull him back out. "Drop me," Drew said.

"You sure?"

"Yep."

Ryan hesitated and then let go.

Drew was swallowed by the darkness and fell several feet before feeling smooth, hard-packed dirt at his backside. He slid and flailed his arms, but there was nothing to grab and no way to stop. Then the floor leveled and he popped out of what had been a tunnel.

He still couldn't see, but his other senses told him he was in a large, cavernous chamber. He was sitting on uneven dirt and could feel rocks and roots beneath him. The air smelled of earth and moisture, and dripping water echoed from somewhere. He climbed to his feet, afraid and disoriented. As he started to shout again, he saw a faint light appear in the distance.

"Sheela?" He stumbled toward the twinkling star and soon bumped into her.

Sheela was holding out the key, and its cold light was growing brighter. As the key brightened, it appeared to activate a blue-white light, like dawn, at the chamber's distant edges, and a large silhouette materialized ahead of them.

The Polar Starship rose like a pyramid. Its white metal exterior reflected the growing light, and the bottom half sat down within a crater while the topmost deck touched the ceiling. It was a starship, but like the cruiser, it wasn't futuristic. It was an ancient alien obelisk, magical and ethereal. A giant cannon pointed off the stern—the Polar cannon that would defeat Malgore's Necrobeast and destroy the Outland gateway.

Screams echoed from behind and Drew pulled his eyes from the beautiful ship to turn and see the others tumble from the tunnel slide. The screams and laughter stopped when they saw the ship.

Sheela was transfixed, and when Drew finally touched her, she jumped.

"Isn't it beautiful?" Her eyes shimmered and she could barely speak. Drew felt numb and smiled so widely every muscle in his face was cramping.

The others joined them, and they clung together in a collective stupor. Then the group charged for the ship. Sheela led the way down into the shallow crater. They ran beneath it; its wide base was well out of reach and the same circumference as Drew's court. They spotted a spiral staircase near one of the great legs and climbed it to a circular hatch.

At a small hole to the hatch's left, Sheela used the blue key. She plunged it in and the hatch slid back. Instead of climbing up, the staircase raised up inside. The group lifted into the bowels of the great ship and the hatch closed beneath them. The air was close and warm, and light emanated from the walls and ceiling in gradients of orange and purple. They finished climbing the staircase and exited up onto the bottom deck.

Sheela led them through a corridor of tan walls with cream-colored conduit. Drew felt like he was deep in the alleyways of some exotic city. The bottom deck was a biodome. A stream bubbled around below the floor and pooled in a lagoon. The plant life was purple and green, and thick vines and other plants grew and glowed across one side of the chamber and ran up the walls and hung from the ceiling. Fungi dotted the landscape, mushrooms glowing red, yellow, and orange, and Drew realized the interior light wasn't coming from the ship but the plants.

"It's an Orelian garden," Sheela said. "This is what they eat on long journeys. The plants also clean the air and filter the drinking water."

They moved past the garden to a spiral ramp, passing the next deck and going to the one above it. It was dark now and Sheela used the blue key to light their way. They exited the ramp and stopped in front of two wide doors. She waved the key in front of the doors and they slid back.

They entered a dark room with a low ceiling. Sheela went to the center of the room, her light revealing a console.

"Polars, with me," she said.

Drew was the first there, but everyone gathered around her. She turned to Drew and held out her hand. He was confused until he realized she was handing him the key.

She whispered to him, "Dimensions and worlds will be forever in your debt. You will be the keeper of the key. It must never leave you."

"Why me?"

"Yeah, why him?" Kevin said.

"I gave over to despair, but you proved yourself a true liaison and brought us all to this moment. The key is safest with you."

Drew took it and inserted it into a hole on the console.

"Everyone, turn it together," he said.

They all took hold of the key and turned . . .

Nothing.

And then a low hum built and grew and vibrated up

through them. Banging noises from the lower decks startled them. The giant ship woke with creaks and groans. Consoles around the room lit with low blue lights, panels flickered to life, conduits glowed, buttons, switches, dishes, screens all winked and blinked and chattered. Then, in a powerful flash, the entire command center of the Polar Starship was lit.

They all stood at the center of the room on a raised quarter deck. The consoles and stations all faced a wide, narrow port window. There was a worn leather chair, creased and stained like an old baseball glove. Sheela approached the chair and placed her hand gently at the back. They all looked on, and she caught them watching as she regained her senses.

She smiled through shimmering tears. "What are you guys waiting for?"

They ran about the command room, finding the same stations they'd been assigned on the cruiser. They found their seats and ran their hands over dials and switches and wheels and buttons. The ship spoke to them, whispered into them, guided them.

Drew stood and watched, soaking in everything until his brain threatened to explode from joy. He felt a weight lift. They were saved! They were going to win this war. They were going to be heroes. Most importantly, *he* was saved. He was getting out of Warfield.

Sheela stood beside him, addressing the crew as they explored their stations. "The ship has three decks and is fully collapsible. It can hyper-fold into something not much bigger than the cruiser. My father told me no one knows how old it is or who constructed it, but it has a portal jumping technology no one has ever been able to duplicate. It protected the floating cities of Gladerian, and explorers used it to discover the dimensions of Zoltron and Astoria."

Sheela spoke, but no one listened. They were struck by the ship's captivating beauty, the dancing light from the waking systems.

They sprinted into the main hallway and down the ramp to the next deck. They found the lab, lit with spectral yellow light from the floor. It was full of test tubes, beakers, and strange alien creatures preserved in yellow liquid. Multicolored vines hung from the ceiling, and more exotic plants sprouted from the walls and floor.

They found the equipment pool stacked high with messy aisles of small vessels, gadgetry, tools, suits, engine parts, weapons, and things for which there was no earthly description. They discovered the medic bay through a hidden entrance off the main hall. It contained six pods with glass shells and mattresses made of healing foam. Sheela explained that the lives of many great explorers and warriors had been saved in these six pods.

Kevin found the mess hall. It was full of foreign fruits, vegetables, meats, and liquids preserved beneath a layer of mist. Gunnery turrets lined the hallways, between stations, and on all three decks. They found the barracks on the lowest deck with its armor and rows of laser rifles. These weren't the old boxy models Sheela had stowed in the cruiser. These were smooth, rounded, lightweight, copper-tinted rifles with strips of blue light lining the barrels, just like her snub nose pistol.

Sheela called them in after a while. "I want you to see the sleeping quarters."

She took them to a wall on the middle deck. She tapped it several times and a circular hatch slid back. The rounded, narrow tunnel was just big enough to walk through. It reminded Drew of the large drainage tunnel they rode their bikes through near Watkins Park.

"You sleep in a tube?" Kevin asked.

Sheela beckoned them and they followed single file through a short run and came out the other side into a dark room, beneath a wide dome. Sheela touched a panel on the wall. The room came to life and suddenly they weren't in a room at all.

They were standing on a beach, under a red sky. A strong breeze rushed over them and they looked down the hazy shoreline to see a magnificent city with twinkling spires. The room projected the images so clearly it no longer felt like a room.

Sheela said, "You can set this to look like whatever you want—whatever helps you sleep or not miss home so much. My father said he used to come in here and bring up projections of us and sit staring at us for hours. He never slept well on long voyages."

The others marveled as Sheela changed scenes by touching the pad and imagining different places. The palace chambers of Orel's capital city. The Zoltarian Star Bridges. The giant cave lagoons of Rexo. Cots were spread around the floor where you could lie down under an alien sky or deep in the jungle city of a faraway world and fall asleep to a gentle breeze.

Drew felt himself getting woozy. The room was warm and comfortable, like a bath, and smelled sweet and calming. His shoulders dropped and his body tingled. The battle with the slore had clenched him in knots, but now every muscle was loosening and releasing, like he could unravel and fall in a comfortable heap on the floor.

He looked around and saw Sonetta stretching out her arms, closing her eyes, and tilting her head as the soft breeze kicked back her hair. Kristen and Missy were leaning their heads on Kevin's shoulders, and Ryan swayed like the breeze might blow him over. He was transfixed by the distant city. Justin was the only one fully alert. He scrubbed his glasses and swished in his windbreaker as he moved about, examining the walls and dome.

"How does this work?" he kept muttering.

A thought washed hotly down Drew's chest. "This can show you anything you can imagine?"

"That's right," Sheela said.

The room dimmed as she removed her hand from the pad. She led the group to the command room, but Drew lingered. He turned to follow the others but then paused. Checking to make sure everyone was gone, he approached the touch pad. He gulped and thought about running from the room. Then he stretched out his hand and placed it flat against the pad's cool surface before closing his eyes.

Even with his eyes closed, he felt the room light up and the air change. He smelled familiar smells. He heard birds chirping. He trembled violently so that his teeth clicked, but he forced his eyes open. It was exactly as he imagined: his room at sunset, the warm red sun casting its last light down over his bed and the mess of clothes and action figures on his floor. He glanced at his dresser and saw the picture. It was propped upright and, in its reflection, he saw her.

He turned slowly and there she was, leaning against his doorjamb, arms crossed comfortably at her chest. She wore the shirt he'd given Sheela, and she smiled at him. Her hair was thick and wavy and beautiful, her eyes bright and full— like she'd never been sick. They didn't speak. She was just a projection of his memory. She just leaned and smiled at him.

Drew finally pulled his hand away.

He hid himself deep in the equipment pool and pulled

himself together by shocking himself on a busted Oren disk. He found the others in the command room. When he entered, Ryan spotted him and grabbed him around the shoulder. "I looked all over for you."

"I was exploring."

Ryan looked in his eyes. "You okay?"

Drew tried not to look away, but his hands were fidgeting. "I'm good." Ryan pulled him over with the others but kept a tight hand on him.

"I got a question," Kevin said, looking up from the wide, colorful comm station. "How the heck do we get this thing outta here? I mean, do we start digging?"

Sheela smiled and nodded as though Kevin had read her mind. She went to the captain's station and punched in some coordinates. "Just like you, I've never been here before, but Father told me how it works. Watch this." She pulled back the jumper lever.

The kids waited for something to happen, but the ship merely groaned and rattled as lights throughout the halls and rooms flickered. Sheela frowned and tried the code again. A soft alarm beeped from the engine console and Justin ran to it instinctively.

"Report!"

"It says the plasma needs to be mixed before jumping. What does that mean?"

Sheela joined him and checked the message. "This is going to take two whole days. We don't have that time." Sheela kicked the console and hung her head. "Malgore's already sent a detachment of gremlins." She sighed. "Start the mixing."

"We're low on fuel?" Drew asked.

"The polar plasma that allows us to fly, jump, and defend

ourselves has been sitting too long and needs to be mixed. We can't get the ship out from under this barn without jumping. The polar plasma also powers the cannon I'm going to use to destroy Malgore and his ship."

"Hey." Drew put a hand on her shoulder. "Malgore still doesn't know we found the ship. Two days gives us time to prep, and when those tanks finish mixing, we'll rescue the warriors and give Malgore the surprise of his life."

Sheela suddenly hugged him. Her cheek grazed his, and he wrapped his arms around her. He wasn't embarrassed or nervous. In that moment, he felt one with her, knowing the weight of her burdens and the strength of her hope. They held each other tightly as the others gathered around them and joined in. There were no words, only tears and laughter.

They eventually exited the ship through the basement hatch. The stairs lowered and the hatch closed. Drew looked up while the others descended the spiral staircase. Something caught his eye—a bit of chicken scratch they'd missed on the way in. He got up closer, and when he saw what it said, he went numb and nearly fell from the staircase. The phrase read: *Mickey Mouse has warts.*

"Sheela." Drew grabbed her before she was off the stairs. As the others kept going, he pulled her back up the stairs and pointed at the scrolled writing. "That was my mom's saying, her password. She was here. She *saw* the ship."

Sheela gently touched the etched writing, marveling at it. "*See.* It's my destiny to come with you, back to your world."

"Drew, I need your help as crew, but then you need to come back here. This is your home."

"You promised. If I found the ship, I could go with you."

Sheela looked at the message again, scratched out by a

young girl, long ago, and nodded. "But if you're leaving for good, you need to tell your father."

"I will."

Chapter 23

Countdown

Early the next day, Drew was thankful to see the invisible cruiser had stopped smoking. They would need to move it eventually, but for now it was represented by a smashed section of corn, like a UFO crop circle. He lay awake all night thinking about the Polar, and it called to him so he could think of nothing but boarding it.

They spent the day exploring, prepping, and learning the ship's stations. The seekers used to find the ship were now pointed at the Warfield gateway to alert them the second anything—like a gremlin fleet—broke through. They cleared out the barn and loaded all the gear into the Polar's storage bay. They rounded up all the Talk-Talks and kept them on board, where the creatures trundled about underfoot and made messes.

"Nothing yet!" Kristen reported for the tenth time that morning. She nervously chewed on her newly painted nails while she and Sonetta monitored the gateway from her radar for any gremlin activity.

The gremlins would arrive in zool ships, large, living organisms the gremlins had converted into ships. The zools looked like slugs and moved slowly, but their gelatinous flesh was covered in a thick membrane that protected them from small arms fire. They were also dangerous in their own right, able to spit acid goo and use their long-spiked tongues to snatch soldiers from twenty feet away and devour them.

Justin sweated over the engine diagnostics console, watching the painfully slow mixing progress. To distract himself from the oncoming gremlin attack, he frequently snuck off to explore the ship's catacomb-like engine room.

Ryan and Missy learned the weapons systems, starting with the ship's giant plasma cannon. Sheela told them the gun's highly concentrated blast of polar plasma would destroy Malgore's nearly indestructible Necrobeast in one shot. With Malgore dead, she believed the adults would be freed from the parasite's control and the gremlins would surrender.

Sheela stood tall at the Polar's helm. Even though she barely slept, the dark circles were gone from her eyes. She'd sworn to Drew she wouldn't touch any more Starlust. Her eyes were fiery and focused, her jaw set.

"I've got Bash!" Kevin said from his station.

Kevin projected Bash in the middle of the room. His transparent form fizzled and waved.

"Hey, sis!" He smiled, even while wearing a bloodied headband and his left arm wrapped in a ratty sling.

"What's happening?" Sheela said.

"Nothing much. They got us pinned deeper in the tunnels." Bash gripped his rifle tightly with his good hand. "Good news: Dimension Warriors from all nine dimensions have reported in. But it's getting hard to hide them all, let alone feed them—"

"—Bash, I lied," Sheela said. "We didn't have the ship, but we do now."

They heard the other warriors cheer in the background.

Bash chuckled. "I knew you were lying. I was just hoping you'd actually find it before we all became slore food."

"Speaking of, Captain Shipley and his Polars killed a slore. It would have killed me and I would never have found the ship without him.

Bash nodded to Drew. "You did good, liaison,"

Sheela smiled. "He's more than a liaison. They're Dimension Warriors. And he's the keeper of the Polar key."

Bash hooted and the others cheered. Drew let his chest swell, showing off the key on the necklace. He was handling this newfound fame quite well, he thought.

"Welcome, brothers and sisters," Bash said. "Life's about to get a lot worse . . . but we're glad to have you." He looked at Sheela. "I can't wait to see the ship. Anything you want to tell me?"

"Bash . . ." Sheela's eyes shimmered with tears. "It worked. We're mixing the plasma and then we're coming to rescue you."

Bash gave her a look. "So you're not gonna tell me about the gremlin fleets on their way to capture you?"

Sheela snorted, "Minor inconvenience."

Bash shook his head. "No, it's not." He began to disappear. As his signal faded, Sheela lunged to grab her brother, but her hands went through him.

"We're coming for you! Barricade yourselves. We're leaving soon!"

His voice cracked through the transmission. "Be

careful—Malgore—an't know yo—have th—Polar. He'll—ki—us all or—old us—ostage. You—ave to fight the Greml—and ake—em by surprise." Bash vanished.

"What'd he say?" Missy asked.

Sheela looked at Drew. "Malgore can't know we have the Polar. He'll hold the warriors hostage or kill them if we get close. If he gets desperate enough, he'll send the human army after us and we'll be forced to fight our own."

Drew saw Sheela spiraling downward with all the horrible possibilities. "Hey!"

Everyone looked at Drew. He went on, "We keep radio contact to a minimum and we don't ever talk about the ship. If the gremlins get here before we take off, we blast 'em before they have a chance to report back to Malgore."

He looked around at the group. "Keep learning your stations. We're leaving in less than forty-eight hours."

Suddenly an alarm sounded and everyone jumped.

"The gremlins are here!" Missy screamed.

Drew's blood turned to ice and all his confidence evaporated.

Chapter 24

The New Girlfriend

"Polars, quiet!" Sheela ordered. She killed the alarm. "Someone tripped one of the sensors outside the barn."

Kristen used a seeker dish hidden among the brush by the barn door. It was fitted with a camera. The monitor flickered to life and displayed the clearing and cornfield.

Drew couldn't believe it. Steve pushed through the cornstalks and emerged into the clearing, dusting himself off. He had a flashlight aimed up at the barn.

"It's just my dad," Drew sighed.

"How did he know we'd be here?" Sheela asked.

They watched as Steve approached the doors and yanked on them.

"I locked the barn doors. If we wait, he'll leave."

Justin paced nervously. "He knows something."

"He's looking for you," Ryan said to Drew. "We're supposed to be spending the night at your house.

Remember?"

"And we're staying at Kristen's," Sonetta said. "We all better get our butts back if we don't want to raise suspicion."

Sheela was back at the engine station, checking the mixing process. "You okay?"

"Yes. Just get back as soon as you can."

Steve jumped when they pulled back the barn doors. "Whoa! Wasn't sure if you guys were here."

Steve went on to tell them the slore fight put Grimes over the edge. Sheela had coated the slore with acid powder, leaving nothing but a gooey, unidentifiable blob in the middle of Chuck E. Cheese. But the damage around town and the multiple break-ins at Book Alcove and Safeway combined with the missing dogs and cats and a random trail of green ooze uptown ignited a panic.

Warfield's two cops were working overtime to patrol the parks, back alleys, and other secluded areas. They also deputized some good ole boys—friends of Willy's—to cruise around in their smoky trucks and make a lot of noise to intimidate who or whatever might be terrorizing their town.

Kristen got permission to have the girls stay the night. She told her dad she was sad about Cooper, who they were still looking for, and she claimed she needed her friends to help comfort her. She wasn't lying. The tears were real and her parents agreed.

Steve was excited when Drew asked to have Justin, Ryan, and Kevin stay the night. "Oh great! We can get a pizza and watch a movie!" Steve said.

The boys agreed to the pizza, but Drew claimed they were too tired to stay up for the movie. All that work on the treehouse wore them out. Drew also invented a new lie, claiming they were now dividing their time between construction and hunting the creature that was eating all the dogs and cats.

Steve listened and gave Drew an odd smile. "Alright, son. Sounds good. I'm proud of you guys." He took a swig of his beer and pointed at them all mid-gulp. "There was talk of canceling the carnival this summer, but people complained and they're gonna have it! I saw 'em settin' it up today over at the high school! It's Friday."

Steve handed Drew a pink printed sheet of paper advertising the carnival. "It's actually kind of mandatory due to the curfew. Sounds like the whole town'll be there."

The boys feigned excitement with grunts.

"I know you guys are probably worried about the wolf or weirdo or whatever is stealing the cats and dogs—the Millers can't even find Cooper—but we'll all be together and all your parents'll be there."

The pizza was delivered but no one had an appetite. The coming astro gremlins wore heavily on their minds and stomachs. Kevin ate two slices out of pity and Steve collected up the nearly full boxes, struggling to squeeze them into the fridge. "Wow, I would have thought a crew of hardworking boys would be famished. You all trying to lose weight?"

"Yes, sir," Kevin said, slapping his belly. "My mom wants me wearing a size five before school starts."

"Well, it'll be our breakfast tomorrow—unless you guys want Anne's famous pancakes. I taught myself how to make 'em. I want Drew to try 'em, but every time I turn around, he's sneaking out the window . . ."

They all looked up at Steve as he caught himself. "I mean, sneaking out the door—and I don't mean sneaking. You guys aren't sneaking anything, you're just going out to work on the treehouse, you know." He sighed. "Anyway . . . get a good night's rest. I'm sure you've got a lot of work to do tomorrow."

He awkwardly tousled Drew's hair as the boys headed upstairs. "I love you, son."

Drew stopped at the bottom of the stairs. His dad's words were slow to sink in, but when they did, they punctured his heart. Drew turned slowly, and his friends waited awkwardly for him to respond.

Drew thought it, but he couldn't say it. "Oh, uh, you too, Dad," he muttered.

They barged into Drew's room. "Why didn't you say you loved him back?" Ryan said.

"It doesn't matter."

"You're scared to say it."

"He just said it outta nowhere. I wasn't ready for it."

"When else would he do it? You're never around."

"Wish my dad would say it to me," Kevin said.

"Are you gonna tell him you're leaving?" Ryan asked.

"No. We can't tell anyone. It's top secret."

Justin plopped on Drew's bed miserably. "I've been trying not to think about that, but Ryan's right. How do we say goodbye to our parents without them knowing?"

"You won't need to. We'll be gone a few hours or a day, tops."

"You don't know that," Ryan said.

Sheela hoisted herself into the window. "When can you all return to the ship? We need to keep prepping and monitoring."

They all clammed up and she narrowed her gaze at Drew. "What?"

"Nothing. We're fine," Drew said.

"Well, my brother's not. I got a call after you left. The warriors are dug in and Malgore has him surrounded. He's looking scared, and Bash doesn't scare easily." Sheela reached into the sack she was carrying and brought out handfuls of small wrist watches. "Everyone take one. These bands are set to the ship's radar and will blink red when the gremlins enter our gate." The team put them on and Drew looked his over, half expecting it to start blinking.

Suddenly, the bedroom door opened and Sheela pulled her gun. Drew grabbed it from her as his dad peeked in with a laundry basket.

"Drew, I have clothes here—oh!" Steve looked Sheela up and down, taking in her head band, scar, warrior jacket, and Anne's shirt.

"Hey, Dad!"

"Hi, son . . . and you are?" He was still looking at Sheela.

Drew was trying to remember Sheela's backstory when she cut in, "Stacey, Kristen's cousin from Arizona."

Steve frowned. "Stacey? You had blond hair the last time I saw you."

"Yeah, colored it—trying something new."

"Uh-huh." Steve dropped the laundry basket on the bed. "Son, I need to speak with you." Drew followed Steve into the hallway.

"Dad, we've been getting together like this to talk about the treehouse—"

"Stop." Steve crossed his arms. "What's going on? Why is she wearing your mother's shirt? Why were you going through our closet? Your mother's journals were pulled out."

"Dad—"

"What is going *on*? I thought I could trust you. I thought you were growing up."

"She's my girlfriend! That's why I've been sneaking around. I was embarrassed. I was looking through Mom's journals to better understand girls." Drew hated himself more with each lie, but he told himself it was all to protect the old man and Sheela. Steve stepped back and blinked. His hardened expression softened and he broke into a smile.

"Wow, a girlfriend. Ha! She's really cute too. Hey, what's with the jacket and headband?"

"She's really into punk rock." Lying was easy once you started.

Steve ducked back into Drew's bedroom. "Stacey, sorry about earlier. Drew just told me you guys were—are going steady, or whatever you call it now."

Drew's friends did their best not to laugh and Sheela played along even though she had no idea what Steve was talking about. "Yes, we're going steady."

"And she's leaving soon to go back to Arizona, so we're trying to spend time together."

Steve blushed, giddy. "Good thing you'll have the carnival tomorrow night."

Drew shook his head. *There was no time to go the carnival, they needed to prepare—*

"That would be great, Mr. Shipley." Ryan glanced sideways at Drew, and the two shot each other wide-eyed looks in a silent argument.

Steve didn't notice but was lost in thought. "The carnival was where I took Anne on our first date." He snapped from the memory. "Drew, you and the guys walk Stacey back to Kristen's."

Steve approached Sheela and she tensed, her hand creeping to her hidden weapon. Then he reached out and shook her hand. "Stacey, it's nice to see you again."

Sheela gulped, her shoulders loosened, and she returned his warm smile.

"You too, Mr. Shipley."

They went downstairs to the door, and just as they were about to leave, Steve called down, "Stacey, come over for dinner tomorrow before the carnival. I'll make Anne's recipe."

Drew again shook his head. *Dinner? Mom's recipe? Why is Dad putting our mission in jeopardy, and why is he torturing me?*

"I'll be there," Sheela said, before Drew could stop her.

When they got outside, Drew pulled his hair out. "We don't have time for the carnival or dinner!"

"I wasn't going to say yes," Sheela said, fighting tears. "But when he shook my hand . . . I saw my own father." She looked at him. "Drew, you have no idea how lucky you are." She left them and went into the corn.

As they walked home, Drew fell behind. He was looking at the stars again, wondering what it would be like to go beyond them. Now that leaving was a reality, doubt crept in.

Kevin and Justin had gone on ahead, but Ryan dropped back beside him. "I heard what you asked Sheela, back at the ship."

Drew looked away from the sky and saw Ryan eyeing the chain for the blue key under Drew's shirt. "What are you talking about?"

"You're leaving. *You.*" Ryan gulped and Drew realized he was trying not to cry. "You want to leave."

Drew didn't need this now, not with his dad telling him he loved him and talking about first dates to carnivals and his mom's recipes. "We're all leaving to destroy Malgore and become heroes—"

"No, you don't just want to leave for the fight. You want

to leave for good. When we found the ship, I heard you tell Sheela she'd promised to take you with her. You want to live in her world."

A single tear dropped down Ryan's cheek, and it struck Drew that the last time he'd seen his friend cry was kindergarten.

"Were you even gonna tell me, or were you just gonna wave when you dropped us all off?"

"You guys could come visit and I could come visit you. All ten dimensions will be safe and . . . and I would come back."

"What about your dad? You're just gonna abandon him?"

"He'll be fine."

"Really?"

"I wrote him a letter."

"*Wow*, a letter. That makes it all better." Ryan turned his hat around and pulled the bill over his eyes.

"Every time my dad sees me, he sees my mom, and it makes him sad. And he makes me scared of growing up. I think we'd both be better off with new lives."

"What's wrong with you, man?"

"What's wrong with me? *Everything!* Kevin and Justin have each other and they're good at school. Kevin wants to be a comedian in Kansas, Justin an aeronautical engineer for NASA. You have your sports teams and you're gonna go on and do great things. Eventually, you're gonna realize you're cool and I'm just a freak. None of you are afraid to grow up. All of you have goals and a place here. I have no place, and finally something happens and I'm not just Drew Shipley. I'm a pilot and a liaison and a Dimension Warrior. I don't belong here, Ryan. When I saw my mom's writing on the starship, I knew this was my destiny."

Ryan angrily wiped his eyes and turned away, heading home. Drew looked down and found he was gripping the blue key in a tight fist. Its soft blue glow creeped through his fingers and he looked from it to his friend until Ryan disappeared into the darkness. Drew did go home, after Kevin and Justin came back for him and asked where Ryan was. Drew lied and said he wasn't feeling well. He didn't know it, but Sheela had been listening, hidden behind a few rows of yellowing cornstalks.

Chapter 25

The Last Supper

Drew woke later that night. He was in bed and about to fall back asleep when he saw his mom standing at the foot of his bed. She held the hand of a boy—the younger him. She looked at him with a sad smile and pointed to the corner of his room where his dad sat, slumped against the wall. He had his head in one hand and the other clutched a piece of paper. Steve had found his letter. He looked small, like a child. Drew looked past Steve to his doorway where Ryan's silhouette had appeared, silently waving to him. Drew waved back until he realized Ryan's limp body was being operated like a puppet by a black slore just behind him.

Drew heard his mom moan and looked back to see her transforming, her hair falling out, her face caving in, the chemo and cancer doing their terrible work in a time-lapse. He heard a giggle and saw the boy holding her hand was no longer him but the boy Malgore projected. Drew tried to look away, but he couldn't. His terror grew as he saw a figure emerging from the darkness, behind her. It filled his room and its hands reached around her and enveloped her. She melted into the thing behind her. It swallowed and became her.

Malgore. He stood at the foot of Drew's bed, putrid and oozing, his deformed face mostly hidden within a red hood. Two small, yellow eyes glowed from deep within the hood.

"Captain Shipley . . ." he said, his hot breath washing over Drew's face.

Drew opened his eyes. He was staring out at the same dark bedroom. His digital clock showed 3 a.m. He was shaking and his heart was pounding.

He quickly felt for the blue key beneath his pillow—but it wasn't there. Panic struck him and he felt Malgore's hot breath wash over him again.

Malgore is here! He took the key!

But when he looked up, he saw the breath was just a humid breeze drifting in through his open window. He hurriedly went back for the key and spotted a soft blue light glowing through his bifold closet door. Now he could smell the faint odor of sweat and leather, and he knew what had happened.

He went to the closet and found Sheela curled up among his dirty clothes, hunched over Anne's journal. She'd taken the blue key from under his pillow and used it to read. She had the journal flipped to the pages about her father. His sketch rested under her free hand. Drew sighed heavily and tried to shake loose from his nightmare.

Malgore felt close and he wondered if he might meet the creature face to face when he left with Sheela. He reached down and gently took the key from her hand and put it around his neck, hiding it beneath his PJs. Protecting it was his one job, and it wasn't going to leave him again.

He wouldn't be going back to sleep, so he went to his desk and used the light to begin the letter to his dad. He started and crumpled several versions, dropping them into his wastebasket. *Dear Dad, by the time you read this, I will be gone . . .* He tried not to look at his mom's picture on the nearby dresser. She had encouraged him to go—with her dying, her journal entry, and her secret code written on the ship. More than that, it was her weirdness and the way she always urged him to embrace his imagination as she did hers. She made him this way, and his dad had never understood him. It was her fault, yet he could now feel her judging him. He placed the picture face down and finished his letter.

"Captain Shipley!" Drew woke at his desk, the pencil stuck to his face. Sheela's voice came over the walkie on his bedside table. The sun peeked above the trees, shining into a now empty closet. He jumped up and grabbed the walkie.

"Is it gremlins?"

"Mickey Mouse has warts," Sheela said.

He felt for the key. It was gone from around his neck again. "Sheela! Stop taking the key! What's going on?"

"I needed it to boot up the ship. Over and out."

He dressed quickly and ran to the barn. The team was already in the ship, manning the command room and crowded around the maps and navigation station.

Drew burst in. "What is it?"

Justin ran to him, practically skipping. "The mixers are nearly done! Eight more hours and we're off!"

"Eight hours is still a long time. Why did Sheela use the code?"

Justin grabbed and dragged Drew to the navigation

220

station. "Kristen located the zool fleet using the Polar's tracking technology!"

"Why is that a good thing?"

"Kristen radioed me at four this morning." Sheela put a hand on Kristen's shoulder and squeezed proudly.

"Who needs beauty sleep." Kristen worked and manipulated the map, spinning and enlarging it. "I thought, the map system can't see ships—especially with Oren walls—but it can identify creatures. So I made Justin give me the code for zools and then I started searching the different dimensions." She looked up at Drew. "Pretty good for a blonde, huh?"

Drew tried to make eye contact with Ryan, but his best friend wouldn't look at him. He tried to focus on the map, fighting a sinking feeling since their argument and his nightmare.

The zool fleet appeared as a collection of red dots within a 3D projection. They shimmered as they crept across the map.

"But they're getting close," Drew said, pointing to a planet on the map. "They're almost to us!"

"They would be, if this were us." Kristen pointed at the chyron below the map. The zool fleet was drifting through Zoltar.

"Okay, what does this mean?"

The flickering map reflected in Sheela's eyes. "Zoltar's big. Zools are slow. We've calculated their arrival time as late tomorrow."

"And the mixers will be completed by tonight!" Justin was back at the engine console.

"There are other zool fleets. Right? How do we know this is the closest one? How do we know this is the one headed for us?"

"The rest are currently stationed in Orel, with Malgore or in Toren, assaulting the Warriors," Sheela said.

Kevin moved to the radio console. He hit play on a recording, and a gremlin transmission played back in gremlin language. "*I locked in on the fleet's transmission and recorded our buddy, ShinFar. Pretty good for a fat kid, huh?*" He winked at Kristen and smiled.

Sheela turned to Drew, doing up her jacket and tightening her belt and holster as if ready to take off at that moment. "I thought we'd be forced to make a stand and fight the gremlins on your turf." She looked at Drew gravely. "And we would have lost."

"Against gremlins? We killed a slore." Drew searched himself for his original exhilaration and tried to emote the confidence he had before, but it wasn't there.

"ShinFar is the leader of the Morg tribe. They're killers—cold, calculating, and ruthless—and they'll probably have slores and other creatures with them. ShinFar himself has killed some of my best Warriors, and I've already told you how dangerous their zool ships are. But it doesn't matter now. We'll launch well before they get here, destroy them, rescue the Warriors, and strike Malgore's Necrobeast before dinner. I'll bring you back before your families even know you were gone." She looked at them proudly. "You will return as heroes, even if no one here knows what you've done."

Ryan crossed his arms, grunting and glaring at Drew with a cocked eyebrow. Drew knew he wanted him to confess he was leaving for good, but the others were too absorbed with Sheela's speech to notice the exchange. Ryan went to Sheela, and Drew was sure he was about to announce it himself.

"Permission to go organize the armory."

"You and Missy already did."

"Permission to double check."

"Permission granted."

Drew watched him go. *Why doesn't Ryan get it? I'll be back. I'll probably have my own ship and return whenever I want and take them on adventures.* But the thought no longer comforted him. He circled the map with his nightmare still clinging to him. "Why wouldn't Malgore come here to capture you himself?"

"He doesn't know I have the ship. He thinks I'm scared and alone and he wants me brought to him."

As Drew looked about him, he no longer recognized his friends. They'd become the crew of the Polar Starship, but somehow he felt confused and small like he had before meeting Sheela. It occurred to him they'd all broken their promises from that night in the cornfield. They'd all grown up.

He shuffled around, the only one without a station.

"Are you all right, Captain?" Sheela asked.

"I'm fine."

They practiced their stations throughout the day as more systems came online. The engines pumped the newly mixed polar plasma into the veins of the ship like a giant heart so that the only system yet to power up was the jumping booster. It also happened to be the most important, as they couldn't go anywhere until it was powered up. When Missy reported that the polar cannon was operational, everyone cheered.

Kevin bumped Missy out of the way, messing with the cannon's controls. "Why wait to jump when we can just blast our way outta here?"

"Because it would probably disintegrate half your planet." Sheela had returned from her nap and was checking the mixer progress.

Missy punched Drew's shoulder and crossed her arms. "What is *up* with you and Ryan? I don't like secrets!"

"That's 'cause you're a gossip." Drew tried to say it playfully, but it sounded more like an accusation and Missy returned a sour expression. When he saw the others were listening in and waiting for an answer, he backed away from them. "Everyone have your portal watches?" He held up his right wrist to show the thin, black monitor.

"I'm not wearing it. It's ugly," Kristen said. "We don't need 'em anymore." The other girls had ditched theirs.

Justin patted him on the shoulder, enjoying the fact that he wasn't the worrywart for once. "Drew, they're entirely unnecessary. Plus, it inflames my eczema."

He knew they didn't need them. The little watch was to show them when something breached the portal, and that wasn't going to happen. But he kept it on just to spite them.

Sheela switched off systems. "Go home, see your families. We'll rendezvous at your carnival before leaving." They powered down the ship but for the mixers and left. Drew placed the key around his neck and squeezed it for reassurance. It wouldn't leave his neck until they left.

As he walked out of the barn, Drew gazed up at the peach-colored sky. He was headed for the great beyond. He finally felt his heart lift, the way it had before, but the thought was interrupted when something pricked his thigh. He reached into his pocket and his heart sank. He pulled out a folded piece of notebook paper—his letter. He would slip it into his dad's briefcase tonight. The idea of seeing his dad was suddenly terrifying.

"How did your father react to your decision?" Drew was startled to see Sheela beside him. She'd quickly changed into some earth girl clothes from Kristen.

"What are you doing?"

She gave him a funny look. "Your father invited me to go with you to the carnival. Remember? I wasn't going to come, but now that we know about the zool fleet . . . anyway, how did your father react? Did he bless it right away or did it take convincing?"

"My decision . . . oh, yeah, he was fine."

"So he knows my true identity?"

Drew gulped and wiped a sudden sheen of sweat from his forehead. "He knows I can come back and visit."

She reached up and pushed his lips into an artificial smile. "I can see why you remind him of your mother. You look like her."

Drew thought, *Wait, did I tell her how Dad gets sad because I look like my mom?* But Sheela was already walking away, so he shook the thought and followed her.

That had been the reason. Somehow, he'd forgotten. His dad was sad and resentful when he saw Drew, but he wasn't anymore.

They came to the edge of the cornfield with the sinking sun at their backs.

"Look, maybe this isn't a good idea—the carnival. It might be better for you to wait on the ship."

"Your father requested I come, but if you want time alone with him, I understand." Drew was relieved when Sheela began to turn and then—

"Stacey! Drew!" His dad stood at the back sliding door. "Ready to go?"

Drew's heart sank, but as long as they headed straight for the carnival, he could make it through this evening without either Steve or Sheela catching him in his lie.

"You're shaking," Sheela said. She grabbed him and

shook him firmly, staring her cobalt galaxy eyes into his. "We did it, Drew. This is going to work."

"I know," Drew said. He wasn't thinking about gremlins at that moment. He looked ahead at his little yellow split-level house and dilapidated deck as the sun painted the discolored siding orange.

"Let's go," he said, planning to take her straight into the garage.

But when they squeezed inside the sliding door, Drew jolted to a stop. The dining room was neat and the table set for dinner with his mom's china. There were glasses of water with actual ice, sweat from the cold water collecting around the glasses and dripping down the sides. There were napkins folded and silverware laid out. There was a cut-up baguette and a bowl of peas. The table hadn't looked this way since well before his mom got sick.

"I thought we'd have dinner before we go!" Steve said as he exited the kitchen wearing oven mitts and carrying a steaming casserole in a glass baking dish. He placed the dish down and surveyed the table with pride.

"What is this?" Drew said in dismay.

"Dinner . . . I think." Steve glanced doubtfully at the casserole. "I tried to follow your mom's recipe." He looked at Sheela and smiled. "I'm glad you're here." He came over and pulled out her chair. Sheela sat and he scooted her in. Drew sat across from Sheela and Steve stood at the head of the table, blushing. "Mind if I say grace?"

Drew paused with a piece of bread halfway to his mouth. "Sure," he managed.

"Please," Sheela said. She followed Steve's lead, folding her hands and bowing her head.

Steve cleared his throat. "Lord, we, uh . . . haven't . . . *I* haven't talked to you in a while. Anne always did this. She's probably laughing at me right now. I thank you for Drew and for Stacey and for new life. Oh, and tell Anne I can't wait to see her again. Amen."

Drew swallowed and crunched his teeth together, holding his tears back at gunpoint. He started eating the bread midway through the prayer. The spongy yeast helped push back against the lump in his throat. He hadn't closed his eyes either but watched as tears squeezed through Steve's closed eyes. They dropped away from his bowed head and hit the carpet with audible thuds. Steve opened his red eyes and cleared his throat again. "Let's eat."

"This is good," Drew wasn't sure if it was, but he shoveled it in as he glanced at the clock. His foot bounced below the table. Steve sat and slowly made his plate. Sheela wolfed down the home-cooked meal. She'd eaten mostly snacks and cold leftovers since arriving in Ten.

"I'm sorry you're leaving, Stacey," Steve said. "Somehow I feel like I know you."

"I feel the same, Mr. Shipley."

"Steve. Call me Steve."

"Steve."

"Drew and I are really gonna miss you," Steve said. "But I want you two to keep in touch."

Sheela paused and shifted a hard glare at Drew, chewing a hunk of her bread angrily. Drew looked at his plate.

"Uh oh. I used to get that look from Anne. Did I say something wrong?" Steve asked.

Sheela looked back at Steve and softened. "No, of course not. You just reminded us of something we *haven't done yet.*"

"Will you be back?"

"I hope so. This is so good. This was Mrs. Shipley's

recipe?"

Drew wasn't hungry, but eating was an excuse to stay quiet.

"Yeah, this was Drew's favorite although not after tonight," Steve chuckled. They both looked at Drew.

"Drew? Anything to add?" Sheela asked pointedly.

"Nope," Drew responded through a mouthful of casserole.

She looked back at Steve. "Mr. Shipley, I'd like to know more about Drew. He's a student of others but reveals little about himself."

Steve chuckled. "If he's not gonna say anything, he leaves us no choice."

"What was he like as a little boy?"

Drew got up and started clearing dishes even before Steve and Sheela were done. He took a stack of plates to the sink. He turned on the hot water and began scrubbing. The blue key hung heavy on his neck.

Steve sat back. "He was adventurous—never knew where he was half the time. I guess Anne always knew because she was the one giving him the ideas. She told him and his friends stories about ghosts and monsters that roamed the woods and the cornfield and barn. She told them if they could brave those things there were amazing treasures to be found out there. She drew them maps and hid little prizes for them to find . . ." Steve trailed off. "I actually don't remember much. I was working a lot and traveling. It was really just the two of them."

"That was admirable of you, providing for your family. My father traveled a lot. Months at a time, but he did it for us."

"What does he do?"

Sheela looked away. "He works far away."

"Well, I'm sure your parents can't wait to see you. When do you think you'll come back?"

Sheela looked back at Drew between sips of water. "I don't know. I'd like to think soon, but I'm thinking it may be a very long time."

"Oh." Steve tried not to look at Drew. "Maybe you two can be pen pals or chat on the phone. We have your number. Right?"

Sheela nodded and looked back at Drew. He was engulfed in a cloud of steam, washing the same dishes over and over. "What else about Drew?" Sheela said.

Steve thought and laughed. "He used to bring home animals, wounded ones that needed help. He was so worried about them. He and Anne would bandage them and try to make them comfortable in a shoe box or something. I would come home and find mice, moles, squirrels, frogs, and salamanders in shoe boxes all over the house. He would stay up all night with them, check their water and food and make sure they were warm." Steve sighed. "I remember getting so angry. You remember that, Drew? I hope not. I used to yell at you to go to bed. Biggest fights Anne and I ever got into were over Drew caring for these stupid animals."

"He's a good caretaker," Sheela said.

Drew came out of the kitchen and checked the clock.

"And when they died," Steve continued, "he was crushed. He cried for days. I think he thought he'd failed them and it was too painful. Anne would make me quietly go out and bury them because Drew didn't want to let them go. She told me once it was because he didn't know how to say goodbye."

The room, the house, the world grew uncomfortably

quiet and small. The old clock in the living room chimed.

"When Anne got sick," Steve said, "Drew started telling jokes and goofing off, leaving doors and windows open and curtains drawn back. He played loud music, destroyed my records he played 'em so much. He created treasure hunts for Anne in the house and made her stay up late so they could tell each other stories. It made me so mad because he was distracting her from getting better . . ."

The silence between words was deafening. Steve's voice was tight, like he was being choked. "I now know he was trying to save her." Steve sniffed and took a sip of water with a shaking hand, "And he's been running ever since."

Steve looked at Drew. "You didn't fail her, bud. I failed you and I'm sorry."

"There's nothing to be sorry for." Drew's mouth moved before he knew what he was saying. He couldn't look his dad in the eye. He couldn't look at Sheela either.

After another moment, Drew managed, "We should probably get going."

As they got up and went for the door, he fell behind. He quickly removed the letter and slipped it into his dad's jacket pocket. He'd read it a hundred times. It was a terrible letter— *Dear Dad, if you're reading this, I'm already gone. Please don't be sad . . .*

The summer carnival glowed neon under the darkening sky. Screams and the clanging and banging of rickety rides echoed across town, and the air smelled of deep-fried dough, cotton candy, and cigarette smoke.

Sheela and Steve talked on the short car ride. He shared about his first date with Anne at this carnival and how he, the cool jock, had wanted to break it off because she was a nerd.

Steve pointed to the Ferris wheel. "We got stuck on that

very Ferris wheel and she confessed she was done with the date because I wasn't interesting enough for her."

As they got out of the car and walked toward the carnival, Drew noticed Sheela was quiet. He finally met her eyes and she no longer appeared angry. She was lost in thought.

The other Polars arrived, trickling in with their families. Drew and Sheela watched as they hugged their parents and said their goodbyes. Their parents had no idea the goodbyes were real.

"You're just riding the scrambler. Why are you crying, Miss Sonetta?" Sonetta's mom asked. She cupped her daughter's face. Drew saw Ryan hug Big Jake. Jake seemed caught off guard but hugged him back.

Deputy Grimes manned the gate. He nodded at Drew with a hardened, blank expression. As Drew observed the looming cop, he felt a compulsion and broke from the group. He went to Grimes with everyone gawking.

"Sir?" he said.

"What do you want, kid?" Grimes looked down at Drew from under the low brim of his hat.

"I just wanted to say I'm sorry you haven't found your brother. I'm sure that's been hard on you." Grimes's broad jaw slackened and his face twitched. "Thanks for protecting us." Drew started to walk away.

"Shipley," Grimes called out. Drew turned. "Just be careful out there."

Drew waved and returned to his friends. He led them deep into the carnival and there they were: the baseball team, the pool kids, their teachers, and the old men who sat outside Pete's Barber Shop. The whole town they were now fighting to protect.

231

Drew called them into a huddle. "Alright, everyone's seen us. Set your watches and split up. We'll meet behind the Ferris wheel in an hour. Do not be late."

They dispersed. Kristen, Missy, and Sonetta were swarmed by all the friends they'd ignored the entire summer. Kevin forced Justin on board the Flying Saucer ride. Ryan's baseball team found him, all of them wearing their Warfield Huskies ball caps.

"Before you leave Maryland, you're trying an elephant ear," Steve told Sheela as he led her to a nearby food stand. Drew was alone, taking it all in, when he noticed the Big Boys. They watched him from a distance. Jimmy wasn't with them.

Drew smiled to himself. *They used to be so big.*

As he turned, he came face to face with Jimmy. The once handsome, horrifying bully now had sunken cheeks and dark circles beneath his eyes. He looked at Drew as if they were the only two people on earth. "There he is."

Jimmy lunged at him and the two of them went to the ground. Jimmy was still quick, grabbing Drew from behind in his sleeper hold. Jimmy squeezed, but Drew's fear and guilt, everything he'd felt that evening, exploded. Before he could think, he sent several hard elbows into Jimmy's ribs and wrenched himself free. Jimmy fell and curled up, gasping.

Drew leapt to his feet and raised his fists, but Jimmy looked up from the dust and smiled, blinking as his breath returned. The burst of adrenaline died away and Drew lowered his hand to help Jimmy up. Jimmy chuckled and spat. He grabbed Drew's hand and Drew hoisted him up.

"You win. At least we got the tree fort." And with that, Jimmy saluted and left him behind the hot dog stand. Drew dusted himself off and looked around. No one had seen the scuffle. It felt like a strange closure to Jimmy Griffin, but a neighborhood bully was no match for a Dimension Warrior.

Drew left the shadows to find Sheela and Steve eating an elephant ear, white powder coating their mouths as they pulled apart the fried dough.

"Where have you been?" Steve asked.

"Just waiting," Drew said.

"Drew, why don't you take Stacey on the Ferris wheel?" Steve said with a wry smile.

"She doesn't want to—"

"That's a good idea, Mr. Shipley," Sheela said. She grabbed Drew by the arm and dragged him toward the Ferris wheel.

Drew checked his watch. "I think we should go back."

"How do you say it in Dimension Ten? Oh, yeah—shut up, Drew."

Kristen had clearly rubbed off on her. They stood in a short line to the Ferris wheel, Sheela still gripping his arm. As he looked at the line, Drew awkwardly realized only couples rode the Ferris wheel. Teenagers and some adults stood holding hands, whispering to each other, resting against each other and staring into each other's eyes.

"Take my hand," Sheela said.

"What?" She'd also observed the protocol. Drew finally reached out and found her hand. They struggled to get the right hold before she forced her fingers in between his, intertwining.

Drew whispered, "Sheela, I can explain about not telling my dad—"

"Wait 'til we're on board," she said. She rested her head on his shoulder to mimic the other couples.

The line of lovers moved and finally Drew and Sheela

were ushered into a red gondola. It whooshed away from the ramp, out and upward.

"I wrote Dad a letter, but it wasn't coming out right. So I rewrote it a hundred times—"

"You're not coming with me." Her voice was calm and she turned her body toward him.

"Wait—what? Sheela, you told me I was made for a greater purpose!"

"Yes, but that purpose might not be what you want right now."

"Sheela." Drew felt his stomach drop as they crested the glowing wheel.

Uptown Warfield sparkled on the horizon and the night sky was clear above them, but neither was taking in the view. Neither saw the mountainous thunderhead approaching from the south, invisible against the darkening sky even with the angry flashes deep within.

She looked into him. "Your dad loves you. He reminds me of my own. You're leaving because you think it's better where I come from—"

"Sheela—"

"Shut up!" Her eyes glimmered like the stars and her twitch was back. "You lost your mom, but you still have your dad and your friends and this world. I had friends like yours too. If you come with me, you'll lose everything and you have no idea what that's like." She sniffled and took his hand. "I want you to listen carefully—and I've already decided so don't try to change my mind—I'm leaving you all here."

Drew went numb.

"I'm taking the Polar beyond your gate and I'm going to seal off the door to Dimension Ten for good. The Polar's cannon can destroy gateways. It's the only way to ensure your world stays safe."

Drew tried to pull away from her. He had no idea he was crying. She held on to his hand and pulled back.

"Hey!" Drew shouted. Some of the couples in the gondolas to the front and back glanced at them. Drew lowered to a hushed yell. "You promised me I could leave."

"You want that because you think my world is better, but it's not."

"I'm your second in command."

Sheela shook her head as a tear ran down past her pink scar. "No, you're just a kid."

She leaned in and kissed him. Her lips were soft, and when they brushed his, the lights from the Ferris wheel glowed brightly and his body floated upward. Drew felt himself press into her and kiss her back.

They kissed as the gondola gently ascended the Ferris wheel's back curve and their lips parted as it slowed to a stop. As the gondola parked, a fat carny wearing a sweat-stained trucker hat and a Margaritaville tank top undid the chain and beckoned them out. Drew stumbled off with his legs numb and wobbly. Sheela grabbed and steadied him.

She was right and he knew it, but even as an immense weight lifted from his shoulders, he fathomed not seeing her again and shook his head. "Sheela, I'm still going."

"Drew. That was goodbye."

Drew wiped the tears away, his heart burning and pumping pain into his veins. The two stood speechless.

"Hey," the trucker-carny called out. Drew looked back at him and the man pointed to his wrist. "Your watch is blinkin'."

Drew and Sheela looked down. The gate sensor on Drew's wrist flashed red. "Oh no," Drew whispered. "This can't be happening! There not coming 'til tomorrow, right?"

Sheela looked up at the sky. "It's not possible . . ." Thunder rolled over her words.

"Maybe the sensor is broken." But it blinked faster and faster.

The gremlins were here.

"Drew, we need to go—*now.*"

Drew jumped up on a nearby picnic table and waved. Ryan saw him and broke from his team, grabbing Kevin and Justin as he passed them. Justin and Kevin handed their elephant ear, complete with strawberry jam and powdered sugar, to some random kids and headed for him. Sonetta tapped Drew on the shoulder. She and Missy had been waiting.

Missy was smiling and pointed at the Ferris wheel. "K-I-S-S-I-N-G."

Sheela yanked Kristen away from some older boys trying to win her a teddy bear.

"Guys!" Drew flashed his wrist and everyone's eyes bulged. "We have to get back to the ship *now!*"

"It's gonna take us forever to run back," Ryan said.

Sonetta huffed, "We shoulda brought the dang cruiser."

"What are we gonna do?" Justin grabbed his face, pulling his cheeks in panic.

"What's up?" Steve approached. From his expression, he'd noticed their sudden erratic behavior.

"Dad, we need a ride."

Chapter 26

Gremlins

"So, you left Kevin's mom's stereo in the treehouse?" Steve asked.

"That's right, and it's gonna get soaked in this thunderstorm," Drew said.

"And that's why you *all* had to come?" The others were piled into the back of Steve's tiny Celica like it was some kind of clown car. They sat on top of each other, anxiously scanning the darkening sky. Sheela was squeezed in beside Drew in the front seat.

They came upon the Big Boys riding their bikes up Sweepstakes Avenue and heading toward Drew's neighborhood. Jimmy was in the lead and swerved his bike so Steve was forced to veer into the other lane. As they passed, Jimmy looked right into the car, right in Drew's eyes, and he smiled. It wasn't Jimmy's normal sadistic smile; it was a hateful joy, and his dark eyes twinkled as if he were harboring some terrible secret. The other Big Boys gave them the bird as they drove on.

"I see Jimmy's still a fine young man," Steve said, shaking his head. "Came from a good family. What a shame."

Drew could feel Sheela shaking. She bit her lip and wore a cold, focused expression. "We need to go to the barn." She sounded like the general she really was, not the girlfriend from Arizona.

"The barn?" Steve frowned in confusion. "Isn't the treehouse out closer to the creek?"

"Dad, just take us up Pal's Run to the old driveway."

Steve took the old one-lane road and pulled up the long gravel driveway. Drew saw the cruiser lying in the field right where he'd crashed it. Its Oren wall had failed and it lay in plain sight but for the dusk and the coming storm. Steve was so preoccupied with the bizarre situation he didn't spot it. Once in the clearing, the kids spilled out the two open doors and Kevin climbed out the hatchback and flopped onto the ground.

"Stacey, it was very nice to meet you," Steve called out.

Sheela was already headed for the barn but stopped and came back.

"It was nice meeting you, Mr. Shi—Steve." She was so flustered she forgot to shake hands and instead pulled him into the Orelian embrace, going up on tiptoe to touch her forehead to his. Then she set off at a run and charged into the barn. Steve looked at Drew, desperately perplexed.

Ryan grabbed Drew and whispered, "This is serious! We need to tell your dad what's going on."

"Affirmative!" Justin hopped about, cupping his face.

"Drew, we're in a lot of trouble here," Kevin said.

Sonetta said, "You heard what Sheela said about making

a stand and fighting the gremlins here!" Missy was shoving sticks of gum into her mouth as she and Sonetta clung to Kristen. They all circled around him, tugging and pulling on him and speaking loudly enough for Steve to hear over the rising wind.

"*Polars*! Relax! We stick to the plan. We still have the starship and they haven't landed yet. Now, follow Sheela and get to your stations!" He shoved them all forward.

"Son!" Drew had forgotten Steve was there. He stopped and turned back as the others ran into the barn. His dad held a piece of paper. His letter.

"Oh no—Dad, don't worry. I'm not leaving!"

"What is this? What's going on? Were you gonna run away with Stacey?" Steve was pale and blinking in the wind.

"Dad, I'll explain everything. I swear on the hair. Mom started something many years ago and I've gotta finish it."

Steve shook his head angrily. "What?"

"You're gonna have to trust me—"

A guttural moan carried above the wind and thunder. Like the night Sheela crashed, Drew felt static electricity as the hair on his arms stood up. Steve's car headlights flickered and went out. Steve and Drew were in darkness when a sickly green spotlight came slanting downward from the thunderhead, hunting over the corn until it located them like actors on a stage.

"Dad, *run!*"

Suddenly, a powerful downdraft sent Steve and Drew flying. Drew hit the barn wall and fell. He looked up to see a fleet of dark masses swimming out from the thunderhead like great sharks. He couldn't make out any details, but the sight petrified him. He forced himself up and rushed to his dad. Steve lay beneath the tree line, where he had been knocked cold. Drew hurriedly checked his pulse.

"Dad! Wake up!" Then hands were on him, yanking him back. "Dad!" Drew screamed.

"He'll be okay! The mixers are done! We must take off and fight back!" Sheela yelled. "Your whole world depends on it!"

Sheela and Drew leapt down into the trap door, sliding and then running. The great Polar Starship stood ready and Drew felt a surge of adrenaline as he climbed up the stairs, up through the hull and bottom decks until he flung himself, heaving, into the command room.

The semicircular room felt hazy, lit only by the ghostly running lights from the floor. The others were at their stations. Just being back in the ship helped Drew regain control again.

Sheela took the helm. "Let's get in the air and take out that fleet!"

"How did they get here so fast?" Kristen kicked her radar station.

"It's okay, Kris!" Ryan said.

"No, it's not! This is my fault!" she screamed.

Drew ran around in front of the consoles. "Hey! We'll deal with this later! Stations, report in!"

"Weapons are ready," Missy called out, furiously chewing her massive wad of gum.

"Morphjump ready and the Oren wall is on," Justin said.

"Navigation is set for the Toren dimension," Kristen called.

"Medic bay and supplies ready!" Sonetta said.

"Communications ready!" Kevin screamed.

Drew's heart quickened. He wasn't scared. He felt excited, confident, and something else—worried for his dad.

He loved his dad. And he loved his stupid little town and the old men and Grimes and the Jimmy Cone. And it suddenly occurred to him: *I have a place in this world. And I must defend it.*

"General," Drew said, turning to Sheela. "We can take them whenever you're ready."

"I preset our jumping coordinates. We'll appear right behind them. We jump on my mark." Sheela held up a hand, waited for a five-count, and dropped it.

"All right, this is what we trained for!" Drew called out. "Commence Polar start-up . . ." Drew went for the key around his neck, but his hands grasped nothing. His hand spidered down inside his chest.

The blue key wasn't there.

He rifled through his jacket as Sheela stepped away from the helm.

"Captain Shipley?" Panic tinged her voice. "Commence start-up."

"Commencing," Drew said absently as he finished grasping through the last of his pockets.

Drew turned to the crew. Everyone looked at him in confusion.

"I don't have it," he heard himself say.

"Drew, we can't fly the Polar without it," Sheela whispered.

His mind raced. He had it on him ever since the slore attack—felt for it every few seconds. It was always with him. He swore to guard it with his life, he never took it off! He was about to rip his own head apart to look for it. Sheela and Sonetta raced for him, tearing through his jacket while the others hunched anxiously at their stations.

Suddenly, the whole story flashed before Drew: Sheela giving him the key after the slore attack. Watching over it.

Sleeping with it. Showering with it. Feeling for it. Living by its soft, reassuring light. When had that light gone out? He felt it before the Ferris wheel—

Jimmy's voice suddenly whispered in his head. *You win. At least we got the tree fort.*

Jimmy saw the key. He stalked Drew and saw him fiddling with it. He heard them discuss it. Jimmy didn't know what it was, but he knew it was important. He wasn't trying to fight Drew.

"Jimmy's got it," Drew exhaled. His brain did backflips and raced ahead of itself. "Change of plan! Everyone to fallback positions!"

Sheela went scarlet red. "No! I'm relieving you of command!"

"I know where Jimmy is! Please trust me!"

"Bad time for a stroll, Drew!" Kevin said.

Drew turned to leave. "The hoverbikes are outside! Everyone, stay here. I'm going after Jimmy."

Ryan tried to block him. "Don't do this."

Drew patted his shoulder. "I'm not leaving with Sheela, but I do need to leave now. I screwed this up. I need to fix it."

Sheela grabbed a rifle off the wall. She was headed for the door when Drew spun on her. "What are you doing? *Stay* here!"

She looked back. "Astro gremlins are about to overrun your town. You get that key. I'm gonna protect Warfield."

Kristen joined her without hesitation, and the two of them left the room. The others looked back and forth, petrified, from Drew to the empty doorway before running and clumsily grabbing laser rifles off the wall.

"Guys! Please don't go out there!" Drew said. None of

them listened. Then Drew saw Justin. His friend still sat at the pilot console, shaking so badly his teeth were chattering and tears were streaming down his face.

"I'm sorry, Drew. I can't m-move." Justin was soaked in sweat and looked like he might faint. He had hit his limit.

"Are you okay?"

"Nope." He sobbed softly. "We're all gonna die." Justin was right.

"It's okay, Jus. Stay here. We'll be back."

Drew left the room and heard Justin pound the console in hopeless anger. Drew chased after the others—out of the ship, to the surface, and through the trap door. His head was swimming as he climbed up into the barn and found them huddled in the darkness. Lightning flashed between the warped planks, and thunder rattled the loose floorboards. They bumped into each other in the dark and clustered at the doors.

Their hoverbikes and the hover couch leaned against the wall just outside.

Sheela and Kristen slowly pulled back the door, and they all peered out. It was dark but for the distant fireworks from the carnival. Sheela beckoned them to follow. She got low and hustled across the clearing to the corn.

"Kevin, shoulders," Drew said and climbed up Kevin's back. He looked out to the cruiser. He could just make out the ship twenty yards off, its back rising above the stalks like some great beast.

They heard two deep moans, like whale calls, and then a flash of lightning revealed them—big as jumbo jets—descending silently just behind the cruiser: two squirming, slimy zool ships. They looked like fat larvae with no faces, just puckered mouths full of teeth. Tiny arms sprouted randomly off their sides and spikes covered their bellies. Small rockets, surgically implanted along the zools' sides, spurted and fired blue flames as they landed.

Chapter 27

The Battle of Warfield

The zools crunched the cornstalks beneath their girth. There was a gooey, crackling sound and green light poured out from orifices on the zools' chests, open hatches glowing through the corn with pale green light. The night, with all its bugs and birds and thunder, was suddenly quiet, as if all the earth recognized it had been violated. Drew squinted through the darkness, straining to hear, unable to move against the deafening weight of the silence. He nearly broke his brain listening. He felt asleep in dread.

Then the soft crunch of dirt and the shivers of drying corn husks woke him. Things were moving out there. And they were getting closer.

A flash of lightning revealed them. Hunched, misshapen silhouettes crawling over the cruiser's exoskeleton like vulture apes. Sheela had described their standard weapons, so Drew recognized them. Red death lights shone on their razor cannons and green-glowing orb grenades hung off their tattered web gear. Sharp, long particle spears and jagged cutlasses jutted off their backs like insectoid antennae. One gremlin, leading the pack, picked along the roof, peering down through the cockpit windshield and aiming its razor cannon. A soft cabin light lit his grotesque face.

"Shee—la," it gurgled. "Gor versh."

"They're telling me to surrender," Sheela whispered.

"They're all over the cruiser," Drew whispered down to them. And it wasn't just gremlins. Drew saw several slores and other creatures.

He tried to get a better look at the gremlins circling the cruiser, but his elbow slipped and dug into Kevin's neck. Kevin squealed in pain and nearly dropped him. When Drew looked again the gremlins were gone.

"Oh no."

A green orb suddenly flew up from the corn. It arched over them like one of Ryan's home runs and exploded the rusted cupola on top of the barn. Everyone watched as green, glowing goo melted the cupola instantly in a bubbling glop that ran down the roof.

Drew toppled from Kevin's shoulders and landed on Ryan. As his friend helped him up, Sheela grabbed him. "We need to split up and distract them. You go for Jimmy!" Before Drew could respond, Sheela screamed, "*Fire!*"

Thwap! Thwap! Thwap! Blue lasers ripped from their barrels across the darkness, exploding against the dirt and the cruiser in showers of sparks. The blasts struck the zools, their slick flesh absorbing the plasma.

They fired their guns so long they ran low on polar-charge and Sheela held up a hand. They ceased fire and their guns hummed as wisps of smoke danced off the barrels. The bright lasers had temporarily blacked out Drew's vision, but he could hear his friends' shallow, quivering breaths.

"Did we win?" Kevin whispered.

Then they heard hissing and the *snap-crack* of breaking stalks.

"Here they come!" Sheela yelled.

Staccato thuds rumbled across the field as the gremlins returned fire with their razor cannons. Red balls of plasma hurtled toward them. The bloody, pulsing light revealed an advancing platoon. Everyone screamed and dove into the dirt. The red, burning balls soared over their heads only to punch holes in the barn and blast through the other side.

Sheela leapt to her knees and took aim. Blue lasers zipped from her barrel. The muzzle flashes flickered in her wild eyes and her body jumped from the rhythmic recoil. Drew found himself too scared to get up. Those red plasma balls had burned real, smoldering holes in the barn. What would they do to him? The others were also petrified, still crouched in the weeds as Sheela swept her gun back and forth, fanning lasers over the field and slowing the advancing gremlins.

She nudged him. "They're on the move! They're gonna pin us down!" Drew looked up. His eyes had adjusted and he saw shifting shapes racing toward them through the corn.

Sheela said, "Drew! We need that key! How are we gonna find Jimmy?"

Drew looked back at the hoverbikes and couch. "I think I know. Everyone grab a bike. Split up into two groups and retreat into the woods! We gotta keep 'em away from town, but double back to the Polar!"

Then he screamed, "Covering fire!" and he blasted the field. When the charging gremlins ducked, the others were forced to retreat to the barn. They frantically grabbed their hoverbikes. Drew grabbed his as Sheela dove onto the couch Missy was pulling behind her bike. They shoved off toward the woods as Ryan, Sonetta, Kristen, and Kevin headed in the opposite direction to Pal's Run.

Drew's heart raced. He was alive, awake, and terrified as he pumped his pedals. It grew eerily quiet until all he could hear was their labored breathing, the hum of their hoverbikes, and the old couch as they soared along the field's edge. Sheela lay facing backward, stretched out on her stomach, rifle resting on the arm of the couch.

Then Drew heard a cacophony of pops as a light show erupted. The field filled with red-glowing projectiles, exploding orbs of acid goo, and their own blue lasers. The orbs erupted, spraying the surrounding corn and causing it to hiss and steam.

An explosion boomed along Pal's Run. Drew looked back over his shoulder. Smoke rose from the ditch along the narrow road. He saw the hoverbikes glowing quickly across the horizon. The red balls of death were launching into the woods and at the road.

"Ha! You're not catching them now," he whispered. Then he saw it—two groups of gremlins catapulting from the corn on black, chariot-like hovercraft. They soared, two to a craft, far above the field, howling and shrieking like demons. On each vehicle, one piloted while the other discharged an onboard gutter gun. Lasers rained down like neon rainbows.

The gremlin craft were faster than the hoverbikes. The smoldering field emptied and the true chase was on. The Polars returned their blue fire. They would be caught soon. This was it. Drew swerved, leading his team into the field. More red plasma balls zoomed around him. Sickening rot filled his nostrils and green steam burned his eyes as it rose from where the acid grenades had eaten patches of corn and left pale, dead earth. Dry leaves and husks slapped his face as he mowed down stalks.

Drew's squad burst from the corn and into the woods.

"Follow me!" he screamed as red balls zoomed past them and struck the trees. Drew found the narrow bike path as everyone fell in behind him. He heard Sheela's laser rifle spitting back at the incoming gremlin craft. Drew dodged trees and ducked branches, some longer and lower than before. They jumped the creek and split up, weaving down the many paths that descended the hill. The five gremlin craft closed in, flames spurting from their black boosters. Their cackles echoed through the woods. The trees hadn't slowed them, but they did just what Drew had hoped. They'd dropped down onto the trail, right behind the Polars. Drew pumped his legs harder.

"Everyone duck!" he screamed. The squad lowered their heads as they passed beneath the invisible fishing line secured between two giant poplars across a twenty-foot area. Their old trap, set for the Big Boys. Drew looked back in time to see the pilot of the lead gremlin hovercraft lose his head. It popped off so suddenly the gunner was still screaming instructions as purple blood spurted from the pilot's headless neck. The hovercraft drifted into a tree and exploded. Two other gremlin ships hit the wire at the base of their carriages and the gremlins went soaring through the air, hitting trees with disgusting crunches. The two rear gremlin craft slowed, one flying above, the other low, as their drivers ducked behind the protection of the black-armored carriages.

The remaining gremlin vessels swept in from either side, their pilots cursing in guttural gremlin language. The gremlin gunners unloaded and red lasers lit up the woods, leaving an erratic pattern of tiny fires along the forest floor. The Polars returned blue lasers, shooting over their shoulders. They pedaled hard, gasping for breath as they tried to keep ahead of the gremlins and not smash into trees.

One gremlin gunner yanked out a jagged black cutlass and jumped from his carriage. He landed on top of Sheela. The couch dipped and hit the ground, jerking Missy's bike so she nearly went over the handlebars.

The gremlin wagged its long, forked tongue in Sheela's face as it brought down the cutlass. She blocked the blade with her pistol and pushed back. Drew aimed but couldn't pull the trigger, afraid he'd hit her. He felt heat as a volley of lasers zipped past his head. Before the gremlin's blade plunged into Sheela's eye, she ripped an acid grenade from the gremlins vest and stuffed it in its mouth. Its sharp teeth punctured the orb and the gremlin shrieked. It smacked Sheela with the hilt of its blade, knocking her out as it melted in a steaming pile of glop and fell off the couch. Sheela lay on the hovering couch as if sleeping.

The other craft dropped down behind them, blowing out the back half of the couch and setting the rest of it ablaze. Sheela lay unconscious, dangling off the hovering furniture as the flames lapped her boots and legs. The gremlin craft shot and hit the backplate of Missy's body armor. She screamed through gritted teeth. Drew's shots flew wildly and his gun started overheating. The gremlins were nearly on them when they hurled an acid grenade at Sheela. It struck her but didn't explode, the green orb churning and swelling—about to detonate.

Then Drew looked ahead and saw the great leaning sycamore, the one ready to fall. He banked sharply, slamming the flaming couch and nearly knocking Sheela over the edge. He snatched the acid grenade as a milky substance seeped out, searing his hand. He screamed and flung it ahead of them. It struck the base of the tree and erupted, engulfing the wide trunk in a rancid, pale mist. Drew grabbed Sheela off the couch as the tree came down on top of them. It slammed the earth, sending up a torrent of mud and leaves before catching the last bit of couch. Missy went flying as Drew and Sheela hurtled into honeysuckle.

Both gremlin hovercraft tried to pull back but had accelerated too fast and slammed into the trunk, exploding.

Drew found Sheela in the underbrush as Missy limped over to join them. "Missy, you okay?"

"Yeah, Drew. I'm dandy!" Her sarcasm had survived the fight, so far. Sheela suddenly sprang up, grabbing them both as if to keep fighting.

"Sheela!" Drew steadied her. "We're good!"

She blinked and shook her foggy head. "What the hell?"

They all looked up to see Billy and the Big Boys crouching behind the tree fort, peering out in shock. Jimmy wasn't with them.

Drew ran wildly at the gang. He yanked Billy out of hiding. "Where's Jimmy?"

Billy, who looked paler than usual, stammered, "Wha-what was all that?"

Drew felt his anxiety rising as he pulled Billy close. "Billy, *where* is Jimmy?" He saw Billy's eyes travel up over his shoulder and heard Missy scream. Drew turned to see Jimmy behind him just before Jimmy hit him in the head with the butt of an old shotgun.

Drew hit the ground and lost his gun. He heard a *click-clack*. "We've been waitin'. I'm taking you to Grimes."

251

Drew shook his head, but his vision was still blurry. "Where's the key?"

"It's a key? What's it for?" Jimmy said.

Sheela and Missy went for their guns.

"Hold it." Jimmy blinked and shuttered. His trigger finger looked itchy. They heard the boom of the distant fireworks at the carnival and the thunder as the wind picked up.

Missy spat out her gum and raised her laser rifle. "Give him the key, Jimmy."

Sheela looked Jimmy dead in the eye. "Boy, you have no idea what you're doing. You're about to destroy your world."

Ryan and the others zoomed in from the south. "We lost 'em!" Ryan shouted before seeing Jimmy's gun. They jumped off their bikes.

"Back!" Jimmy shrieked as the other Big Boys crawled away, out of the line of fire.

Drew glanced at the crazed bully. "Jimmy! We need that key *now!*"

"The key powers a spaceship. Doesn't it?" The corners of Jimmy's mouth curled up with amusement. "That's it. You're aliens and now you just want to go home. You abducted Willy and took all those animals and tracked slime all over town."

He got a wild look. "Always knew you were an alien, Drew. My parents always said that about your mom too. And if you're aliens, it's my civic duty to shoot you—"

"Drew!" Sheela dove over him as Jimmy was squeezing the trigger.

Then a clicking sound rippled through the dense canopy of trees. They heard a tapping and creaking of branches and hissing. Drew recognized the sounds even before Sheela whispered in his ear, "Slores."

"We're out of time!" Sheela said. "They're here!"

The Big Boys looked at each other, terrified. Jimmy's insane smile waned. "What was that?"

Drew got up. "The real aliens, jackass."

Brandon, a broad-shouldered maniac and the largest of the group, was hiding in the honeysuckle when something big and cloaked by the dense leaves scaled down the vines and yanked him beneath the foliage. They followed his screams as he was hoisted all the way back into the treetops. Then his screams stopped and one of his shoes fell beside Jimmy with a thud.

The Polars raised their guns, backing into a tight formation as they peered into the dark canopy. They couldn't see anything, but things were moving up there, crawling around and chuckling in horrid wheezes.

"Brandon!" Jimmy raised his shotgun and blasted buckshot over his head. He spun on the Polars. "What was that? What took Brandon!"

The Big Boys, Billy and Tyler, took off at a run.

"Guys, no!" Drew called after them. He saw glowing eyes further up the path. The gremlins were moving in.

Then Billy and Tyler screamed out and were gone.

A tortured moan filled the silence, and Drew could just make out a zool ship lowering over the trees, its giant sucker head slithering down and searching for them. The pale, sickly green light seeped down through the trees. The spotlight moved, throwing shadowy patterns over the forest floor and centering on them.

Jimmy dropped his gun in shock and Drew shoved him hard against the tree. "The key—*now*!"

Sheets of rain started pouring from the sky. Jimmy stared

upward, his mouth unhinged and eyes fluttering. "It's, uh, it's . . ."

Drew saw the key glowing from Jimmy's pocket and dug it out, but before he could shove it in his own pocket, Sheela snatched it away.

"I'll keep this," she said, shoving the key into her jacket.

"What are those things?" Jimmy asked.

Drew looked him right in the face. "Come with us if you want to live." He looked back at Sheela. "Let's go!"

"It's too late," Sheela said.

At that moment the forest went red. With howls and cackles the gremlins opened fire with their razor cannons and gutter guns. Red plasma balls hurtled through the trees, smashing trunks and branches and erupting in sparks. The Polars went to the ground as Drew tackled Jimmy.

"Stay down!" Drew fired back over Jimmy's head. The Polars were surrounded and pinned down by the constant barrage of artillery. The slores—Drew counted four—crept down the trees toward them.

"Ryan! Shoot at the trees!" Sheela ordered. "Missy, concentrate on the gremlins!"

But it was no use. Ryan's lasers bounced off the slore shells and ricocheted back at the huddled group, striking Kevin in the chest. He fell onto his back, grimacing as his breast plate smoked.

"Kevin! I'm sorry!" Ryan pleaded.

"We surrender!" Jimmy yelled.

"Jimmy, don't!" Drew tried to hold on, but Jimmy fought him off in a panic and stood.

Suddenly, a gleaming purple tongue shot down from the zool, its faceless head poking through the treetops. It caught Jimmy by the leg and upended him. He clawed the earth, sobbing as the Polars reached for him. Drew grabbed his hand, but not before he was yanked upward. Drew was shaken loose as the zool slurped Jimmy into its puckered mouth. The Polars opened fire on the zool, but its thick skin absorbed the lasers, which did no more damage than if the Polars were tickling it.

"We gotta get outta here!" Drew yelled. But they had nowhere to go.

Ryan grabbed him. "Drew! I'm sorry. I shouldn't have gotten angry."

Drew hugged him. "It's okay."

What would happen now? Would the gremlins attack Warfield and release the parasites? Would his dad ever find his body, or would slores carry him off? What would death feel like? How slow would it be?

The gremlin and slores closed in, and the Polars were forced to drop their weapons. They grabbed and held each other. Drew closed his eyes.

Chapter 28

General ShinFar

As the rain pounded down, lightning flashed again and again followed by gremlin shrieks. Drew opened his eyes. The lightning wasn't lightning. Blue lasers whizzed down from the sky. The gremlins were no longer advancing on them but retreating into their hovercraft, and the slores were climbing back into the trees. The zool drifted above them with its terrible head lowered when suddenly a flying object collided with it. The zool groaned, jetting backward, but its head was trapped in a tangle of vines. It snapped branches and uprooted trees as it reared back.

The flying object was…the cruiser! Drew couldn't believe it. He had never seen a more beautiful hunk of metal! Drew and the others cheered as Justin lowered the ship into the top of the large boxelder tree. He got stuck in its thick limbs and screamed through the shattered windshield, "Climb up!"

The Polars hurriedly scaled the tree.

"Hey, Justin! You got your treehouse!" Drew called out.

The side hatch opened and the group scrambled on board. Drew brought up the rear, returning fire at gremlin hovercraft and slores climbing after them. The ship lurched and nearly took off without him. Drew jumped in, hearing rain and gremlin artillery striking the exterior. The ship was murky from whisps of smoke emerging from the engine room, and it smelled of burning circuits. It creaked and shuddered as Ryan and Missy loaded into their turrets.

Sheela stood at the front with Justin as rain fell through gaping cracks in the windshield. The others fired their rifles through open hatches. Gremlins and slores dove onto the top of the ship. They shot inside and swung swords and claws through the cabin.

"Hold on!" Sheela threw them into a barrel roll, shaking off the creatures clinging to the outside while the crew inside grabbed hold of rigging.

The gun turrets blazed. The gremlins returned fire but were scattered, sparking, and exploding as the blue lasers struck them. The cruiser rose above the woods as the gremlins regrouped and swarmed overhead in their hovercraft. They dove at the cruiser, hurling acid grenades and firing gutter guns.

Drew grabbed Justin, but all he could manage to say was, "How?"

"I chased you guys but you were gone and the gremlins had followed you. Then it dawned on me, the cruiser was just lying there."

Missy dove in and kissed him before yelling, "You saved us, Jus!"

Justin puffed up and then spotted sparks in the engine room. "Kevin, help me back here!" Justin was limping and his leg was bloody from the battle.

"You need a medic, little buddy!" Kevin said.

"Engines first!" The two of them grabbed tool vests off the wall and charged into the tight rear compartment.

"Justin!" Drew took him by the shoulders. "You did it!"

"Almost died doing it too. Gotta go!" He shoved past Drew toward the engines.

Drew passed Missy, who had grabbed the dual triggers and was swiveling herself in a three-sixty spin, unleashing lasers into the oncoming gremlin craft.

Drew climbed up to the front, pulling Sonetta with him. He forced Sheela out of the pilot seat. "Check on Sheela. She inhaled a lot of smoke."

Sonetta checked on Sheela, who'd fallen back against the wall hacking and coughing.

Drew took the flight controls as raindrops smacked his face and stung his eyes. He took them up, and everyone rocked and fell as he banked sharply over the woods.

He looked back and saw Sonetta patching a burn on Sheela's shoulder. "I told you I'm fine!"

"Girlfriend, sit your butt *down*!" Sonetta ordered. Kristen helped hold Sheela against the wall while Sonetta hit her with the healing foam and pasted on a bandage.

The cruiser shook as they took more fire. Drew took them down into a sprawling neighborhood. They flew along the empty streets with the gremlins chasing them. Missy and Ryan cheered as they picked off gremlin ships one by one.

"We're almost to the Polar! We'll be back in business!" Drew said as he pulled the blue key out from his jacket.

The gremlins buzzed around them, dodging cars and hacking the tops off the mailboxes with their blades. A few gremlins sprang from their hovercraft, black daggers in their teeth like pirates. Drew heard them hit the roof and scurry about. One peeked its ugly face in the broken windshield and took aim with its hand-cannon. Drew shot it. Other gremlins banked in front of him, shooting back at them. Drew pulled back, but the cruiser's engine was damaged. The ship was losing power.

"Justin, engine status?"

Justin and Kevin emerged from the smoky engine room, hacking. "Getting there!" Justin stole Sonetta's healing foam and used it to put out a tiny fire.

They navigated the neighborhoods and flew past uptown. Far above, more zools had detached from ShinFar's mother zool ship and chased them, unloading gremlins on four and two-seater hovercraft. They switched on their Oren walls and disappeared.

"I don't understand!" Sheela leaned in beside him, her breaths raspy and labored. "They shouldn't have Oren technology and they should never have been able to get here so fast. Turn on our Oren! We won't see them otherwise!"

Drew switched on the Oren, and the zools and hovercraft came back into view through the windshield. The laser blasts would look like lightning to anyone returning home from the carnival.

They soared over town and out over the woods. The Gladhill barn was right in front of them, but the cruiser's engines were failing. Alarms went off as one booster died. The ship shuddered violently.

"We're almost there!" Drew yelled as he fought the controls. Then the great mother slug ship lowered right in front of them, blocking their path.

"Call comin' in!" Kevin said from the comm station. He answered and a life-sized projected gremlin wearing a red helmet with horns appeared in the cabin. Sonetta screamed and sprayed the image with foam.

"Sheela, tarlock krull!" the gremlin general growled.

"No, ShinFar, you surrender to me," Sheela said.

The gremlin shrieked and swung at her with a large misshapen blade. The projection went through her. Sheela shot the comm station with her pistol, killing ShinFar's projection.

Drew flew around the slug mother ship as it spat glowing goo from orifices along its body. "I can't get around it!" he said, rolling away from the slug. It blocked their path and the cruiser's damaged engines meant he couldn't outmaneuver it. Their guns didn't have any effect; the beast ship's thick, slimy skin easily snuffed out the blue lasers and plasma.

"How much fuel do we have left?" Sheela said.

"A Big Gulp's worth!" Drew said, switching off alarms for multiple system failures.

Sheela squeezed his shoulder. "Punch through it."

"What?"

"Lasers are ineffective against the outer membrane, but the skin is soft. Aim for the head. It's the command center."

"Have you done that before?"

"Oh, yeah. Sure."

He looked at her and she grimaced back. "Liar," he said.

She squeezed his shoulder again.

Drew took a breath. "Justin, route all auxiliary power to engine two! Everyone, brace for impact!"

Ryan climbed up and Missy dropped down as they dove for their seats. Everyone held on. Sheela twisted her right hand around some rigging and gripped it. Drew shoved the throttle forward and punched the thrusters.

The cruiser launched forward and Drew was thrown

back in his seat as they hurtled toward the slug. They hit it and the cabin filled with sparks and blown circuitry. Drew fell forward against the controls. Warm slime splashed over his face and purple, red, and green entrails filled the cabin through the broken window. They burst through the skin and into the red-lit main command room.

Drew saw ShinFar's horrid face for one moment—his gremlin's snake eyes bulging and razor-toothed mouth gaping—before they smashed into him and his crew. More entrails and hot slime. The cruiser pitched forward. Drew left his seat and hung in the air before slamming back down across the dash as they hit solid earth.

Chapter 29

Malgore

Drew found himself on the floor, wedged between the seat and dash controls. He pulled himself out and crawled to his feet. The cabin was dark.

"Everyone okay?" he called. His voice, hoarse and broken, didn't sound like his own.

In the silence, Kevin said, "Can we go home now?" This was followed by weary grunts and moans. Justin turned on a lantern and the Polars emerged from the chaotic, dark cabin as if they'd been spelunking.

Sheela got up off the floor and looked around hurriedly. "That worked? I wasn't sure if the impact velocity against the zool's membrane would kill us." She wiped slime on her jacket and yanked a laser rifle off the wall. "Come on! We're not done."

The others sifted through the mess of supplies on the floor, grabbing rifles and whatever pieces of body armor were visible. They stumbled from their smoldering ship. Sheela and Drew looked at each other, covered in multicolored entrails and dirt.

"You look good," Drew said, and Sheela returned a wry smile, her hair slicked up from the slug ship's snotty membrane. "Is everyone okay?" Drew turned back to the crew. They looked rough, but everyone gave the thumbs up. He could hardly distinguish between them except for Kevin.

They heard a groan, like a distorted whale call, and looked up. The wounded beast undulated its mortally wounded body upward into the sky, retreating for the gate. With ShinFar and the gremlin crew dead inside, the creature was making its own decision. The other zools followed it.

"The creature ships are running back to Malgore! We need to destroy them before they escape and warn him!" Sheela yelled.

"To the Polar!" Drew ordered. They ran for the barn—for the ship. "Let's blow these suckers out of the sky!" Drew screamed. His body pumped with adrenaline as he ran.

They made it to the doors—not the way he'd planned it, but this was going to work! Drew pulled back one door and began to enter when Kevin grabbed and yanked him back.

"Watch out!" Kevin yelled. They all looked up. A white ship dropped from the sky directly above them. They retreated into the corn just as it crushed the barn's roof and landed in the clearing.

Drew sat up from where Kevin had dragged him. They were hidden among what few corn stalks were still standing. The white ship, a sleek jet-looking vessel with inlaid gold along the fuselage, steamed. Then a hatch opened on its side.

"Who is that?" Drew said. "Let's run for the barn."

Sheela shook her head. She stared at the ship with

recognition. "We're gonna take these out first! Everyone ready to fire?"

They took aim as a gremlin platoon spilled down the gangway. They saw not only gremlins but vivisected creatures with insect jaws, snake eyes, and robotic appendages. Eels, ghostly creatures that drifted about on the wind. Space pirates and other mercenary types in furs and horned helmets toting twisted, black guns.

A black slore descended the ramp. It hunched, bigger and fatter than any Drew had seen. It had deep red spiraled etchings and patterns carved across its body. Even at this distance, Drew could hear its low, guttural growl from beneath the bulbous abdomen and its hydraulic sounding hiss, spraying steaming saliva through its razor teeth. Its entire exoskeleton flexed and shuttered with anticipation.

They hadn't seen the kids and looked around at the alien environment, the barn, and corn.

"Fire on my command," Sheela growled. Everyone readied themselves, their guns humming. Drew aimed for the slore's lower half. The Polars' combined firepower and ambush might give them the edge they needed.

Drew squeezed the trigger, but before he could fire, Sheela suddenly tackled him and pinned him to the ground. "Hold your fire," she whispered. The others froze, fingers hugging their triggers.

"What are you doing?" Then Drew followed her gaze and saw what she'd seen. His heart stopped.

A man exited the ship and descended the gangplank. Drew recognized him from the many projections he'd looked through on the cruiser.

Sheela's father. Mayzon.

He was handsome and dressed in a white uniform. He

peered out into the darkness. "Sheela!" he called, his voice deep and kind.

Drew heard cackles behind them and looked back to see a squad of gremlin hovercraft landing in the cornfield.

"Sheela, we're surrounded. We need to shoot our way out—now."

"Hold on, I'm thinking." Sheela knew it too. Her moment of indecision had cost them. They were finished.

"There's no time." Drew took her by her shoulders and she blinked at him like a frightened child. "*You* cannot be captured. You're the only hope." Even as Drew squeezed her tighter, he felt her slipping through his fingers like water.

She focused on him a moment. "Drew, I'm not the only hope . . . but if I stay, we'll all die." She whispered, "Stay here."

"You're not going out there," Drew said. The other Polars looked at Drew to do something.

Her father called out, "Sheela! Where are you?"

Drew went numb. It was all over. His brain tried to understand as it cycled through blame, guilt, and disbelief. They were about to be captured, tortured, and hauled away to Malgore.

Sheela said, "Drew, look at me. Captain Shipley?" Her voice sounded faraway. Hopelessness dulled his senses. He gazed out at the cornfield, his eyes dim and ears crackling. Sheela grabbed him by the collar and forced him to make eye contact. "Stay here and don't make a sound," she said.

"Wait." He clutched at her. "Where are you going?"

"Just keep the others quiet and don't come out. You must swear to keep the ship hidden."

"What?"

She yanked him. "Swear."

Unable to speak, Drew nodded and blinked. Sheela released him. The fierce blue storm in her eyes calmed and a tear fell. She placed her forehead to his, hugged him tightly, and released him. She looked back at the others for a moment as they all clutched each other, petrified. With her rifle slung over her shoulder, she got to her knees and crawled away along the row of corn.

A moment later, as her father and the creature horde looked on, Sheela emerged from the corn. She had her laser rifle raised, aiming at her father. He saw her and smiled warmly. The gremlins and other creatures encircled her.

"Sheela, my love," her father said, smiling. "You can drop the rifle."

"So that's how the gremlins got here so fast. That's why they have Oren technology. *You* gave it to them."

"The gremlins would have taken ages to get here without my help. And I wanted to see you."

"Promise me you'll take me and leave," Sheela said in a quivering voice. Her hands shook as she advanced. The rifle was trained on his chest.

"I promise, my love." Her father stepped off the gangplank and strode to her. She faltered and slowly lowered her rifle.

Drew was frozen. The man with the plan, always with an idea or a way out, was completely at a loss. Worse, the fear he thought he'd overcome swallowed him in black panic. He could feel the others looking to him, but he had nothing.

Sheela's father came up to her without hesitance. He never broke eye contact, never looked at her rifle. His eyes were deep azure, almost black. His hair blew gently in the exhaust from the ship. She looked exactly like him. Drew saw Sheela's shoulders drop. Her body was limp and the hardened warrior was gone. She was a little girl seeing her father for the first time in a long time. All else had been an act. He came so close her rifle's short barrel pressed against his chest. He gently moved the rifle aside and embraced her. She fell into his arms.

Drew could barely hear the man's low voice. "My darling. I've missed you so much." He caressed the back of her head as she dropped her rifle in the dirt. Then her father looked up and out the field. "Did you have a liaison or make friends here?"

"No. I paid mercenaries, but they betrayed me and retreated. There's nothing here."

He looked down at her as she pulled her head from his chest and looked up at him. He cupped her face. "My darling, where is the Polar Starship?"

"Don't you know, Father? You're the one who hid it."

The man's smile faded a bit. "That I did, but I can't remember." He stroked her cheek. "If you give me that ship, all the wrongs will be forgiven and you and your Dimension Warriors will be free."

Sheela paused. Drew watched her quiver before him. "I . . . I haven't found it." Sheela stepped away from her father. He twitched and cocked his head. His jaw slackened, and when he spoke again his voice was high and inhuman. "Give it to us, my child!"

"I don't have it . . . *Malgore*."

The man smacked his lips and his tongue flicked. His carefully brushed hair fell out of place. "You must know where it is."

"It's not here."

He sighed, glanced back, and nodded. The slore sprang into action. It scuttled at Sheela and grabbed her up in its claws. The demon platoon cheered with cackles and howls as the slore choked her and stretched her arms and legs, pulling her into the shape of an X. Sheela screamed in pain.

Drew lunged forward, ready to shoot, when the panic and dread took hold of his gut and he froze. He looked out at Sheela, her body held fast and stretched like a rag doll. He felt himself shrinking. He saw his mom in the hospital bed, gritting her teeth against pain and nausea, fighting to live just long enough to see him.

He'd run then, when his dad had taken him to say goodbye. Even when she'd reached for him and tried to smile like everything was okay, he couldn't say it. He'd been too afraid—afraid of her pain and terrified of the final goodbye. He couldn't save her, so retreat was the only option. He would never get that chance to say goodbye. He dropped the laser rifle and crawled backward like a frightened animal.

As the slore stretched her, Sheela's father looked up at her and smiled warmly. "Do we know where the starship is now?"

Her breath came sharp and quick as she moaned against the pain. "Nnnoo!" she gasped.

Her father sighed again. The gremlins growled and hissed at her, flicking their forked tongues and playing with their twisted knives. Her father stiffened and twitched. "Your brother's base will soon fall. Where is the Polar?"

Sheela looked down at him hopelessly. "I never found it."

"Let us search out this dimension," her father called to his troops. Sheela spat down on him. The slore stretched her further and she screamed.

"There's nothing here but useless humans!"

"It doesn't mean the ship isn't here."

"If I had the ship, I would have used it to destroy you. But I know where it is! And Bash and the other Warriors will stand down if I order them to. I'm the key to finding the ship and ending the war!"

Malgore looked hungrily at her from her father's eyes. "Yes, Sheela, and I am very . . . *eager* to meet you. Let us go, child. You will do all of those things." He looked at a nearby gremlin. "Collect the dead and their vessels. Leave nothing for the scavengers."

The Polars shivered and wept, holding each other as the slore carried Sheela aboard the ship. The ship lifted off, smashing through the remaining walls of the barn. It rose higher and higher and disappeared in a twinkle as it passed through the gate. The zools disappeared in Oren shrouds and traveled quickly around, collecting dead gremlins and their hovercraft.

Sheela was gone.

The others lay there in the mud, stunned, as the rain died away. But Drew had run. He'd left his weapon and fled.

Chapter 30

First Day of School

The first day of school was abuzz with excitement. Everyone was talking about their summer. The luckiest kids had gone to Disney World while most of the others ended up at Ocean City, at sleepaway camps, or on dreaded road trips to visit grandparents. There had been sleepovers, pool parties, fist fights, and summer romances, but nothing out of the ordinary.

There was still some talk of the tornado. Even though they only saw the aftereffects, city officials and weather experts said a massive EF4 tornado, with winds up to 166 mph, must have touched down just to the west of Warfield the first night of the carnival. Strangely, it only destroyed some mailboxes before ripping through a cornfield and the old Gladhill barn. Much stranger were the blackened scorch marks along Mary Street. Some older residents said they saw lightning strike the street and some trees. One man claimed the lightning was so close and flashed so brightly it temporarily blinded him. The important thing was that no one had been injured—or so they thought.

Jimmy Griffin and three of the Big Boys had been missing since that night, last seen leaving the carnival at seven o'clock. The gossip among the kids was that Jimmy and the others had run away. Some said he and the others might have been swept up by the same tornado that smashed weird, erratic patterns throughout the Gladhill cornfield. Police discovered one of Jimmy's Converse shoes hanging from a branch out in the woods. Besides that, they found no trace of the boys, so the curfew was still on and anyone with information was encouraged to contact a tip hotline.

After Sheela was taken, the Polars scattered and hunkered down in fear. But Sheela's father and the gremlins and slores hadn't returned, and nothing dropped from the gateway in the sky. A group of convicts picking up trash along Route 108 did find a strange piece of twisted black metal thought to be a gun. It was evaluated by authorities and tossed in Willy's junkyard when they couldn't determine what it was. Willy's was now under new management.

The Polar Starship still lay buried below Warfield, under the remains of the Gladhill barn. The group once referred to as the Polars had no key to power it even if they wanted to. So, as helpless, stupid kids, they fled to their homes. They all had sleepless nights and night terrors and acted strangely. After a few weeks, the town acted as if nothing had ever happened, but the kids were broken.

They couldn't find their way back to childhood now. Missy started hanging out with friends she'd neglected during the summer and chewed more gum than usual. Sonetta volunteered to help in her mom's small law office, stapling

271

depositions and shredding old documents. Kevin developed a stutter and shut himself in his room, listening to comedy records until his parents threatened therapy. Justin hid away, rebuilding his giant Rube Goldberg Erector Set catapult. Kristen went with her family to their beach house in the Outer Banks, as they did every year and would return the second week of school. Ryan started basketball and went to the gym every day. He shot free throws late every night on their driveway until his dad came out. Ryan wouldn't stop shooting, even when called, and often had to be tapped on the shoulder. He jumped every time.

Steve had woken up in the field, questioning his memory of what happened. The tornado sounded better than everything else he remembered, and no one else had seen anything. So instead of thinking he was crazy, he accepted the EF4 story.

Drew Shipley was in hiding. Ryan would knock and ask for him and Steve would shake his head and shrug. Every time, Steve asked, "What happened that night? Did Stacey get off okay?"

Ryan would shake his head, shrug, and leave. He even gathered Kevin and Justin a few times and stood in the backyard, below Drew's room, tossing twigs at his window. His shade was drawn and he never pulled it back. They tried calling him on Justin's walkie, but there was nothing but static.

So it was weird to see Drew the first week of school. He drifted in quietly. He wore a faint smile and didn't talk to anyone. Ryan tried to stop him, but Drew slipped in and out of classes too quickly. At the end of every school day Ryan looked for him, but Drew was gone. Kevin and Justin didn't have any luck either. Drew was a ghost.

Drew felt wonderful. His mind was clear and full of sunsets and bronzed clouds and pirate ships. He'd been reading *Peter Pan* and comic books as well as watching cartoons. He spent time playing with action figures, stretched out on his stained oval, braided rug—the one his mom had in her room growing up. Sometimes, he drew treasure maps of the woods and cornfield, the places his mom used to call Weird Space. He no longer had a problem remembering her. To help him imagine Weird Space, he paced about his room wiggling a pen or pencil. He knew it looked strange, but he'd done it since he was little. Once lost in his imagination, Drew could pace and wiggle for hours. He kept his door shut so his dad wouldn't see him.

But sometimes, at the end of a day, Drew began to feel weird. His heart quickened. He broke into a cold sweat, and his stomach did flips and threatened to toss his dinner. Drew would pause from TV or wiggling or comic books and sneak to the black stuffed monkey on his bed, the one his mom had bought him at Toys "R" Us. The monkey had a small rip at the back of its neck where a bit of white stuffing often stuck out. Drew would reach in and feel around where a leather pouch of shiny black pills was hidden inside. He knew to fish one out and he knew to only take one for some reason, having the faint concern that they would eventually run out. In another moment, he would feel right as rain.

Right as rain. What does that mean? He thought that every time before diving back down to the oval rug to read.

One night, Drew was perched on the tan toilet in the upstairs hallway bathroom. He'd been there a while, somewhat constipated and prairie-dogging a large bowel movement. The hum of the old ceiling fan, beige walls, and warm light from the fixture over the sink had mesmerized him, and he sat thinking comfortably about life. Suddenly, his heart began racing and a cold sweat broke out over his face. He forced himself to poop, wiped the blood from his butt, and ran for his room.

He froze in the doorway. A boy wearing a basketball jersey stood in his bedroom. The window sat half open with a gentle breeze blowing in the curtain. The boy stood by his bed, holding up the old stuffed monkey. In his other hand, he held up the pouch. Drew eyed the pills. His brain screamed for them.

"This is what Sheela was taking. Wasn't it?" the boy said.

"Who?" Drew had no idea who he was talking about.

The boy nodded, finally understanding. "So. They make you forget."

"Give 'em back, Ry . . . Ry . . ." Drew struggled with the name.

"You don't remember me either, huh?"

"Just give 'em back!"

"No. You don't get to forget. Not if I have to remember. I'm not letting you do this again. I need my friend back."

Drew lost himself and rushed at Ryan. They crashed into the end table, smashed the lamp, and fell to the floor. Drew fought for the pills, but Ryan crushed the remaining twenty in his hand. A wispy black powder blew away in a sudden billowing breeze.

"No!" Drew screamed. He spun and punched the side of Ryan's face, but Ryan didn't defend himself or retaliate. A moment later, Steve hoisted Drew up and pulled him off Ryan.

"Drew!" Steve shouted, wrestling Drew back.

Ryan got up, his basketball jersey torn and a red mark blushing below his left eye. He'd have a black eye for the next week and say he got it from a stray baseball. He looked at Drew another moment and left through the door.

Drew fought back against his dad. Steve wrestled him to the bed and shoved him down. "Drew! What the *hell* is going on?"

"Nothing."

"Something." Steve said as Drew glared up at him. "Is this about Stacey going back home?"

"Who?"

Steve sighed angrily. "Or was it about this?" He yanked a piece of paper from his pocket and opened it. Drew didn't recognize the paper. "Dear Dad," Steve read, "by the time you read this, I will be gone. Please don't look for me or call the police. You won't find me. I'm helping do something important, and I think I'm where I am supposed to be. I want you to go and live your life and start a new family." Tears filled Steve's eyes and he gulped. "I'm sorry about Mom and I'm sorry I wasn't a better son. I love you and . . . I hope I will see you again someday."

He tossed the letter at Drew. "Why would you ever think I want a new family? You remind me of her. And I love that."

Her. Drew saw a silhouette in his mind, but it wasn't Anne. It was her. Sheela.

"Please don't, Dad."

"Where were you going?"

Drew sank to the floor, sobbing. Steve crawled down beside him and put an arm around him as he wept.

"I'm sorry. I'm so sorry," Drew said through tears. He could barely breathe, and with each gasp for air, he saw her more clearly: dark blue eyes, wild black hair, pink scar, smile. Her gaze, like she was looking into his soul.

Drew had failed her like he'd failed his mom, his dad,

and his friends. The memories returned and crushed him under the weight of pain, guilt, and sadness.

Steve wrenched Drew back from the precipice. He held him tightly for a long time as they cried together.

Drew woke up. His face hurt from crying, and his throat stung. Steve was still asleep, curled up on the floor beside him. Drew's letter lay nearby. He remembered writing it. He remembered it all now, and he thought about her. She eclipsed everything in his mind. He watched her betrayed by her father and taken away over and over, dragged off by the slore. He could do nothing to save her. He remembered running. His heart still burned, his brain locked in the dark— no ideas, no way out, and nowhere to run. He sat there in the deafening silence, surrounded by his horrible thoughts with Sheela's scream echoing from far away. He had to move or run, otherwise he would lose his mind.

Then Drew had an unthinkable thought to do something he'd been determined never to do.

He got up quietly, so as not to wake Steve. He snuck to his closet and uncovered his Dimension Warrior jacket buried beneath clothes and books. The jacket still smelled faintly of acid grenades and smoke as he put it on.

He left his house when it was still dark outside and walked across town. He didn't look at the cornfield or rubble where the barn once stood. The area was still roped off due to safety concerns. He passed through the woods and emerged behind the old Presbyterian church as dawn lit the horizon. He heard the distant whoosh of morning rush-hour traffic on the highway and saw blankets of dew on the grass.

He entered the graveyard at the back of the church and went to her grave in the far-right corner. He stood over it. He was no longer afraid of her or of this place. He knew she wasn't there. This hadn't been the end of the road for Anne Shipley. He believed that now.

"I'm sorry," he whispered into the morning.

The graveyard quieted his thoughts. He looked up and whispered, "What do I do now?" He stood a while, waiting for an audible voice, for his mom or an angel or God to open the morning clouds and speak to him. The only response was a cool breeze to remind him the summer was over. He didn't know what he thought would happen, but it wasn't going to.

He turned to walk away and shoved his hands in his pockets—and felt something. He froze, feeling the object with his fingers. Then he slowly pulled it out.

The blue key glowed in his hand.

He stared at it, expecting it to disappear. But it remained.

This is a dream. This can't be real. I've lost my mind. I'm hallucinating.

He turned the object over and over in his hand and then looked up for that break in the clouds in case his mom had tossed it down to him. Sheela took it from him. It was on her when they took her . . .

Her hug. All at once, he remembered. Sheela had grabbed him before sacrificing herself.

She'd given him the key.

Chapter 31

Mickey Mouse Has Warts

The church basketball league had a short season starting at the end of summer and ending in the fall. All six teams played out of the same dusty old gym connected to the Methodist church on Kline. After the competitive summer sports, like baseball, this was just for fun. Even Big Jake relaxed, sitting in the stands to talk and laugh loudly with his friends. The players weren't all that good, and the coaches and refs were volunteers. People from the community used it as an excuse to visit with each other while waiting for the high school sports to start.

But at this evening's game, Ryan Wilcox charged up and down the court, stealing the ball and rushing it back for layups. He was flushed and sweat-soaked. His torn jersey and his shiner made him look scary. His coach and the refs joked about him needing to slow down and take it easy.

"He's still upset about blowing the baseball season," Jake

quipped with others in the stands.

His team was confused, collectively deciding to stay out of Ryan's way. He scored twenty-four of his team's twenty-six points, and that was only because another kid on his team had been fouled. Ryan had not missed a shot.

"Pass the ball, Ryan!" Big Jake shouted from the stands. "Where was this during baseball?"

His coach prepared to take him out, readying a substitute off the bench. The other team grew timid, passing the ball quickly before the demon, Wilcox, bore down on them to block their path. Ryan stole the ball again and was fouled when one of the other players got fed up and shoved him. He didn't react but went to the line. He dribbled at the line, not taking his eyes from the basket. *Swish*. He hit the first. He readied himself for the second when—there he was.

Drew stood just behind the pole of the basketball hoop. He wasn't smiling or waving or angry or sad. He was just there, watching.

The two stared at each other. Ryan glared at Drew before wiping the sweat on his forearm. He shook his head, dribbled, and took the shot.

It missed by a mile, falling three feet short of the basket.

Justin was in his unfinished basement, perched at his dad's workbench below the migraine-inducing fluorescent light. He was using his dad's soldering gun on the same radio he'd taken apart and put back together five times. The exercise made him feel better at first but had begun to remind him of repairs he'd wanted to do on the cruiser—

Something struck the back of his head. Justin shrieked and jumped off the stool, startled. He heard giggles and spun to see his little sister sitting on the steps with her tongue sticking out. She'd ripped the catapult cup off his Erector Set and used it to launch a marble at him.

That's when the call came through.

Kevin was in his room, sitting at his desk and pounding his head lightly on his math textbook. He heard the crackle over his walkie, heard the password whispered.

"Mickey Mouse has warts."

"Did you hear that?" Kevin was on his walkie with Justin a second later.

"I did."

Kevin and Justin arrived at Drew's house in ten minutes. They'd both been running when they met each other on Mary Street and sprinted together onto Angela Court. The others were in the backyard, standing in the dark shadows of twilight and whispering to each other.

"What took you two so long?" Sonetta said. "He wouldn't tell us anything until you got here."

They joined the others and Missy smacked them both with their own hands as she chewed gum. "Hey, it's Tweedledum and Tweedledumber!"

Ryan was there, still in his jersey. "Ryan, what the hay is going on?" Kevin asked. Ryan said nothing but smiled.

"Oh, thanks a lot, you're a wealth of knowledge," Kevin snorted.

Suddenly, Drew emerged from the field. He wore his burnt black Dimension Warrior jacket and a gun belt strapped around his waist with a laser pistol occupying the holster. He had his school backpack slung over shoulder. He saw Kevin and Justin, dropped his bag, and ran to them. He pulled them all into a group hug.

"I'm sorry," Drew said. "I abandoned you guys."

"We forgive you," Justin said with more confusion than sincerity.

"I snuck out for an apology?" Sonetta frowned.

"That's all this is?" Kevin twisted his face in disappointment. "I thought you had a plan or something."

Missy blew an enormous bubble as Justin turned to Kevin. "There's no plan, Kevin. We don't have the—"

Drew pulled the blue key from inside his shirt. They gasped, the glow illuminating their shock. They crowded around as Ryan leaned in to inspect it. "But Sheela had it . . ."

Drew shook his head. "She gave it back so it wouldn't fall into Malgore's hands."

Sonetta said, "Why didn't she tell you she was giving it to you?"

"Because I would have given it to them to save her."

Justin looked at Drew with a freshly horrified expression. "What does this mean?"

"We're it. We're their only hope." He looked at them all somberly. "I'm going after her. I just wanted you guys to know I didn't abandon you again."

Ryan said, "Maybe she just wanted you to keep it secret like your mom did."

Drew shook his head. "She needs my help."

Sonetta poked him in the chest, "I'm sorry, are *we* not invited?"

"Helping Sheela find the ship was one thing. Going out there—" Drew looked up to the stars. "Going out there is another."

"You can't pilot the Polar alone," Ryan said.

"No, but if I can get it into the Toren dimension, I can pick up the other Warriors."

Justin grunted as he cleaned his glasses, "That's if they're even still alive. Drew, you saw these things—gremlins, slores, space pirates. *Malgore*?"

"That's why he can't go alone," Ryan said.

"This is crazy." Missy chewed. "I love it."

Sonetta said, "Our parents . . . people are gonna flip."

"Then let's make it a quick trip," Kevin said.

Drew sighed. He was afraid of this, but instead of fear, he felt relief. "Alright, who's in?"

Everyone's hands shot up. Justin shoved his glasses back on. "Only because you wouldn't make it off the ground without your engineer."

"Guess we better start digging," Ryan said as he glanced back at the field. "It's gonna take us hours to get down to the trap door."

Drew shrugged with a smile.

"What?" Ryan asked.

"Already did it." Drew turned and they all followed his gaze into the empty sky behind them.

"Wait!" Ryan dropped his baseball. "It's up there now?"

"I'm going tonight."

Ryan grabbed his shoulder. "*We're* going tonight."

"But we're stopping by my house," Sonetta said. She blushed. "I at least need underwear."

"Me too," Missy said.

"It would be good for us all to say goodbye," Justin said.

Drew looked back at Steve. The moment felt dangerously like his dream. His dad wasn't hunched in the corner with his letter, but Steve was about to lose the only other person he had.

Drew had left him another letter, but this one promised he'd come back.

Kristen was on her last night at the beach. She wandered the lonely shoreline, her feet sinking into the cooling sand as the crabs scuttled about her toes. She'd done away with the makeup and worn the same baggy Outer Banks sweatshirt nearly the entire two weeks. She hadn't gone in the water and only strayed out at night.

She struggled with anxiety, always watching the sky. The loneliness was crushing—never more so than when she was on the beach under the stars and moon. She watched families hunt ghost crabs with flashlights, laughing and talking and holding hands. It reminded her of night tag. The people on the beach were blissfully unaware of what worlds lay beyond and the reality of Malgore.

Kristen was sure she was the worst of her friends. After Drew disappeared, she had run, leaving the others behind. She'd learned a lot about herself. She'd learned she would abandon those she loved to save her own skin, and she could never face them again. She had also been haunted by thoughts of Sheela, the alien girl. Sheela must have known what she was. Somehow, she knew she would end up a crazy old cat spinster, babbling about aliens and government conspiracies. Her life, whatever it would be, would look very different from what it might have been, and she deserved it.

As she sat in the cool sand listening to the surf, someone

sat down beside her.

"Hey." She recognized the voice, but it couldn't be. She turned her head slowly and blinked. Her mind was playing tricks. Drew had just plopped down beside her. He was wearing normal clothes and sitting comfortably, as if he had just appeared out of thin air.

"What? How?" she stuttered.

"We can't rescue Sheela without a navigator. You're the best one I know. You in?"

"What are you doing here?"

"We just need to know if you're in."

She narrowed her green eyes and hit him in the shoulder.

Nearly a month after Jimmy Griffin and the Big Boys disappeared, six more kids from Warfield were reported missing, one of them from six hours south of Maryland, in the Outer Banks.

No one knew what was going on, but to the old men outside of Pete's Barber Shop, it was all very weird.

Sign up for my author newsletter at WeirdSpaceBook.com

And don't forget to review *Weird Space* in Amazon!

ACKNOWLEDGMENTS

I want to thank my wife, Heather: my inspiration, champion, creative partner, and most honest critic. To my boys, Gabriel, Uriah, and Gideon for listening to early drafts of the story and telling me it "was really good" even when it wasn't-I will forever love you for that. Two of my dear mentors, who have sadly passed away. My aunt Anne, who always encouraged me to read, write and revise. My dad, Steve, who filled our home with great music, books, films, and other works of art. To my brother, Dan, a gifted artist who created the amazing book cover and website. To Tim Scott, one of my closest friends and a champion of this story. To Caitlin Anselmo, who composed the perfect piece of music for the audiobook. To Janie Townsend for a fabulous copy edit and Amanda Brown for proofreading the final manuscript. To Sophia Rundell, who read the story in three days and gave me her wonderful feedback, thank you! There are others who have been along for the ride. It's a team effort and I am humbled and eternally grateful!

ABOUT THE AUTHOR

Andrew Michael Wiley is a writer and video producer at the National Institutes of Health. He lives with his wife and three sons in Maryland. Weird Space is his first novel.

Made in the USA
Las Vegas, NV
13 December 2023

82707089R00173